Scaoil do ghreim agus ar aghaidh

leat ag eitilt!

THE
IRISH CASTLE

THE IRISH HEART SERIES,
BOOK 4

THE
IRISH CASTLE
KEEPING ELIZABETH

THE IRISH HEART SERIES, BOOK 4

BY JULIET GAUVIN

The Irish Heart Series

TABLE OF CONTENTS

To La Tia Luisa, my own great-aunt and part of the inspiration for Mags, who passed away as this book went to print. She was 95 years young.

THE IRISH CASTLE

THE IRISH HEART SERIES, BOOK 4

PROLOGUE: UNICORNS & MARGARITAS

A white house stood atop a green and brown hill overlooking the San Francisco Bay. The setting sun cast a magical glow over the massive structure, hitting the white pillars and glass wall. The golden light effect gave the illusion that the house was on fire and imbued the dwelling with a grandeur that went beyond its imposing size.

A small child played in the blue waters of a sparkling pool which seemed to stretch all the way to the ocean. The white and rainbow inflatable unicorn toy floated majestically alongside the girl.

The two women of mature years and young hearts sat sipping margaritas at the intricate wrought iron table some distance from the pool.

"Elizabeth is growing so fast." The woman with a short silver-haired bob and thick accent remarked.

"She is indeed," Magdalen replied, glancing in the direction of the infinity pool where her great-niece played happily. "I can't believe she's five today."

The two women looked again towards the small girl as she splashed around the pool, dancing and jumping with her new toy, frequently falling off of the unicorn and then scrambling back up again.

Magdalen chuckled softly as she watched, "What a wonderful birthday gift. You're very good with her." She turned towards her friend in time to see Camille's smile falter.

The decades of friendship between them had taught the two women many things about life and about each other.

Magdalen hesitated before speaking because she knew well what her friend was thinking. But she asked anyway, "What's wrong, Camille?"

"Oh, the usual, Magdalena." Camille took a breath before sipping her margarita. She stared out at the horizon and the Golden Gate Bridge. "I've made so many mistakes with Isabelle. I never knew how to be a mother. My mother was not . . . well you remember. She was not *loving*. I received more love and attention from your father, Alejandro, than I did from Adriana, rest her soul. Your father was a good man."

"Yes, he was," Magdalen agreed.

They both took a sip of their drinks and sat in silence.

"I know I've said this to you many times, but I don't blame you, Magdalena," Camille looked at her friend thoughtfully. "I'm glad Isabelle had you to turn to all those years ago."

Mags swept a long strand of hair out of her eyes, "It was nothing." She thought carefully before continuing, "Have you spoken to her recently?"

"Not since she made it clear she didn't want me at her wedding a year ago," she paused remembering something else, "I'm told that they're expecting a child."

Mags nodded, confirming what Camille had already been told by the man she employed to keep her informed.

Camille's lips set in a line, her jaw tensed. "She wants nothing to do with me . . . and perhaps that's as it should be. My life . . . has never been easy, and she felt it more than anyone."

Elizabeth fell off of her unicorn once more with a splash that demanded the women's attention.

They were grateful for the interruption.

"Lizzie loves coming here, you know."

Camille smiled, "Your visits are delightful and your life-long friendship invaluable." She reached across the table to squeeze the weathered hand of the woman who had known her since birth. Magdalen was twelve years her elder, but they'd grown up together, they were more like sisters than friends.

Magdalen thought again of the question she'd intended to ask, "Camille, if anything should happen to me . . . well you know our situation . . . I'm all she has. Could you—?"

3

Camille held up a hand, not letting her finish, "Of course, I will always be here for Lizzie."

The two women looked back towards the five-year-old as she launched herself out of the water and back onto the unicorn. Elizabeth shrieked with delight.

Camille spoke softly, "I hope she has an easier time than we did finding our way in the world."

Mags considered for a moment, imagining what her great-niece might see or do or accomplish in her lifetime. "I think she'll be all right. I look forward to seeing what life has in store for her."

"As do I," Camille agreed. "Although I hope she doesn't make a mess of it as we both have in our own ways."

Magdalen's voice took on a mischievous tone, "Oh, I don't know. Life can be quite the glorious mess."

The two women exchanged a knowing look and laughed. They clinked glasses and looked to the sky, enjoying the pink and purple hues left behind by the dying light.

1

IRISH HOMECOMING

*S*he made the final turn just as the sun broke through the clouds and the golden light spilled out onto the rolling green hills.

The trees stood on either side of the little house—the guardians of Rhia's cottage and the lough that lay beyond. They swayed in greeting just as they'd done all those years ago.

Elizabeth took a deep breath and released the steering wheel of the rental car she'd hired at the airport. It had taken nearly a month to go through Magdalen's house in Berkeley before the sale.

It would have made more sense to pay someone to take care of it all, but she couldn't do it. Couldn't have strangers going through her great-aunt's belongings.

Mags had been gone for nearly five years and it had taken

her all of that time to go back.

"Five years . . . ," she said to herself.

She stared at the cottage in front of her.

Five years.

Five years since she'd pulled up to this very cottage and her life had changed forever.

Double semi-lancet arched windows flanked the bright red front door. The pitched roof was a dark black-gray color with a chimney. The lake was there peeking out on the right side waiting for her.

It was quintessentially Irish. Every bit of it was blissfully the same.

She tried to remember what she'd thought then.

What had she thought she would gain there? Peace? Enlightenment?

She shook her head, laughing at the memory. How wrong she'd been . . . *and how right.*

She got out of the car and grabbed her luggage, there had been a reason she'd come to the cottage first and not told anyone she was coming home early.

Her brain was filled with the memories of the past, memories of California, of the house, of the strange business with Camille, of Mags, of the life she had spent a decade building . . . and then after Mags' death, mere weeks tearing down.

The large shipment she'd sent herself from California, which included some of Mags' personal belongings, the picture albums, the diaries, the porcelain dishes, along with some of the larger furniture pieces from the house in Berkeley, including her favorite blue couch, wouldn't arrive in Ireland for a few weeks. There would be time to finish processing it all. Finish going through the boxes of papers and hard drives, and all that remained.

She thought of what it would mean to finish. To get to the end of all of Mags' mysteries—nothing left of the woman she loved. It was an unbearable thought.

She shook her head and took another deep breath, trying to change the direction of her thoughts. She was home in Ireland now. All she needed was a shower, a glass of wine, and the gleaming waters of Lough Rhiannon. They would work together to relieve her tension and soothe her soul.

She set her luggage down, leaving it by the car and took the small undefined path to the right of the house as she had done all those years ago, again careful not to look inside.

The sky had turned purple and gold, a tingling sensation ran up her spine—she anticipated the scene that awaited her on the other side of the cottage. The breeze found her, greeted her, beckoned her forward to the beautiful lake that had changed her. She could hear her footsteps quickening, even as she began to lose control of her body. Lough Rhiannon called her.

And then it was there, stretching out in front of her in all its glory. Four or five golden rays broke through the purple expanse of clouds, hitting the water, setting it alight in a delightful display. The green below her feet and indeed everywhere that was not sky or water was greener than green, a green which she'd only ever found in Ireland.

She breathed it all in, let it bathe her in its magic.

California was still home. It was where she grew up, where she'd shared a life with Mags. But Ireland? Ireland was a home for her deepest self . . . her soul.

It had always been thus, she just hadn't known it until she'd stepped foot on the Emerald Isle.

"Hi Rhia, hi Mags," she said faintly, letting her words be carried by the breeze.

The wind kicked up, caressing her face and blowing her long brown hair out behind her in wild waves.

They were finally coming home to live again, permanently.

There would be visits to her French Château and visits with family and friends—they would still travel—but after spending the better part of four years flitting from place to place, never spending more than a couple of months anywhere, they'd decided to come back to live in Ireland.

To take up permanent residence at Castle Bannon and be still for a while.

"A while," she said under her breath. Mulling the words over in her mouth.

That was the plan . . . settle down in Ireland in their beautiful castle, the castle that had once held so much darkness for Connor, and now held so much light.

He had redone it from top to bottom himself after his father had died, trying desperately to rid himself of that man's darkness, but only succeeding when Elizabeth had waltzed through his door, healing old wounds and giving him the life he'd always wanted.

Now they had renovated the castle again, this time not to rid themselves of darkness, but to create a life that they both wanted together.

That was the plan . . . to settle down. That's what they had decided, that's what made sense.

Even as the thoughts crossed her mind her hand went reflexively to the letter in her back pocket. The offer.

She shook her head trying to clear her mind, trying to be present. There would be time for that. Time to figure out what she wanted. Time to reconnect with her voices.

It had been so long; the buzz and bustle of life had taken her all over the world. She had all the beautiful memories and experiences of a life well-lived. And the photographs to prove it.

But now what she wanted was to be still and hear those glorious inner voices again. The ones that never failed her, the ones that always knew the right way—her direct line to the Universe.

Elizabeth closed her eyes and took in the sounds of the lake, the calm water gently swaying and lapping against the shore, the birds whistling their familiar tune, and the breeze rustling through the trees.

The air left her lungs all at once, a deep sigh that signaled peace, like Shavasana at the end of a long yoga session.

She opened her eyes and gathered herself, turning back to the cottage and making her way around the other side of the house.

She had passed the first window without looking inside, but when she came upon the second a flash of movement caught her eye. The defined flesh of a naked chest filled her vision first, and then she looked up towards a face and found the electric blue eyes she knew so well.

Connor was standing there in only a pair of old jeans, his eyes fixed on her, confusion colored his features and then a glorious smile transformed his already beautiful face. His Christmas morning smile.

Butterflies danced in her stomach and a warm sensation crept into her chest, her breathing came faster, and she felt her mouth turn up instinctively, mirroring his expression.

She was suddenly running alongside the cottage, making her way to the front, she was sure he was doing the same.

She reached the red front door just as it opened and found her bare chested, barefoot Irishman standing there waiting to wrap her in his arms.

Either she jumped or he bent down and picked her up, but they were suddenly enveloped in each other's arms.

Connor let her go just long enough to bring his strong

lips down on hers, tasting her, and letting his love show in the way his lips moved and his tongue tangled with hers.

After a few seconds or a few minutes, they released each other, their faces flushed, their breathing fast.

He beamed down at her, "What are you—I mean how are you . . . ," he shook his head, trying to process her sudden apparition.

"I changed my flight, came a day early." She raised her eyebrows, "Good surprise?"

His jaw dropped, "Brilliant surprise!" His Irish accent was thicker when he was excited.

She bit her lip trying not to let out a little scream. Her time in California had been filled to the brim, so much to do at Mags' house in Berkeley, and her flat in the Marina, and her brief but intense secret return to the law on Camille's behalf, she hadn't allowed herself to think of Connor or their reunion.

Now that he was there holding her, kissing her, her happiness spilled over, making her want to jump in place or scream or attack him and hold onto him until her limbs went numb and tingly. She wanted nothing more than to be bound to him for days, weeks, months.

"Why didn't you tell me?" Connor scolded.

She raised her eyebrows. "Then it wouldn't be a surprise, would it?"

He ran his fingers through his hair, "I suppose not," he agreed.

Elizabeth bit her lip again. She'd come a day early because she'd hope to have peace at the cottage first. Hoped to collect herself before dealing with all the bustle and voices of others. Have a chance to process everything before life got in the way.

She hadn't been sure how Connor would fit into that equation. Perhaps she would've taken a few hours to herself and then walked up to the castle to surprise him then.

Or perhaps she would've taken the entire evening to herself and stayed the night at the cottage.

She would have probably taken a few hours and then walked up to the castle, unable to resist the pull of her husband sleeping a couple thousand feet away.

The truth seemed too complicated to explain. "Wait, what are you doing here?" She looked down again at his bare chest, jeans, and bare feet.

She noticed for the first time that part of his jeans were wet. "Oh no. Don't tell me the plumbing has gone haywire again! I thought they were supposed to finish the week I left for California?"

He let go of her completely, realizing all at once that he stood to get her wet as well. "That would be correct. They *were* supposed to finish nearly a month ago. The truth for the delay lies somewhere between us having an extended issue with the bathroom on the ground floor and the fact that the men aren't nearly as afraid of me as they are of you." He chuckled to himself.

She raised an eyebrow.

He stopped laughing. "They'll be finished by tomorrow, I promise."

"Uhuh, sure." The day she'd spent traveling had taken its toll, the words came out harsher than she'd intended.

A few years ago, when she'd first stepped foot in the cottage, she remembered having the same thought, that her words came out harsher than she had intended because she had been exhausted from traveling.

Her lips turned upwards at the memory. She softened, "I'll believe it when I see it, Bannon."

Connor could read the thoughts as they crossed her face. He had made the connection as well. His features transformed as he remembered her bursting into the cottage, holding a long umbrella, and demanding to know who he was and what exactly he thought he was doing crashing her much needed break from reality.

His energy changed, his brows knitted together as he gave her a more intense look. A look of longing and lust. "I remember having other thoughts that day," he said. Taking her in his arms again. "You were so . . . ravishing—"

"No, I wasn't! I was a mess and completely exhausted." She protested.

"Well I didn't notice," he fibbed.

Elizabeth rolled her eyes. "Uhuh, sure," she said, this time in a light and teasing tone.

"OK, I noticed a smidge, but I had other thoughts that

day that completely overtook any observations I might have had about your demeanor." He leaned in and kissed the nape of her neck, slowly tracing his lips up towards her jaw.

Her breath caught in her chest. Accepting his intention and remembering that her thoughts had dipped that way as well, if only for a moment. When presented with a glistening, naked Irishman as gorgeous as Connor Bannon, anyone's thoughts would lean in that direction, no matter how weary the body or how broken the soul.

And she had been broken then. They both had.

His lips left her skin for a moment, "You're ravishing," he growled. He moved his mouth back to her lips, taking her deliberately. He made no attempt to disguise his growing need for her. Each kiss was more unhinged than the last.

"Mmmm . . ." a moan escaped from her chest. How easy it was to lose herself in him, in his body, in their passion.

He broke away then, the heat and love burned in his eyes.

Elizabeth stared up into his beautiful face, allowing herself to feel everything he was trying to convey. And then his electric blue eyes burned deeper, wilder.

His voice was somewhere between a growl and a whisper, "Come 'ere, wife." He moved his hands down to her backside and kneaded her before moving them lower and picking her up so she was straddling him.

They'd been married for four years, but she always delighted in hearing the word "wife."

It had surprised her. She'd never been one to dream

about her wedding day. In fact, she'd never thought much about marriage in the first place.

Connor had changed all of that.

He flexed his hands, using his strength to crush her to him for several moments before he started walking towards the bedroom.

Elizabeth was on fire for her husband, but some remote thought kept trying to rise, trying to break through the fog of their undeniable need for each other. "Wait, wait, wait," she managed between kisses, "I need . . . to shower."

"No you don't, Luv."

She kissed him a few more times before managing to contradict him, "Yes, I do. I've been traveling for almost a day, I've been on a plane, I'm gross."

She kissed him one last time and jumped down, her wedge boots connected with the wooden floor with a thud.

"I don't care!" He tried to reach for her again.

She put her hands on her hips, "I do!"

They looked at each other for a moment, both stubborn in their resolve.

He put his hands on his hips, trying to convince her with his eyes.

Elizabeth stood anchored to the spot.

Connor relented with a quick shake of his head, "Jaysus woman! What you do to me." His blue eyes had turned electric with a raw emotion she understood all too well. His jaw was clenched, "Fine, then. Go shower."

Elizabeth tried to hide her amusement, "That's exactly what I intend on doing." She patted his bare chest lightly in consolation and made her way to the bathroom.

She looked back, intending to blow him a kiss, just as he declared, "It's lucky that I made that shower big enough for two, because I'm joining you."

She could tell from the expression on his face and the tenor of his voice that there was no arguing with him, which suited her just fine. The corners of her lips turned up slightly, she bit her lip trying to suppress a smile.

He flashed her a wicked grin, taking pleasure in his wife's attempt at hiding her delight, before noticing something else. "Did you come home from America with nothin' but the clothes on your back, Luv? Or is the luggage coming later?"

"Ahhh, I forgot my bags by the car."

He nodded, stepping into dutiful husband mode. He gave her a quick salute, calling out behind him, "You go ahead and start without me, I'll be with you in just a moment, Miss Lara."

She turned on the shower and quickly undressed. The letter that had been in the back pocket of her jeans fell to the floor. She bent down to pick it up, holding the small ivory envelope in her hands, running her fingers across the lettering as she had done several times over the last week.

It was a great honor, but she wasn't sure it was one she wanted.

Was she home in Ireland for good? Or would the call of

the offer be enough to take her away again?

She heard the door of the cottage open and close. Quickly, she placed the letter back in her jeans and stepped into the shower, letting the drops of water wash away the exhaustion of travel, and the complicated choices of life.

Connor stepped into the bathroom just then, undressing in a flash. He took his wife in his arms, pressing their flesh together. With a kiss to her nose and in his heaviest Irish accent, "Miss Lara," he began, his words an enticing caress, "welcome *home* to Ireland."

The Dingle Daily News
"Lord Bannon and Lady Lara Set to Settle in Ireland
Permanently"
By Reuben Hurley

After four years of travelling the globe, with stints in several countries including France and England, Lord Connor Bannon and Lady Elizabeth Lara are set to move into their newly renovated 4,000 square meter residence at Castle Bannon.

The town is much abuzz about what having nobility, albeit honorary nobility as their titles are in fact merely honorary (Ireland royalty has been absent from our country for hundreds of years), back in permanent residence might mean for Dingle.

It's been more than thirty years since Lord Bannon's father, Lord Keanan Grail, and his wife, Lady Madison Grail, inhabited the Castle on a permanent basis. Lord Bannon himself has lived on and off at the Castle for a number of years, but never for more than a few months at a time.

His time in Dingle decreased even further after the passing of his mother, Rhiannon Bannon, seven years ago.

After falling hard and fast for American attorney, Elizabeth Lara, Lord Bannon's travel schedule intensified. Many hoped the couple would settle in Dingle after they were married, but the Lord and Lady have continued their globetrotting lifestyle throughout their four-year marriage.

In the past, the Lord and Lady of the Castle would often host events for the community and sponsor numerous events in the town. Townspeople are excited to see what the new couple will do to establish their legacy.

Local resident and pub owner, Fitz O'Leary remarked, "It is very exciting indeed. To have a lord and lady back at the Castle. You know they're very good people and it's been grand when they've been at home here in Ireland, but it will be different, you know, now that they're living here year-round. I'm personally very excited to see what they will do, especially our new Lady Lara who has proved herself to be a true force."

When asked how he thought that Lady Lara's being American would affect her ability to find her footing in Irish society, Mr. O'Leary said, "Oh I think she'll do well. Some might find her wonderful candour off-putting, but I think her American zeal will reinvigorate this town."

Whatever their influence might be over the town, sources say they've already put their stamp on Castle Bannon. It was established in the 17th Century and has been renovated multiple times by many generations. Lord Bannon renovated it himself after his father died, but the couple have once again decided to remodel the Castle to take into account their new life and to properly incorporate Lady Lara's style.

Sources say the new renovation is stunning and includes twelve bedrooms, three studies, a formal sitting room, dining room, great lounge, library, a conservatory, a cinema, and a full wine cellar, among other delights. The Castle and grounds sit on more than 400 acres and encapsulate all the property surrounding Lough Rhiannon, which includes a former gate lodge, now a cottage, a large garage and warehouse, as well as a guardhouse.

The town of Dingle eagerly awaits the couple's next move. All eyes will be on them as they attend their first public event since announcing their permanent residence at this week's Summer Festival.

In Related News:

Rock star Kilian O'Grady, best friend of Lord Bannon, and frequent collaborator of Lady Lara, is to perform at iconic Croke Park stadium at summer's end. Tickets go on sale on June 30th.

2

THE IRISH CASTLE

The large door closed behind them.

Elizabeth registered the silence. "Where is everyone?"

Connor set her bags down briefly to answer. "Declan left last week for his annual combat and medical training refresher course."

Elizabeth shook her head in disbelief. "He's like sixty something, when do you think he'll stop going to training?"

Connor made a tut-tut, "Now if he were a woman, would you still think he should stop because of his age?"

Elizabeth was properly humbled. "No, you're right. I'm glad he still does it. It's clearly part of what he needs to feel himself."

Connor beamed. "I love being right."

Elizabeth swatted his arm affectionately. "Shouldn't he be back by now?"

"Oh, that. I gave him a couple of weeks after his training as well. Mona hasn't been in for a week either since I wasn't expecting you until tomorrow. Aidan or Henry or someone might be at the guardhouse, I don't know. And the workmen have all gone of course."

"And is there much left to do?" She held her breath. Hoping the renovations were finally over. She couldn't deal with anymore construction noise.

Connor smiled triumphantly, "Tomorrow they'll just pop in to put in the new tap in the bathroom by the kitchen, then that's us completely done with the house . . . unless of course we ever decide to refresh the cellar which hasn't been touched except for the update to the electrical I did a few years ago." He smiled, teasing her.

Elizabeth's eyes grew wide as she shook her head furiously, "Please, no. We're done." She held up her hands.

"Then, after tomorrow, we're done with our house!" he agreed.

Elizabeth exhaled all at once. A sense of deep relief hit her, until his last word registered. "You mean *Castle*," she corrected.

"Yeah, house, castle . . . same difference," he called behind him as he ran her bags up the stairs to their master bedroom on the second floor.

"Not the same!" she yelled.

He ignored her, "So it's just you and me!"

Elizabeth relaxed. She looked around at her new home and relished in the peace of it. The silence.

The sitting room to the left of the foyer had been transformed. Bookshelves continued to define the space, but an updated chandelier and newly installed recessed lighting illuminated ivory couches and pale blue walls.

Elizabeth stood there for a moment, trying to take it all in. Trying to imagine what their lives would be like if they lived out their years together in this beautiful place.

Connor reappeared in a flash. "All right then, bags in the bedroom, check. Mind-blowing reunion with wife, check. What would you like to do now? Unpack? Or are you hungry?" His excitement could not be contained.

"Why Mr. Bannon? Did you miss me?"

His smile was wide, his eyes full of mischief and emotion. "Very much." He took her in his arms again, this time for a bear hug. The kind of hug which could make your soul feel good.

Elizabeth breathed him in. Relaxed into his strong arms. Wherever they ended up living out their years, Elizabeth knew that Connor's arms would always be home. The rest was just background noise. Window dressing.

He released her, but kept her hand. "I am at your disposal m'lady."

Just then a soft growling noise filled the massive foyer. They both looked down. It was Elizabeth's stomach.

Connor chuckled, "Well that answers that. What do you think, I can cook, or we can order in?"

Without another word they walked through the dining room and into the kitchen to take stock of their options. With Declan and Mona gone, the contents of the fridge, or lack thereof, resembled that of a helpless college student instead of a forty-something lord of a castle.

Elizabeth glanced at her husband and raised one eyebrow. "Been ordering out a lot?"

Connor just shrugged and looked guilty. "What? I've been busy! I just eat out when Declan's not here."

Elizabeth's stomach growled again, "Let's order pizza."

He flashed her a confident grin, "Now that I can do." He disappeared to make the call.

Elizabeth grabbed two wine glasses and opened a bottle from the massive wine fridge they'd had installed in their new kitchen.

Connor was back at her side by the time she'd finished pouring. "All right, that's that. Large pepperoni extra sauce."

She went to sit at the table. "Perfect. Now, what have I missed? What's happening in our fair Dingle?"

Connor regaled her with tales of the people and places that made up their beautiful community. Which always seemed to include a healthy dose of scandal and intrigue.

"Barnaby O'Hanlon has just hired his nephew Alfie to be the new paper photog and reporter, even though he has the attention span of a bag of spuds, poor bloke. The decision raised a few eyebrows and turned a few heads."

Elizabeth tilted her head, watching as her husband spoke animatedly about the town.

"Joe Hill's pet pig Ruthie got out again, it took him half a day to catch her, but not before she'd had herself a proper stroll through the whole town."

Elizabeth shook her head. "Poor Ruthie, Joe's ex-wife, not the pig! I still can't believe he named his pig after her."

"Oh, she's got herself a pet peacock and gotten her revenge, finally."

Elizabeth took a sip of her wine, "Let me guess. She named him Joe."

Connor laughed. "She did indeed."

She listened eagerly as he continued to update her on what she'd missed.

He leaned forward. "And I spoke to Kil yesterday. We had a good catch up."

"Yeah? How is our favorite rock star doing?"

"He's grand! Still livin' the high life and walking around like he's in a dream. He can't believe what happened this last year."

It had been a whirlwind. Seeing their friend finally succeed in the music industry, had been thrilling to watch.

Connor took a sip of his wine, "He says he has a new song for you to listen to."

"Like a full song or just an idea that he wants to work on?"

Connor shook his head, "I don't know."

Elizabeth pursed her lips. "Well did he say he wanted lyrics for it . . .?"

He shrugged, helplessly. "I don't know. He just mentioned that he had a new song. He's coming into town for the music festival tomorrow night, going to play a surprise set, I think."

Elizabeth sat forward, "He's coming to Dingle tomorrow? Is Dree with him?"

"Yes, and actually they're in town today, I think. He mentioned something about maybe dropping by."

Elizabeth considered Kilian and Dree for a moment. Kilian was Connor's best friend and Audre was Elizabeth's best friend. They'd met at Elizabeth and Connor's wedding four years ago and had hit it off.

She and Connor had both thought that they would get together, but for whatever reason they hadn't. They had seen each other often through their best friends over the years, but their story hadn't really begun until Audre accidentally overheard one of Kilian's songs.

Elizabeth had been setting it to lyrics and blasting it throughout her French château in Méré when Audre had flown in from London for a surprise visit.

There was something about that song that struck a chord with Audre and the next thing any of them knew she was quitting her digital curator museum job and offering to be Kilian's manager.

It had been one year since she had taken over his career and made him famous.

She'd had no real experience in the music business, but she was business savvy and she had a keen understanding of the digital world. When Elizabeth had asked her what had compelled her to quit her job and start a brand-new career, Audre told her that when she'd heard Kilian's song she just knew she could make him a star.

"I don't know how to explain it Babes, I just knew. And I was getting bored with the job at the museum. It had just stopped being exciting. I made the change. Not really all that surprising for me is it?"

Elizabeth had thought for a moment, her friend had always been wonderfully unique and multi-talented. She had always marched to the beat of her own drum. "No, you're right I guess it makes sense that you would switch gears and hop into something else, as crazy as it might seem to the outside world."

Within a month of that conversation, Audre had gotten one of Kilian's YouTube videos to go viral. Another month after that she cracked radio stations in the UK.

It had been six months since they'd cracked the American market.

And for all that success, intelligence, and talent between them, it had become glaringly obvious to both Elizabeth and

Connor that Kilian was desperately, madly, and deeply in love, with Audre.

She on the other hand, seemed to be completely clueless.

At least that's how it appeared.

Elizabeth took another sip of her wine and shook her head in frustration, fighting the urge to drag them both into the castle and shake them until they came to their senses.

Connor shrugged and gave her a sympathetic smile. He shared her frustration.

"Besides the career stuff, how is he doing?" she asked.

"You mean the whole Audre and the new guy?"

She rolled her eyes, "You know his name."

"Fine. Yes, I meant *Julian*." He said it like that was his name, allegedly.

"I mean we're guys, we didn't actually talk about it. But for my money he's having a rough time with it, just trying to focus on the music, I suspect."

Three months ago, Audre had met Julian Brooks, a business manager for a top music label, at a benefit concert and they had been a couple ever since.

They'd met him a couple of times now. Elizabeth thought he was nice enough, but perhaps too on the dull side for her vibrant friend.

She prodded her husband, "What's wrong with Julian?"

"Nothin' . . . I'm sure he's a perfectly fine lad. But you know, *he's English*."

Elizabeth laughed. "So is she!"

"Yeah, but he's *really* English." Connor scrunched up his nose.

"Seriously? For crying out loud you went to Cambridge." She gave him a look that said, *really? really?*

"All right, all right. It's not that he's English, it's just that he doesn't strike me as the type of bloke that could keep Audre's interest for long at all. It's not that he's English," Connor considered, "it's that he seems as fun as an uptight English accountant. And Kilian is my best mate, I'm not supposed to like the guy who's involved with the woman of my best mate's dreams."

Elizabeth's ears perked up, "Has he actually told you that he is into her?" she almost squealed.

"No, the last time I saw him I really tried to get it out of him. I don't know what he is so afraid of or what he's waitin' for."

Connor shook his head. "You'd think becoming a rock star would give him more confidence, but he's still the same old Kil, humble and never assuming or believing that he can get the girl."

That part of Kilian's personality had always baffled Elizabeth. It was part of what made Kilian, *Kilian*. But it had never added up in her mind. "Why is that do you think?"

Connor considered. "I don't know. He was a bit on the heavy side growing up." He took another sip of his wine, "I think that stuff from our childhood stays with us."

They sat in silence, both lost in their own thoughts. Lost in the stuff from their childhoods that stayed with them.

The room had grown heavy with the past.

Elizabeth refocused her thoughts on their friend. Remembering the obvious, the bit that didn't add up. "Yeah, but . . . I mean no offense my love, but . . . your best friend is beautiful, and from what I can tell he's been that way for a while now." She admitted with a laugh.

Connor raised an eyebrow.

"What? Kilian *is* gorgeous!"

He jutted out his lower lip, a pathetic attempt to look sulky, jealous.

She quickly added, "But no one is as beautiful as you, husband."

He rewarded her with a quick grin and a wink. "That's better," he said with all of his swagger. "What about Audre? Do you think he has a chance there, because it seems to me—"

He was interrupted by the doorbell.

They exchanged guilty looks, like they'd been caught talking about someone who had overheard everything they'd just said.

Suspecting that the man of the hour was now, in fact, standing outside their house, they made their way to the foyer.

Connor opened the door. Standing there in all his glory

was Kilian O'Grady. All six foot two of him. The mop of curly brown hair nearly reached his chocolate eyes.

He wore a sleek black leather jacket and expensive looking jeans, otherwise he was the same old Kil.

"Awww there he is! Dingle's very own rock star in the flesh." Connor grabbed him by the shoulders and brought him in for a hearty hug.

Kilian's eyes fell on Elizabeth next, "Liz! What happened? I thought you weren't coming in until tomorrow?" He scooped her up into a bear hug, lifting her off the ground. "Ahhh it's grand to see ya! How are you then, how was California? Did you get the track I sent you last week?"

He didn't wait for her to answer his barrage of questions, he just swung her around and squeezed her until she couldn't breathe. She batted his biceps in an attempt to get him to put her down.

Elizabeth had just found firm ground and was regaining her breath when someone behind them cleared their throat.

Kilian wasn't alone.

3
VISITORS

A woman's voice came from behind Kilian near the door. "Gosh he's never that excited to see me! What's your secret, Babes?" She sounded like Mel B from the Spice Girls.

Elizabeth looked around Kilian and found her own best friend, Audre Bright standing there in a sleek olive green dress that set off her dark glowing skin, blue eyes, and perfect curves.

Going into the music business had suited Audre, perhaps more so than her former life as a digital curator at the Natural History Museum.

"Well it might have to do with the fact that he doesn't spend every day with me." Elizabeth flashed her friend a welcome smile before wrapping her in a bear hug that threatened to dishevel Audre's uncharacteristically smooth locks.

"Come in, come in!" Connor beckoned.

The foursome made their way through the foyer and into the sitting room.

"Oh wow, you have been busy," Audre said as she took in the room. "It's so much lighter."

The dark brown tufted couches and dark paneling which Audre had remembered from previous visits, had been part of Connor's renovation. The castle had been beautiful then, but still carried the heaviness of Connor's past.

The plush cream couches and the pale blue walls which greeted them all now, were part of the latest revamp. They'd managed to maintain the historical integrity of the room while making it feel more like a home.

Elizabeth smiled. "Thanks, yeah we think we're basically done. Which is a relief."

"I'm afraid we have nothing to offer you," Connor began, "we ordered a pizza, but I think now I'll go and order a second, does that sound OK to everyone?"

Audre nodded, "Sure."

"Sounds good," Kilian agreed. "I'll come with you."

The men left the room to go order the food, leaving Audre and Elizabeth to catch up.

Elizabeth took Audre's hand and pulled her quickly to the biggest of the couches facing the window. There was no telling when Kilian and Connor would return, and she needed some answers.

About one topic in particular, but she suspected she would have to lead up to that.

There was no time to waste. "All right Dree, tell me everything. How's the tour? How has everything changed since you hit the American charts? Tell me about Julian, how's that going?" She spoke so quickly she found she was out of breath.

Audre held up her hands in mock defense. "OK, *wow*, what's gotten into you, Liz? Two seconds in the door and you've my head spinning with questions!"

Elizabeth rolled her eyes. "Dramatic much? It was literally three questions."

"Still! At the rate you're speaking you're going to drive me barmy." Audre pretended to be annoyed.

"Noted," Elizabeth shook her head. "Now, tell me everything."

Audre took a deep breath, giving up the pretense of annoyance and smiled at her friend. She looked up and thought about where to start, and then her eyes lit up, "OK, well the tour is going great. I think I'm going to revolutionize the music industry with my new touring model."

"What do you mean?"

"You know, how we don't have one tour bus and we don't have a set of musicians who travel with us, or a bunch of gear?"

Elizabeth nodded.

"We just setup the tour dates in advance, hire local musicians or if there is already a band Kilian can easily fit into, then we hire them . . . they learn the music before we get there and we have the use of their gear or again hire gear locally—except for Kilian's guitars of course—you'll never separate him from those, thanks to you and Connor. I think they're his most favorite things in the entire world."

Elizabeth and Connor had gifted him a Fender American Original '50s Stratocaster and a Brian May Red Special two years back. He'd been left speechless.

It had been hands down one of the best ways either of them had ever spent their money.

"Anyway, so we travel light, it's all very modular and flexible. But it's all Kilian and it's his music and we're able to really harness social media. He's really gotten known for putting on last-minute secret shows . . . you know, it's just a whole new model."

Elizabeth considered, "It's a lighter, independent, 21st-century rock star tour."

Audre slapped Elizabeth's leg, "Exactly! That's it. I don't know if it will work forever, but it's working great for us now and probably for the next few years."

"Wait," Elizabeth began, "it's just you and Kilian on the road the entire time? You don't have anyone else? PAs, assistants, people handling gear, nothing like that?"

"Well, mostly. But I do hire an assistant, a sound technician, and a couple of guys for road crew—but again that's location dependent. They are all freelance, and they're with us for the dates we've got scheduled in say New England, or the West Coast, or like the small team we've hired for the UK and Ireland."

Audre took a breath. "I've got a fantastic network of people to tap into—all independent for whatever reason. They welcome the freelance work." She paused, staring off for a moment, "And I have my full-time PA, Angela, she does a lot of the heavy lifting, but she doesn't leave London or tour with us. Well—except she'll come out to help with Croke Park, of course, because bloody hell—it's a beast."

"Right . . . wow, Dree, that's quite a set up. Leave it to you to throw the regular model out the window and come up with something completely different."

Audre beamed. "I love getting praise," she sighed. "I mean I know how brilliant I am, but I love to hear it from other people—especially other brilliant people—and I'm not afraid to admit it!" She tossed her hair over her shoulder in a dramatic gesture, clearly hamming it up.

Elizabeth laughed. "Oh Dree, you haven't changed a bit in all these years."

"And thank God for that!" Audre finished.

For a moment Elizabeth forgot what she had been thinking and then she remembered the tenor of her thoughts, "So it's just you and Kilian mostly?" she asked carefully.

Audre's phone buzzed from somewhere inside her bag. For some reason, she pretended not to know where it was and made a show of trying to find it.

But Elizabeth would not be deterred. "Alone together?"

"Yes, mostly," Audre answered absently.

"And you guys still . . . get along?"

"Of course!"

It was difficult for Elizabeth to get any kind of read on her while she was averting her gaze.

"So you're friends?" Elizabeth continued.

Audre finally extracted her phone from her bag. She looked up briefly, "The best!"

"*Just* friends?" Elizabeth ventured, hoping not to scare her off.

She started texting someone back. "What do you mean?"

"You know what I mean. Dree, Kilian is such a good guy —not to mention gorgeous in case you haven't noticed."

Audre looked up, finally setting her phone down in her lap. "Well of course I've noticed. Those eyes and those curls? He's a heartthrob—drives the fans mad. And on top of that, he's super humble about it, which drives them even more mad. It's like he has no idea how good looking he is." She shook her head in disbelief.

"You should see how they throw themselves at him. It's mental." Her phone buzzed again. "Sorry, I know I'm being an arse, I just need to send this text to confirm something for Croke Park," she paused, before saying the rest under her breath, ". . . we've taken a big gamble, we'd better sell enough tickets. God, I hope we don't lose our shirts!"

Elizabeth stared at her friend, puzzled by what she'd just said. She tucked it away for later.

She shook her head, trying to refocus on Kilian. Audre had managed to agree with her and completely side-step her question at the same time.

She tried again. "And that doesn't bother you, the women throwing themselves at him?"

"No," Audre frowned, "Why would it? It's all great for his career and par for the course. And it's not like he's had any true nutters being aggressive or anything. Although, there was one woman—completely harmless, just wanted to connect with something I suspect—she followed him to every show we did on the Eastern Seaboard. That was *twenty* shows, Liz!"

Elizabeth flashed back to when an obsessed admirer of Connor's had once taken things too far. If you could call drugging and kidnapping Elizabeth going too far. She shook her head free of the memory and considered whether to continue with this line of questioning or to find another opportunity in the next couple of days. Her friend didn't appear to be budging on the subject.

She knew Audre well, and there was something about the whole situation that irked her. Her gut was telling her there was more to the story.

Her friend was either keeping something from Elizabeth

or flat out refusing to admit something to *herself*. Dree was being too coy, too adept at side-stepping.

The Audre she knew and loved would have just bluntly stated that there was nothing between them, that she didn't care for him in that way, and be done with it.

She decided on a new tactic, "So how's Julian? Everything going well?"

"Sure, I guess so," Audre answered, disinterested. "We see each other . . . *enough*. It's fine."

"*Just* fine?" Elizabeth prodded, confused by how vague her best friend was being.

Audre looked up, her eyebrows furrowed together. "Babes, you know I've never been one for girl talk and this is starting to sound a lot like girl talk. What's going on?" she asked defensively.

Elizabeth leaned back into the couch. "Since when?! You love all the salacious details and want to know everything." She eyed her friend suspiciously, but tried to sound innocent, "I'm just taking an interest in my best friend and her life is all. Is that so bad? And what's wrong with girl talk anyway? What *is* girl talk? Is it just women sharing their thoughts, and their lives, and their hopes and fears?"

Audre opened her mouth to respond and then stopped. "I guess there's nothing wrong with girl talk is there? We've just been conditioned to think that it's somehow daft." She considered for a second and then with a wink and a smile, "And I do love the salacious details," she admitted. "Thanks for keeping me grounded, Babes. I don't know what I was thinking!"

Uhuh. It all seemed like a distraction. A deft maneuver, but her thoughts were interrupted by the sound of footsteps which echoed from somewhere nearby. Big booming voices, thick with delicious Irish accents grew louder as the men reentered the room.

Their reappearance put a stop to all questions on the subject of Audre's interest, or non-interest, in Kilian. Elizabeth sighed, careful not to show her disappointment. Only Connor noticed.

He acted quickly, throwing himself completely into entertaining mode, telling an old Irish joke while pouring the wine.

And so the foursome sat together in the front room of the castle. They opened the curtains so the purple night with its bright stars could shine through and mix with the golden light of the chandelier overhead.

By the time the pizza had arrived, Elizabeth had convinced Audre to change out of her beautiful, but restrictive olive green dress and into a pair of comfortable leggings.

"You can pick up the dress tomorrow, or we'll have it sent over, come on it's time to be comfortable, you're amongst friends," Elizabeth had insisted when Audre had protested. "I'm going to put on my PJs as well." And when that hadn't worked, "Do you really want to risk getting pizza sauce on your Hervé Léger dress?"

Audre began undressing immediately.

The magical combination of food, wine and friends worked to create a euphoric feeling felt by all.

Audre and Connor sat on the couch while Elizabeth and Kilian chose the floor. Elizabeth sat leaning against Connor's knees and Kilian sat close to Audre's legs.

"Which bit did you like best then?" Connor asked Kilian.

Kilian had just taken a mouthful of pizza, "Of America?"

Connor nodded.

"Definitely California," he answered, mouth still full, "New York was pretty great as well."

Red pizza sauce had found its way to the corner of Kilian's mouth.

Without a second thought Audre leaned over and removed the sauce with her thumb in an intimate gesture that had Elizabeth and Connor exchanging meaningful looks.

Kilian smiled up at her, his curls falling across his face. Without the mouthful of pizza, he was every bit the model. His eyes turned warm as he gazed into Audre's face.

Audre returned his smile and his warmth. They held each other's gaze for a few seconds, seeming to forget the friends sitting next to them.

The intensity and emotion of the moment was palpable.

Connor took Elizabeth's hand and squeezed.

It was Audre who broke the spell. With a shake of her head, she cleared her throat, and leaned back against the couch. "This is really good pizza," she took a bite, and made a show of examining her slice of pepperoni.

Kilian looked down, his shoulders drew together a degree.

"Hey mate, didn't you say something over the phone about a new song? Miss Lara over here was asking me about it." Connor nudged Elizabeth.

"Oh yeah, I was," Elizabeth took the cue, "but true to form my beautiful and intelligent husband could tell me absolutely nothing about it." She patted Connor's knee, trying to lighten the mood.

He perked up instantly, as he remembered the song. "Yeah, it's a little different for me. I was hoping you would take a look, I sent it to you last week but I'm sure you were really busy."

"Ahhh yes," Elizabeth remembered the strange business with Camille, it had taken up most of her last week in California, "I haven't checked my email in a couple of weeks, sorry."

"No worries, I figured it was something like that."

"Do you want to show it to me now? We could go to my office, assuming it's still there, I haven't had a chance to inspect the rest of the place yet."

Connor chuckled. "Oh, it's still there," he said before asking Audre about the tour.

Kilian helped Elizabeth up off the floor. Her foot had fallen asleep, she winced as the feeling returned. "I can't believe I'm almost forty," she joked with Kilian. "I miss the times when I'd be able to spring up like a cat."

She turned back towards the couch, "Think you guys can fend for yourselves for a while?" But Audre and Connor were already deep in conversation about marketing strategies.

Upstairs Elizabeth's office was still intact. She had chosen a large room off the library with big arched leaded windows. The walls were the same pale blue as the sitting room.

She'd installed warm lights in every corner and a simple, but elegant, glittering chandelier as the overhead light. Her large desk with dual monitors sat against the wall of windows.

As she approached the desk, she noticed the piles of messages and mail that must've come in while she was gone.

Mona's curly elegant handwriting adorned a small stack of papers from people who had called and left messages for her. She picked up a few, a request to host a charity dinner, and another to judge a writing contest, and something about joining a ladies' society.

She rifled through the remaining stack quickly, it appeared that many people wanted something from her.

She let the air out of her lungs all at once.

"Are you all right, Liz?"

Elizabeth sighed, "Yeah. I guess I forgot for a moment how much there would be to come back to."

Kilian gave her a sympathetic smile, "Are you sure you're not too busy to work on this with me?"

"Kil, please. Collaborating with you on a few songs is always fun. I love the creative stuff, you know that. It's nice to just be me and use my brain and have the thoughts I have. Does that make sense?"

"You mean instead of being what everyone else wants you to be? And falling into the trap of thinking the way you should think?"

Elizabeth nodded, "Exactly. It's like coming home to Ireland for good . . . means that I'm suddenly having to be this 'lady' again." She used air quotes when she said *lady*. "Like it was in the beginning, when we first started dating, but then we traveled so much and I think the people and the press just got used to us being this oddball couple who was always gone, but now that we're back at the castle for good . . . I dunno, you know?"

Kilian nodded. "Yes, I do. I'm loving my life right now, but I definitely feel the danger of losing myself because I'm playing this role, this image."

Elizabeth felt ridiculous. Kilian's life was evolving on a global scale, and it had happened quickly. He actually had to be what people wanted him to be—all Elizabeth had to contend with were the warm local townspeople and the Dingle Daily. The rags had mostly left them alone since they'd gotten married. "I know it's not even remotely the same thing. I can't even imagine how crazy this last year has been for you."

Kilian shook his head, "Liz, it is kind of the same thing.

You coming back for good, it's not just coming home, it's playing a role like I play the role of rock star."

His face changed. His eyes grew wide and his mouth went slack, "God! Can you believe it, Liz? *Rock star.*"

Elizabeth smiled, truly taking Kilian in for the first time that night. He'd had a dream, it had taken years, but he'd finally made it. She was so proud. "Yes, I can believe it, Kil."

Elizabeth's eyes welled up with tears. She threw her arms around him and squeezed. When she released him, she could see the emotion in his face.

Kilian wiped his eyes. "Why does this only happen around you, Liz? I don't get weepy with anyone else." He took a few deep breaths.

"I make no apologies for taking a moment to savor the good stuff of life, and I certainly don't apologize for helping to get you in touch with your emotions." She dabbed at her eyes. "If only I had that power over Audre," she said quietly under her breath.

He didn't hear.

The two friends composed themselves, before Kilian continued, "And anyway it *is* kind of the same thing, but the only difference is I actively pursued the role of rock star. You're this 'lady'," he copied her air quotes, "just because you fell in love and married Connor. You chose Connor, not a title."

Elizabeth considered that. It was true. "Yeah, and I mean

it's really just an *honorary* title here so why couldn't I just be myself?"

Kilian gave her another reassuring smile, "Exactly."

"Yeah," Elizabeth nodded, trying to convince herself.

"Yeah," Kilian repeated.

Both of their expressions faltered infinitesimally. Somehow, she was sure it would not be that simple.

Kilian had learned to read her face almost as well as Connor, "I think you'll find a way to write your own rules, Liz."

She bit her lip, "I hope you're right."

Elizabeth turned her attention to the matter at hand. "OK, let's hear this new song of yours."

They sat down at the desk while Elizabeth pulled up the email that contained the song.

The first few notes filled the room. It was an acoustic guitar playing a slow, sweet melody.

"It's a lullaby?" Elizabeth asked.

"Something like that."

"It's beautiful." She let the song take her away. It *was* beautiful, but it was also something else . . . *heartbreaking*.

"Thanks," he let the last few notes linger in the air before continuing, "I was hoping you could help me with lyrics."

She smiled at him, "I'd be honored. What do you have so far?"

Kilian took out a piece of paper from the back pocket of his jeans. It had only four lines on it.

Elizabeth read it.

"What do you think?"

"I think it's a great start." She looked up at him. "It's a love song?"

He nodded.

Elizabeth examined her friend's face, and it was in that moment that she knew who had inspired such a beautiful and heartbreaking song. She didn't need to prod him for information to figure out his feelings.

She only hoped that the real love story between Kilian and Audre would have a happier ending than the current direction of his new song.

The first few notes of his acoustic guitar filled the office as the song began again.

They listened to it once more in silence, allowing the story of the song to marinate.

"What about this?" Elizabeth turned to her computer screen, typing the words as they came.

4

THE HOUSE ON THE HILL

The following morning, Elizabeth settled into her office for the very first time. She had a slew of photographs to edit and she was looking forward to getting stuck in. Looking forward to losing herself in the pictures, the moments frozen in time, the living history of it all.

She connected the hard drive and waited for the pictures to transfer into Lightroom.

The messages she had briefly rifled through the previous night were still piled on the corner of her desk. None of them were really for her, they were for *Lady Lara*. Her talents, her interests, her opinions—none of it mattered.

It didn't matter who she was or what she wanted, any woman or person really could have fulfilled the role she was being asked to play.

Join this group and *chair this committee* and *host this dinner.*

How was she ever going to find her place when it seemed that all the community wanted from her was a Stepford wife, a prim and proper role model who could dress up, look pretty and honor everyone with her mere presence?

The people she knew and loved in Ireland were full of life and vigor and love and laughter, she wondered where this traditionally proper sensibility fit in with the life fabric of the town.

She doubted very much whether the attributes she'd reconnected with when she'd first come to Ireland, mainly speaking her mind, cursing, drinking grown men under the table, letting her hair down and dancing, and overall living an unapologetic live out loud lifestyle, was what anyone had in mind when they had invited the lady of the castle to sit on their committees and host their dinner parties.

Her computer binged.

The pictures finished loading, giving her the first look at the images she had taken in California over the last month.

Her screen was filled by the Golden Gate Bridge at dawn and sunset. By the meadows and lush trees in Golden Gate Park. The Marina, the skyscrapers, the fog.

The restaurants she loved on Clement Street and in the Mission. The quirky house in Berkeley where she'd grown up, where she'd had a life with Mags, surrounded by the wonderfully unconventional California community.

There wasn't a day that went by that she didn't miss her great-aunt. Didn't miss her vivacity, her badass nature, her thirst for knowledge and for life. She was Peter Pan and Yoda rolled into one amazing woman.

Elizabeth bit her lip, trying not to let that ache, that hole that Mags had left in her life, overtake her. She had dealt with her loss long ago, but there were days when small waves of grief took her by surprise, like painful echoes.

She continued to scroll through the photographs, marking some as favorites and adding them to a shortlist that she would edit later, while other images she fixed easily on the spot.

The last few photographs were of a huge white building set on a hill overlooking the bay. The pristine white columns and larger than life windows reflected the golden light.

The sun hit a sparkling blue pool while a slender woman with tanned skin, the same color as Mags, stood in a sleek red suit in front of the house. She was half looking back at the structure so only her silver bob of hair and a partial profile were visible. Camille hated candid photographs, Elizabeth had managed to sneak it in when she'd started to turn away.

Elizabeth examined the house where she'd had many happy memories, playing in that very pool and listening to the grown women talk. She remembered many afternoons where Camille and Mags had taken in the sunset on the patio with margaritas while Elizabeth played in the pool or did cartwheels on the lawn or took pictures of the butterflies and flowers which adorned the house.

She quickly started editing the photograph to bring out the red of Camille's suit, the green of the plants, and the beautiful California blue sky.

Her brain went into a relaxed flow state, where only the image in front of her mattered.

There was a quick knock at the door, which she hadn't even fully registered before Connor was in the room, standing by her desk.

She jumped.

"Good morning, Luv!" He bent down to give her a quick kiss.

She shook her head, trying to remember where she had left off in the image. "Morning," she answered absently.

He picked up on her tone immediately. "Is something wrong?"

She considered.

She loved her husband, loved spending time with him, loved *mostly* everything about him, but she had just started to feel at home in her new office. "No, nothing. I was just finding my stride doing these edits and it felt good."

Connor nodded, understanding dawned, "And then I burst in here, not even giving you the chance to answer the door and disrupted the flow."

Elizabeth looked up into his cool blue eyes and nodded.

"I'm sorry, would you like me to leave?"

Elizabeth sighed. "No," she leaned in and hugged his torso, "I like having you around."

He wrapped his arms around her and squeezed. "Glad to hear it because I missed you."

"I missed you too."

He sighed. "I don't like being apart for so long. I know you had to go and sort out the house, but I should have come with you."

"You have your business to run. The Rome auction house needed you."

"Yes, but I set up the houses in the first place because it was fun and it was what I wanted to do. Now I seem to resent anything that takes me away from you." He hugged her more fiercely.

"I'm glad you still like me after four years of marriage," she chuckled softly with her face pressed against his stomach.

He removed her arms from around his torso so he could tip her chin up and look into her eyes, "Like you? Lara, I love you more every day." He leaned down and kissed her softly, deliberately.

"Mmmm . . . I missed those lips." She broke away and looked up into his face. He still took her breath away.

He turned his attention to the screen, "What are we working on?"

"They're just snaps really, not sure anything would work in an exhibit. But that's not why I took any of these so . . ." she trailed off.

Connor let out a low whistle, "That's some house!" His

eyebrows drew together as he took a closer look. "Is that the Camille you've mentioned? The one who couldn't come to our wedding because you only gave Audre a month to plan it?"

"Yes."

"And she was a friend of Mags?"

Elizabeth nodded, "A lifelong friend. Their parents were very close, so they basically grew up together, even though Camille is twelve years younger than Mags."

"Do you know her well?"

"Fairly well." She thought about their relationship, and then qualified her previous statement, "As well as anyone can really know Camille, but I'd say she's family."

She played with the contrast of the photo as she explained, "I spent a lot of time there, at her house, when I was a kid. Less so as a teenager and then more regularly as an adult. We would all go to lunch, she kept tabs on me as my career progressed, you know kind of like an urban auntie."

She finished tweaking the photograph and looked back at her husband. "We weren't as close as Mags and me, but it was good to see her. I guess it felt like having a little bit of Mags back, you know? Camille is just as fierce and just as much of a character as Mags was." Elizabeth couldn't help but smile at the memory of the two women and the effect they'd had on her life.

"Why wasn't a month enough time to make it to our wedding again?"

Elizabeth sighed, remembering her disappointment, "Camille . . . works a lot."

Connor was still examining the picture closely, "Didn't you say you gave her a hand with something while you were away?"

"Yup."

Connor's voice changed, he was hesitant, "Did you have to wade back into the law? What did you have to do?" He knew what havoc even the slightest exposure to the law could wreak on her personality.

Elizabeth bit her lip, she technically wasn't allowed to tell him what she'd done, "Not exactly, although she is one of the only people left on the planet who I would wade back into the fray for, but no . . . it was more . . . I represented her in some negotiations. Helped her navigate something to do with her business."

Connor's jaw dropped suddenly, recognition dawned on his face, "Wait . . . is your Camille, Camille *Hennings*?" His voice crescendoed in disbelief.

"Yes," Elizabeth answered simply.

"Your urban auntie is Camille Cortez Fairhurst Hennings? Of Cortez Holdings, the self-made billionaire?" His voice had made its way into another octave.

Elizabeth nodded, surprised by his reaction.

"Well feck me!" His eyes grew wide.

She watched as his face turned red. "You OK? I kind of thought you knew . . . I mean I've talked about her a fair bit over the years."

"Yes, I'm just a little speechless. You weren't kidding about her being fierce, she's known for being a real—" Connor stopped himself.

Elizabeth's eyes narrowed and her eyebrows scrunched together, "Finish that sentence, I dare you." She could imagine what he was about to say. It had been said many times about Camille over the years.

She stared him down.

He put up his hands and shifted his weight backwards.

The blood rose to Elizabeth's face, "She's eighty-two and she's been the head of her own company since she was in her twenties. You try making it in a man's world for sixty years by being the nice girl and not ruffling any feathers."

Connor was appropriately contrite, "You're right, Luv. I'm sorry."

But Elizabeth was still seeing red, she couldn't stand it when men labeled strong women and cast them in a negative light. Watching her own, intelligent, educated, self-aware husband nearly fall into the trap of labeling a strong woman close to her was unnerving.

She took a few deep breaths before continuing, "I think the 'B' word you're looking for is *badass*."

Connor nodded, "That's exactly the word I was thinking of," he said much too innocently.

Elizabeth didn't move.

He jutted his lip out and made a face that was both silly and contrite. "Too right. I'm a bad, bad man."

Elizabeth softened, "You're not bad," she let the beginnings of a smile show, "you just need a little more training is all."

"Is that right? I thought after four years I'd attained the rank of appropriately house-trained," he joked.

Elizabeth bit her lip, trying not to laugh, "It seems we still have some work to do."

"Seriously though, Luv, I'm sorry. You know I love strong women. I mean look at you, you're the strongest woman I've ever met and you are spec-ta-cular."

He looked down at his feet, before bringing her into his arms, "*You* never fail at anything."

He kissed the top of her head, "I'm sorry I was a git," he whispered into her hair.

"Apology accepted." Her words were muffled, but he understood.

He kissed her lightly once more and left the room.

Connor was good at making her feel better.

Still smiling, Elizabeth refocused her attention on the screen and moved on to the next picture. It was of Camille's kitchen which was fully stocked with a beautiful and equally delicious lemon cake and decadent chocolate chip cookies. Cam always hired the best chefs.

She'd just about settled in again, blissfully surrendering

to the process of making the image the best it could possibly be, when there was a tap at the door. She waited, half hoping that the person would go away.

She wasn't so lucky.

Another knock came, now louder than the first. Elizabeth begrudgingly left her desk and crossed the room to open the door.

Mona Porter was the pinnacle of cute. Her short, plump, sixty-something figure was made even more delightful by the light blue dress she wore. Her hair was slightly more gray than when Elizabeth had first met her, but she was essentially the same.

She held a phone, her hand over the receiver. When Mona registered Elizabeth's face she smiled and temporarily forgot the purpose of her visit, instead bringing Elizabeth into a bone-crushing hug, a Mona hug.

Elizabeth returned her strength, over the years she had learned how to get the most out of a Mona hug . . . also how to survive them.

"Oh dear me! I've forgotten!" She placed her hand over the receiver once again, and lowered her voice, "Lara, how are you? Don't answer that, we'll catch up later," she waved the hand covering the microphone and then quickly replaced it again. "There's a lady on the phone for you."

She lowered her voice another degree, and changed her tone to one of conspiracy, or reverence, Elizabeth couldn't tell. "She's from the Dingle Ladies Society," Mona smiled excitedly. "She'd like to talk to you about becoming a member and hostin' a to do."

The name rang some bell, but she asked anyway. "What's the . . . *Dingle Ladies Society*?" She tilted her head wanting to hear Mona's take.

"Oh!" She jumped in place, excited to share. "They are a revered group of women in the community who have a high social standing and are very well respected," she nodded sagely. "It's a great honor to be invited."

"Are you a member, Mona?"

Mona turned bright red, "Well no . . . you see," she cleared her throat, "I'm not exactly the sort of woman they're lookin' for. . . ." She looked down, "I mean I did try once, but it wasn't to be . . ." she trailed off and looked embarrassed.

Elizabeth instantly disliked the society. Any association that would refuse the delightful woman standing in front of her should be disbanded. Over the years, Mona had become family, and Elizabeth was fiercely protective of family.

She took the phone from Mona, kissed her cheek, and walked down the hall to the sitting room off the library. She closed the door behind her, turned the TV on, and quickly put it on mute.

If she had to listen to someone go on about dinner parties and expectations, she would need something to preoccupy her brain or she would tune out completely. She didn't bother changing the channel, the American cable news channel they paid for would do.

She sat down on the couch, and held the phone to her chest, making sure to cover the microphone. She took a deep breath and tried to smile before placing the phone to her ear.

"Yes, hello this is Elizabeth Lara, I'm so sorry to have kept you waiting," she began.

A woman on the other end cleared her throat, "Yes, Lady Bannon, my name is—"

Elizabeth closed her eyes and shook her head. *Not this again.* "Excuse me, I'm going to have to stop you right there. My name is Lady Lara, as you well know, I did not change my name." Elizabeth had spent the better part of a year fighting the local media and getting everyone to acknowledge her name.

It had shocked her, how many people had felt entitled to completely disregard her wishes. She'd been made to declare her name again and again. It was like no one was *listening.* She was born Elizabeth Lara and she would die Elizabeth Lara. That choice had no bearing on how much she loved Connor or how much she loved being his wife. He had never been bothered by her choice, she could never understand why it appeared that the entire world did.

"Yes, well. . . ." The woman's Irish accent was more haughty than Elizabeth was used to, it seemed to come unhinged a degree.

"Yes," the woman's voice was strained, but she continued, "my apologies. Lady Lara, my name is Rose Faith Byrnes and

I'm with the Dingle Ladies Society. I'm calling to formally invite you to join our organization."

"Thank you, that's very kind. I—"

Rose Faith Byrnes cut her off, all her dignity restored, "We are a group of highly respected women in the town, who oversee the moral fabric, the very standards of our community, and provide aid to worthy causes. As you have taken up permanent residence at Castle Bannon, we expect that you will also take your place within the community and join us."

Elizabeth considered. Whenever someone mentioned, "moral fabric," or "community standards," her eyes tended to glaze over. It all just sounded like people trying to control people.

"Would you mind telling me more about your organization?" She kept her tone light and sweet.

Rose Faith answered in the same tone, "Certainly. What would you like to know?"

Elizabeth took her time and then hit her with a barrage, "How many women are part of the society? How often do you meet? How do you determine who receives an invitation?"

Rose took each question in turn, "There are five of us in the governing committee and we meet for tea once a week to discuss our plans and the direction of the society. There are approximately thirty women in the larger organization. A woman may be invited to join if she has proved herself a strong leader, or set herself apart in some other way, and is, *of course*, from an appropriate family."

Hmmm . . . Elizabeth's skin crawled at the "appropriate family" part. In other words, they were a group of stuffy women who liked to exclude others and bring their judgment down on all of womankind.

Still she doubted very much whether she wanted to start her time in Dingle by upsetting these women, and so she held on to her sweet voice, "And what is the purpose of your society?"

"Purpose?" Rose faltered.

"Yes, purpose. As in what do your members gain from being a part of your organization and what is the benefit to the community?" Elizabeth clarified.

Rose hesitated. She cleared her throat, "Members who are *fortunate enough to join our ranks*," she said pointedly, before her voice grew more strained, "gain the benefit of the guidance and wisdom of our more mature members, they find solidarity within the society."

Elizabeth correctly surmised that Rose Faith Byrnes was not accustomed to being questioned.

She continued, "The community benefits from our annual Spring Ball fundraiser along with our flower planting program, which aims to beautify the green spaces in and around town . . ."

Rose continued to prattle on about the supposed benefits of the society, but Elizabeth tuned out. She stood up and walked to the window, the phone still to her ear.

She watched as the swing under the ancient Oak tree

across the lawn started to move with the breeze. She watched as Mona tended to the flowers she'd planted off the patio.

It was a beautiful day and she suddenly wanted to be out in it.

She paced around the small sitting room, impatiently waiting for the woman to stop talking.

Elizabeth was just about to interrupt Rose when she turned her body in the direction of the TV and caught something out of the corner of her eye.

A white building, a shimmering pool.

She turned her complete attention to the TV, where a familiar sight filled the screen.

Her stomach plunged to her feet. "I'm sorry," she managed breathless. "I'm going to have to call you back." Elizabeth didn't wait for the woman to stop talking or for her to process that Elizabeth was about to hang up on her. She hit the off button and tossed the phone onto the couch.

She walked to the TV, taking in the house she had known well all her life. The sparkling blue pool that usually reflected the sun, now reflected something else.

The news helicopter footage zoomed out, revealing the image the pool had reflected more fully. Camille's big, beautiful white house, the very same one she'd stared at and edited in the picture on her computer only minutes before, was now completely engulfed in violent, red-orange flames.

A news announcement label appeared across the screen. It read: "Billionaire CEO Camille Hennings dead at 82."

5

THE BLUE BUTTERFLY

*E*lizabeth fell to the floor, knocking the lamp off the small nesting table with a crash.

She crawled to the stand where she'd left the remote. She unmuted the TV and turned up the sound.

"We can now confirm," the American newscaster began with a grave voice, "that Camille Cortez Fairhurst Hennings, CEO and founder of Cortez Holdings International has passed away in a fire at her home in Belvedere Tiburon. While the fire is not yet contained, officials suspect foul play. Ms. Hennings began her company, Cortez Holdings, out of her studio apartment in The Mission district of San Francisco, when she was only twenty-three."

Connor burst through the door, "Lara?" His voice was full of alarm. "What—"

The newscaster continued, "Her company evolved from

fast fashion to real estate and everything in between. Over the course of sixty years, Ms. Hennings grew her empire, today valued at more than fifty billion dollars." The newscaster stopped, gulping before reading the next part, "She is survived by no one." He cleared his throat. "We'll keep our viewers updated as we learn more about this developing story. In other news. . . ."

Connor reached over and turned the TV off.

He sunk down next to her, pulled her into his arms, and started to gently rub her back.

"I don't, I don't—" Elizabeth could not find the words.

"What happened?" Connor was confused.

"There was . . . fire . . . I don't know . . . arson?" Her thoughts were a jumble, she tried to reach for something to hold onto. Something that made sense.

She tried to hold onto Connor, but it was all too much. There was no strength in her arms, the world was spinning. It seemed impossible. She'd just talked to her, just held her hand. Last week she had been as alive and as fierce as ever. And now she was gone?

Elizabeth's mind rejected the idea. It *wasn't possible*. Her breathing became labored, each breath came a little quicker than the last, she could feel herself starting to hyperventilate.

Before she knew what was happening she stood up, swaying on the spot. Connor reached out to steady her and then she was moving, leaving Connor to chase after her.

She ran to her office grabbed her cell phone and then ran

down the stairs stopping only to put on her shoes and grab her jacket.

"I need to go for a walk!" she called behind her, knowing that Connor would be there to hear.

"Do you need me to come with—" Connor called, his voice strained with concern.

Elizabeth couldn't stop to respond, the door to the castle closed behind her, the cool air filled her lungs and before she knew what she was doing she started to run towards the nearest path through the woods that ran alongside Lough Rhiannon.

She breathed in the trees of the mature woodland. The blood pounded in her ears, the browns and greens of the trees were a blur.

She deftly maneuvered the uneven path, averting the tree roots and the muddy puddles that sprung up occasionally. A gentle breeze moved through the forest, making the trees sway. Sunshine permeated the canopy intermittently, no rhyme or reason to where the golden spotlights appeared.

She ran until she was completely out of breath. Her head was pounding, the blood was rushing through her ears. She doubled over, hands on her knees, gasping for air.

As soon as she could breathe again, she ventured off the path touching the bark of each tree as she passed. The trees were her sanctuary, her repose from the world. She walked through the thick forest until she spotted a tiny hill in a small clearing that was enveloped in sunshine.

The tiny hill, turned out to be a rock, covered in green moss. She climbed it and collapsed on the small plateau at the top. She drew her knees into her chest and hugged herself thinking through all that had come before.

Two weeks ago Camille had called to ask a favor. She had her over to the big white house on the hill for dinner to explain.

A few of her companies had undergone a series of attacks, from local hacks, to information leaks. The US government believed it was part of a more nefarious terrorist plot intended to destabilize certain markets.

Camille hadn't been convinced. Still, she had wanted outside counsel from someone she trusted. Someone who was not part of her company. Elizabeth had represented her at the table when she'd met with the FBI, the SEC, and the NSC.

But there hadn't been anything to suggest Camille was in any danger, and if she were, surely the government agents would have told them. Wouldn't they?

And even barring that, Camille was no sitting duck. Even at eighty-two. She'd studied martial arts since the age of ten, devoting much of the time she wasn't working on her business to learning and mastering several different styles. Karate, Kung Fu, Kendo, the list went on and on, it would have taken something extraordinary to take Camille down.

And for her to die in a fire?

The woman she'd known would have found a way to MacGyver herself out of the burning building.

It didn't make sense.

She'd just decided to phone the FBI to find out what she could, when she spotted something moving in the trees.

A man in his seventies wearing a flannel shirt, khakis and walking shoes stepped into the small clearing in front of her.

Elizabeth couldn't imagine what she looked like, hugging herself and rocking back-and-forth, thinking through the puzzle that was Camille's death, on top of the rock.

Whatever the man saw, it alarmed him.

As he drew closer, she noticed that he resembled the actor Bill Nighy. His pale blue eyes were shrewd, but kind.

"Are y'all right, lass?" he asked. His accent was thick, beautiful.

Elizabeth couldn't speak, she nodded, trying and failing to give him a reassuring smile.

"Are you *physically* well?"

Elizabeth nodded.

The man examined her. He nodded in acknowledgment, correctly guessing that she wanted to be left alone. And made his way out of the clearing and into the woods behind her.

She heard the man walk through the woods, and then heard his footsteps stop.

She glanced back and out of the corner of her eye saw

him stop in front of a large oak tree and take a seat at the base of it, leaning back against the trunk.

Elizabeth returned to her thoughts, feeling strangely reassured by the man's presence. Before long, her brain was a jumbled mess again. Her mind raced, her thoughts were erratic—she couldn't hold on to anything long enough to make sense of it. She felt more than a little insane.

The minutes passed until she wasn't sure how long she'd been out there, sitting on the rock.

Although she never glanced back again, she knew that the kind old man remained in the woods behind her, watching over her and making sure she was OK.

When her limbs were several degrees passed numb, she peeled herself up off of the rock and made her way to the woods in front of her until she found another path that led back in the direction of the castle.

She walked back slowly, deliberately, letting her mind wander and get lost in the smell of the trees, the song of the birds, and the sunshine that managed to pass through the gaps in the canopy and warm her skin.

It was in this zombie-like state that her eyes caught something blue. At first it was a simple flash and then a blue blur. She began to look for it, to catch it again. Her eyes finally settled on the butterfly just as it began flying towards her. She held her breath as it circled her and then landed gracefully on her thumb.

Carefully, not daring to breathe, she lifted her hand to

her face. The bright blue wings were framed by black tips, they opened and closed delicately as she watched. For several seconds nothing existed except those wings. They opened and closed and that was the entire world.

The butterfly left her hand and Elizabeth breathed in, the air filling her lungs all at once. She watched as it flew up the path. Her feet took her automatically forward, she followed with no question or thought in her head other than to keep going.

After ten minutes, it left the path and plunged into the woodland.

Elizabeth's pace quickened, some part of her registered the urgency. She couldn't lose the butterfly—it was showing her the way somehow. It was as though losing sight of the butterfly would seal her fate and she would remain lost forever.

It flew through the woods, into a large clearing, and there it remained, circling the space and flitting from flower to flower. Elizabeth took in the scene in front of her.

The ground was flat and covered with the greenest of grass, wild flowers grew near the edge, and the entire meadow was surrounded by mature trees—majestic Oak trees, Ash trees, and Dogwoods—even some Pine trees that smelled like California. They created a soothing barrier from the outside world.

She walked to the middle and closed her eyes, letting her head fall back so that her face met the sky. For several long moments she bathed in the sunshine and breathed in the wild jasmine wafting towards her from somewhere nearby. She continued in this way until she felt something land on her.

She opened her eyes to find the butterfly on her arm. It remained there as she walked around the circular clearing taking in the trees and breathing in the cool June air. Maybe it was the trees or the sunshine or the butterfly, but the green meadow felt magical.

Like a fairy glen.

Elizabeth felt at peace.

Where was she?

She looked up, past the tree tops, trying to orient herself until she caught a glimpse of the castle to the northwest. She could just make out one of the turrets. Castle Bannon could not have been more than a seven-minute walk from where she stood, and yet, she had never stepped foot in the clearing before.

She walked along the edge where the grass met the trees until she found a small footpath, barely noticeable beneath a layer of grass and earth.

It seemed to lead back to the house.

As she took in her fairy glen one more time, the butterfly left her arm and settled on a purple flower. She stepped onto the footpath, something in the back of her mind clicked into place. It was a thought for another day, a better day. If it could be done, she thought it might just be exactly what she needed to find her new place in Ireland.

Feeling much more herself, Elizabeth Lara walked back to the castle ready to find answers.

The door opened just as she reached it, Connor came barreling out at that exact moment. His forward momentum was so great that he couldn't stop himself from running straight into her. She fell backwards, but he managed to catch her before she fell all the way to the ground.

6

THE IRISH SUMMER FESTIVAL

*W*hispers and giddy faces seemed to follow them everywhere.

Connor and Elizabeth had become accustomed to some measure of constant attention over the years, but walking into the Summer Festival, or *Féile an tsamhraidh*, as it was called in Irish Gaelic, with Kilian and Dree was unlike anything they had ever experienced.

Girls squealed. Boys tried to look cool but lost it once Kilian passed them.

Grown women grew bright red and kept stealing furtive glances in their direction. Even grown men nodded their approval as they passed, looking impressed and proud that one of their own had made it.

"Oh my God! It's him, it's really him!" A teen girl in a

green dress screeched at her friends and hid her face in her hands.

A twenty-something woman wearing a red shirt and jeans announced, "He's just looked at me!" Then quickly turned her back to them and proceeded to start chatting animatedly to her friend, pretending to have the most interesting conversation.

Just then, a slender looking man with short dark hair appeared in front of them, blocking their path, "A photo for the Dingle Daily, if you please?" the man said abruptly. He didn't wait for them to respond.

A flash went off, blinding them all. He disappeared just as quickly.

Elizabeth blinked wildly and tried to look up at Connor. "That was weird."

"Alfie O'Hanlon, he's the new photographer for the paper. He's the editor's nephew I was telling you about. Bit of a gobdaw and an arse." Connor squeezed his eyes shut in an attempt to regain his own sight.

"What makes him a gobdaw and an arse?" Elizabeth whispered.

Connor leaned in, "Well, he's a creeper. He went around spying on girls as a teen, was caught once, but his uncle Barnaby greased some wheels and got him out of it. There are other things as well . . . I don't know he's just an entitled little prick."

Elizabeth felt like she'd been slapped. "Ewww . . . what

do you mean he got away with it? Did he see someone naked?" She was appalled.

Connor thought for a moment, "No, I don't believe it was quite that serious. Was caught before he could see anything, but I don't know the particulars. Surely if it had been worse he wouldn't have gotten away with it!" he said with a certainty his wife couldn't share.

She shook her head, trying not to dwell on the injustice. She knew all too well how much men could get away with when it came to crimes against women. She'd seen it throughout her life, in the courtroom and in the world. It was a burden most women shared.

Connor put his arm around Elizabeth. She leaned into him, allowing herself to focus on the feel of his body instead of the strange details she'd just learned.

The crowds parted to let them through at the start, but as they ventured further into the festival where the food and drink could be found, people seemed to leave them alone.

They were far too busy eating and drinking and being merry to gawk. It wasn't unless Kilian accidentally bumped into someone that they received any attention. He'd instinctively turn to apologize and then the person would fall into some form of adoration.

The men shook his hand and clapped his back. The teens asked for selfies, which he graciously agreed to, and the women were a mix of selfies, shy smiles, and uncontrollable laughter.

Elizabeth was happy that the attention wasn't on her and Connor. The last thing she needed was the intense scrutiny that came with being placed under a microscope. She was grateful for the escape in more ways than one.

The music from a nearby fiddler and a DJ further on contributed to the lively atmosphere. The buzz of the crowd was infectious. It was easy to lose yourself in the smiling faces and the enticing stalls.

"Right, well then where should we start?" Connor asked the group as they walked.

Elizabeth looked at her phone, "Well, we have an hour until we have to judge the music contest so I say we hit the Guinness cake and sugary treats before making our way to the booze."

Dree interjected, "So long as you don't get blitzed. We need you two," she pointed to Elizabeth and Kilian, "to be coherent and show some measure of decorum in front of the good townspeople. We can't have our judges totally smashed."

Kilian objected, "When do I ever get totally smashed?"

"Or me?" Elizabeth protested.

Dree rolled her eyes, "Never. But still, just a reminder. And since this is the first time you've been back in Dingle since making it big," she gave Kilian a knowing look, "I just don't want it to all go to your head and you end up celebrating a little more than you should."

Kilian put his hands up and smiled at her. With a quick nod of agreement, he yielded, "You're so wise."

"I know," she said with a certainty that made them all laugh.

They found the stalls of general savory and sugary goodness on the left. Connor and Kilian chose the "Cheese's of the World" stall, while Elizabeth and Audre were drawn to, "Chocolate Delight + Guinness," which showed off a range of chocolate in various treats. Brownies, cakes, cheesecake— everything you could want in chocolate form.

Elizabeth went for the Guinness cake first, she took a bite and was immediately transported. "Oh, Ida you've outdone yourself," she said to the round woman with puffy cheeks behind the table.

Ida's cheeks went pinker than usual, she clasped her hands, "Thank you so much Lady Lara." She bowed her head, trying to hide the extent of her delight, "Please have as much as you like."

Elizabeth, took another bite. "Mmmm. . . ." She let her head fall back slightly, letting the sounds of pleasure escape her mouth.

Audre narrowed her eyes and pursed her lips. "What are you doing?"

Elizabeth looked up from her cake, "What do you mean?" she managed between bites.

"Why does it sound like you're having sex with that cake?" Audre chided.

"What? You've heard me enjoying food before. I'm sure you have!"

Audre looked both annoyed and amused. "Yes, of course I have," she paused, "it's just been a while, Babes."

Elizabeth tried a cupcake with green frosting next.

Audre leaned in and whispered into her ear, "Yes, of course I remember your foodgasm sounds, but I don't think that I've ever heard you do it in public before. And to such a degree. Liz, you're a *lady* now." She gave extra weight to the word.

"So?" Elizabeth gave her friend a blank look. "It's only honorary. What's the big deal?"

Audre lowered her voice again, "I just mean that as much as you might want to continue behaving the way you normally behave in public, the people here might see you differently now. You might not get the choice. I mean, I love you and your foodgasms, but they could get you into all sorts of trouble if you don't watch yourself."

Elizabeth could not process her words.

Audre kept trying, "Trust me I know. Managing Kilian's image and the perception of the public is everything!"

Some part of her brain registered that Dree was only trying to look out for her, but Elizabeth felt an overwhelming desire to be defiant.

She took a big bite of the cupcake, so big the frosting covered the tip of her nose, and then moaned loudly. Several people around them turned to look.

Audre sighed and looked away, "Just having your back, Babes."

Elizabeth didn't question her best friend's intentions, but still, she couldn't help but be riled. Every time someone brought up her being a lady and how taking on that role permanently meant that she had to behave any differently or be any less herself made her want to scream and rebel at every turn.

Audre raised an eyebrow and waited for Elizabeth to see things her way.

She finished the cupcake and registered the concern in Audre's eyes. She softened, "I know you are just looking out for me, Dree. But I won't change who I am."

"Babes, I would never want you to change. I just want you to realize that you might have to tone certain things down, in order to avoid unpleasantness. The press can be unforgiving."

Connor and Kilian were suddenly at their side.

Connor leaned down and kissed Elizabeth's nose, "Mmmm...tasty." He kissed away the frosting.

A laugh escaped her chest. She took a napkin and made sure all of the frosting was gone.

They walked further into the festival, Connor put one arm around Elizabeth's shoulders and leaned in to whisper into her ear, "How are you doing, Lara?"

Elizabeth bit her lip and tried to keep her breathing in

check. She hadn't been sure she was going to come out, wasn't sure she could face all those people.

She'd spent the afternoon calling various US government officials and trying to find out what had happened to Camille. What had changed in the circumstances surrounding the investigation since Elizabeth had left California and how any change could have put Camille's life in danger.

But she got nothing.

Only condolences and *we're so sorry for your loss*, and *we can't comment on an open investigation*.

She finally managed to get through to Agent Seth Jackson, the man in charge of the investigation and the person they'd met with at the FBI. He assured her that nothing material had changed, and that they had no previous knowledge that Camille's life was in danger. He confirmed that they suspected arson, and would be looking into her death with every resource at their disposal.

That's all she would get from them. It had been an exhausting day. She'd decided that staying home would lead to a downward spiral of unanswerable questions and an endless onslaught of *what-ifs*.

It would have driven her mad.

It still threatened to drive her to the brink.

The festival would serve as a distraction. She had agreed to come out so that she might get lost in the sights and sounds—allow the food and music to take her away—to give her a break from her brain.

She'd been trying to pretend that everything was fine, because she needed a few hours of fine.

"I'm fine," she said, her voice strained.

Connor read her face, he sighed, "I'm sorry, Luv. I won't ask again tonight, let's just have some fun." He kissed her head and tried to redirect her mind. "Look at them." He motioned with his head towards Kilian and Dree a few feet in front of them.

Their friends were walking so close together half their bodies were touching.

Just then Kilian's hand grazed Audre's for a prolonged moment.

Elizabeth held her breath as she watched.

Kilian slowly extended a finger outward more deliberately. For a moment it looked like he might close the distance completely, and take her hand in his.

Audre left her hand where it was, within his reach. She was either oblivious to his touch, or . . . Elizabeth could only guess.

Kilian reached out with two fingers this time, skimming the back of her hand and for an agonizing moment, it appeared Audre might extend her hand and press it into his caress.

The crowd thickened, making it more difficult to see what was happening. Elizabeth extracted herself from

Connor, quickly taking his hand instead. She pulled at him, leading him forward through the throng in an attempt to stay behind their friends.

She lost sight of them and their hands for a few seconds, only to find them again just as it looked like Audre might close the distance between her and Kilian. Mentally, she urged her best friend forward. "Come on, Dree," she said under her breath.

"What was that, Luv?" Connor asked absently.

"No, nothing." Elizabeth kept her eyes firmly on their best friends. Just as it looked like Audre might extend her hand towards Kilian and perhaps finally lace her fingers through his, a big man with a boisterous laugh intercepted them.

Fitz O'Leary, the proprietor of their favorite pub, and in fact the very pub in which she and Connor had first had dinner and a dance together, was all smiles. "Kilian O'Grady, as I live and breathe! It's good to see you lad. You know I've got your picture and autograph on the wall in the back room where you use to play. It would be a real treat if you came by some night and sung a few songs for us."

Kilian turned bright red, first at the unwelcome interruption, and then at the thought of being put on a pedestal in the place where he'd gotten his start.

"You bet, Fitz. If I can swing it, I will come by." He shook the man's hand and clapped him on the shoulder. "Perhaps next week."

Fitz nodded and smiled, "Wonderful!" he said before making his way towards someone else.

Kilian turned back to Audre, but she was nowhere to be seen.

Elizabeth cursed under her breath. Of all the times for Fitz to appear! They'd been so close. . . .

She craned her neck, trying to see over people's heads. But even in her three-inch wedge boots, she couldn't find Dree. She left the men without a word and darted through the crowds.

Being short had its advantages, mainly being able to weave through throngs of people quickly and without much of a fuss.

She found her friend at a gin tasting stall. She was making her way through a flight called "The Gins of Ireland and Scotland".

By the time Elizabeth reached her she was on her third shot.

Elizabeth put her hand on Audre's back, "Everything OK?"

Audre pursed her lips an imperceptible degree, imperceptible to anyone but Elizabeth. "Why wouldn't I be?"

"Ummm . . ." Elizabeth stared as Audre went for the third shot. "Didn't you say that we should avoid getting sloppy drunk?"

"No, I said *you* and Kilian needed to avoid getting totally smashed because you are judging the music contest. I very clearly did not say anything about myself."

"Dree, it's me. What's going on?" Elizabeth whispered. "This is not like you. You're avoiding something."

Audre was silent.

She tried again, "You're either avoiding something, or outright lying to yourself." She tilted her head and gave her friend a knowing look.

Audre looked down at the flight again, "Oh all right!" she huffed. "I know it's going to sound completely barmy, but . . . how do I even say this? Errr . . . I think maybe I'm in—"

But she was cut off by the untimely arrival of Connor and Kilian.

Elizabeth sighed in frustration and put a hand to her forehead. Audre may have finally been ready to admit the truth to herself and to Elizabeth, but then the men had to come and ruin it.

Elizabeth tried to salvage the situation, "Honey?" she smiled at Connor and spoke through gritted teeth, "And Kil? Could you give us a minute?"

Audre was quick to interject, "No, please join us! In fact," she turned her attention to the person manning the gin stall, "another flight please."

"Dree!" Elizabeth tried to stop her.

"Relax, it's for my friend here," she extended her arm and grabbed Connor so that he was standing between her and Kilian and then turned to Elizabeth on her left, "besides I said that *you and Kilian* couldn't get totally smashed, I said nothing about me and Connor."

Connor looked to his wife. Elizabeth just shrugged. Connor seemed to understand.

Audre picked up her fourth shot while Connor took his first. They clinked glasses and shot the liquor back.

After glancing at her phone and realizing the time, Elizabeth paid for two portions of gin and handed one to Kilian, "A bit of fire for the road." Kilian and she clinked glasses and took the shots.

It wasn't the smoothest of gin. Her eyes grew wide and her mouth contorted as it went down. "Come on," she started once she'd recovered, "we're due on stage in ten minutes. We better begin making our way there in case you're stopped by more adoring fans."

She turned to Connor and stood on her tippy toes, reaching up to kiss him on the cheek and whispered, "You got her?"

"Yes, don't worry. I'll get her started on some water after we've finished our flights." He whispered back.

Elizabeth wasn't worried about Audre over drinking and becoming ill. She worried that for someone as self-aware and blunt as Audre, whatever she was avoiding and however she might be lying to herself . . . it was taking its toll.

"I'm sure she'll be fine. She can hold her liquor. But yeah, water wouldn't hurt. Thank you." She kissed his cheek a second time and then followed Kilian to the stage.

. . .

Fifteen minutes later they were on the stage with one other judge, a large man both in height and relative size with mostly silver hair and black spectacles, editor of The Dingle Daily, Barnaby O'Hanlon.

The judges' table was set off to the side of the stage, allowing for a microphone to be placed in the middle with the live band taking up the space behind it.

Thousands had gathered. A general buzz of excitement hung in the air. The organizers had strung warm café lights across the entire area, their glow becoming more pronounced as the sun set over the Atlantic.

A tall thin man with shoulder-length brown hair in his thirties ascended the steps to the stage, microphone in hand. "Welcome, welcome everyone to our Summer Festival music contest."

The man waited for the applause to end.

"My name is Evan Morris and I will be your host for tonight's festivities. It'll be a craic, I promise." He flashed the crowd a winning smile and nodded as people cheered. "Now I'd like to introduce you to your judges. First, we have Barnaby O'Hanlon, editor for The Dingle Daily."

A few people applauded.

"Next we have world-renowned photographer and lyricist, our own Lady Elizabeth Lara." The crowd erupted in applause and cheers.

"And finally, fresh off his triumphant US tour, our very own hometown rock star," he paused for effect and then his voice crescendoed like an announcer at a boxing match in Vegas, "Kilian O'Grady!"

The crowd erupted in thunderous applause. They whooped and cheered and sent a wave of love that hit Kilian fiercely. There were *welcome homes* and *good on you lad* and *we love you Kilian.*

The applause lasted for so long that Kilian himself had to stand. His face was bright red, he bowed his head in a gesture of humility. He clasped his hands in thanks and nodded a few times and then motioned for them to all stop clapping.

"Yes, that's right ladies and gentlemen our very own Kilian O'Grady, who's here judging thanks to Lord Bannon who graciously gave up his spot at the judge's table." The announcer nodded to Connor who was now standing next to the stage with Audre.

Elizabeth was relieved to see that Dree was looking much more herself, completely calm and composed. Ever the professional.

"And," Evan knew how to use a dramatic pause, "as a special treat, Kilian has agreed to play a three-song set for us directly after the contest."

The crowd erupted in a new wave of whistles and cheers, with people chatting animatedly about the surprise show.

"Now then to the contest," Evan cut through the commotion. "These three new artists have been selected from over one-hundred entrants this year. They've made it through three rounds to be here with you today."

He began reading from the cards. "Please welcome to the stage, singing "Somebody to Love" by Queen, our first contestant, Poppy Patterson!"

Poppy sang her heart out in a way that would have made Freddie Mercury proud. Next was Jay Marshall singing a nice rendition of "Moves Like Jagger" by Maroon 5, and finally there was Lacey Walshe who sang an ethereal, yet rock-infused version of "Dreams" by The Cranberries.

In the end Kilian and Elizabeth chose Poppy as the winner. Barnaby had disagreed, voting for Jay instead. Elizabeth had been perplexed at best, until Kilian had leaned in to whisper and explain, "I believe you'll find that Jay is dating old Barnaby's granddaughter." He raised his eyebrows and looked down.

Elizabeth nodded, understanding dawned. *What a guy, that Barnaby.*

After Poppy was presented with her plaque and all the requisite pictures with the judges were taken, the stage was cleared.

Kilian went behind the elevated bandstand to prepare while Elizabeth joined Connor just off the side of the stage. Audre went to find Kilian and speak to the sound technician.

A few minutes later, Kilian was back with his guitar.

Without any faff or introduction, Kilian began to play a

few bars on his acoustic guitar. The crowd fell silent. "This is for you my home, my heart, my fair Dingle."

There were a few whoops and whistles, but mostly people remained silent as they took in the slow, soft melody that made everyone feel alive and very much in the moment.

Kilian sang into the mic, "I fall asleep and dream of last summer. When we were young and the world was fun. . . ."

Connor moved closer to Elizabeth, wrapping his arms around her and finding her cheek with his. They swayed gently to the music and were every bit as affected as the rest of the town.

They listened to Kilian in that way until the song was finished.

Booming applause met the last line as everyone showed their appreciation.

The band didn't skip a beat, they launched into the next song almost immediately. The big rock chords and upbeat tempo of one of his best-known hits came blaring through the speakers and the crowd loved it.

Kilian quickly swapped his acoustic guitar for his electric Red Special as the band covered him on the first few opening bars.

Connor leaned into her, "Come with me," he whispered, taking her hand and leading her through the crowds and out of the square.

"Where are we going?" Elizabeth asked, trying to keep up with him.

They walked briskly for a couple of minutes until they were a block away from the crowds and the music, but he didn't stop there. Connor urged them both forward for several more minutes until there was no one in sight.

He kept moving until he found what he was looking for, until finally he led them to a small space between a bright green building, and a yellow restaurant.

It was a small alley.

"What are we—?" she began, but he didn't let her finish.

His eyes had grown dark, thirsty. She understood immediately.

It was that look she'd come to know.

He moved towards her, pinning her against the brick wall of the alley.

"But we can't—," she started, as he closed the distance and brought his mouth down on hers, kissing her hungrily, desperately.

The familiar warmth permeated her insides. She responded to him instantly, but her brain wouldn't let her surrender.

She put her hands on his chest and pushed him away a degree, "We can't, people will see!"

He turned towards the main street. There wasn't a soul in sight. "There's no one here, just you and me," he growled, leaning in to devour her again.

It *was* true that they hadn't passed anyone in several

minutes. Her body began calling for him as she registered his need for her.

He moved in slowly now, deliberately. His eyes never leaving hers, requesting her permission at every inch. She invited him forward, slowly giving in to what her body needed.

It had been an exhausting day. Her brain had been on overdrive for so long—desperately trying to make sense of everything that had happened. As Connor closed the distance, she slowly let go of her brain and gave in to her body, until she surrendered completely.

With overwhelming relief she gladly accepted his kisses. Losing herself in his full lips and the movement of his tongue on hers.

He moved his hands down to her backside, kneading her through her dress. Her head fell backwards as he kissed down her neck, moving her white cardigan down past her shoulder as he went.

Quickly he moved his hand down further to hitch her knee up around his hip and then leaned his body into her. She could feel every inch of him.

Some part of her brain registered a noise. Footsteps.

Just then, a bright flash of light filled the narrow alley.

Elizabeth pushed Connor away instinctively and turned towards the source of the light.

The small frame and dark hair of Alfie O'Hanlon, stood at the entrance to the alley. His camera at the ready.

Connor reacted quickly, nearly closing the distance between them as Alfie clicked his camera throwing another bright flash their way, blinding them.

Elizabeth managed to grab Connor's arm before he could physically reach the creepy twenty-something photographer.

Alfie ran away, clutching his camera to his chest. He reached the crowd of people still entranced by Kilian's music and then it was too late. They couldn't follow or it would be more of a scene.

Elizabeth smoothed her dress.

Connor reached for her and wrapped her in his arms, they held each other tightly, both breathing heavily and still trying to process what had just happened.

In the distance, they heard the thunderous applause that followed Kilian's last song.

The Dingle Daily News
"Lady Lara Lures Lord into Lurid Love Liaison"
By Alfie O'Hanlon
[A picture of Elizabeth and Connor in the alley filled the front page. Elizabeth's cardigan was falling off of her shoulder, her knee was hitched up around Connor's hip. His lips were on her neck.]

The whole of Dingle turned out to witness their own hometown hero, Kilian O'Grady, play a surprise set of songs for the Summer Festival. Everyone took part in the craic last night except Lady Lara and Lord Bannon who were seen disappearing into a dark alley between two businesses on Main Street where they engaged in a scandalous tryst.

Lady Lara, if she can be called a lady, was seen luring Lord Bannon into the alley just after Kilian's first song. It appears the lady of the castle could not even do her husband's best mate the courtesy of staying to cheer him on as he took the stage in Dingle for the first time since becoming a bonafide rock star. The leggy American was too busy seducing her husband in a back alley to care about being seen by the public or give credence to any societal notions of decorum.

The Dingle Daily has reached out to Kilian O'Grady and his team. No word yet on whether Lady Lara's callous snub will create a lasting rift between Lord Bannon and Mr. O'Grady.

7

THE "ARTICLE"

*E*lizabeth was fuming.

She stared at the torrid picture of her and Connor wrapped in an embrace which the paper had cast in a light so blistering that it made the heavy make out session seem *pornographic*.

She read the title again. All she could see was red. *Of course* it was she who seduced him.

She quickly riffled through the small paper. It was as she suspected. "The entire Summer Festival only gets a small paragraph on page five?!" She threw the paper down on the kitchen counter.

Connor handed her a steaming cup of Earl Grey.

She took a sip, but it was still too hot. "And they placed a tiny picture of Kilian singing on stage on page 2 with an even smaller paragraph?!"

Connor remained silent.

"It's the first time he's played here and all he gets is a tiny paragraph and a ridiculously small picture?! What are they playing at?! Oh and I'm not doing enough to show Kilian support?" Her voice had started to rise, crescendo up into screeching territory. "I bloody wrote the lyrics to half the songs he sang last night!"

Connor moved to sit on the stool beside her. "You know Kilian and Dree are as upset as we are. And they know the truth of it all."

Elizabeth set the tea down and let her head fall into her hands. "It doesn't matter. I know they're on our side and I know that they weren't in the least affected by our leaving the concert early. It's the lies, the making me out to be some slutty American who seduces you to such an extent that you lose all sense of propriety. I'm the Jezebel who's leading you astray!"

Connor chuckled softly, he checked his email on his phone, and then looked up. "And all the while it's me who seduced *you*. If only they knew how truly devious I can be." He wiggled his eyebrows like a villain.

She looked up and narrowed her eyes, staring daggers at him.

He stopped immediately. "Sorry. I'm trying to lighten the mood so I don't turn dark again. We've got to take this in stride." He took a sip of his tea, kissed her head, and with a,

"It will all blow over before you know it," he quickly left the kitchen.

She heard his footsteps on the stairs.

He always tried to find the humor. It was something she loved about him, but the situation was beyond humor for Elizabeth.

How could he think any of this was amusing?

She picked up the paper again and examined the title. "It's sexist bullshit is what it is!" She fell immediately into her legal brain, quickly going through all her options.

She continued spiraling in silence for several minutes. She'd practically resolved to hold a press conference when the sound of the phone ringing made her jump off the kitchen stool.

She wasn't used to having a local area line anymore. They'd gotten it for the house only recently and so far she wasn't impressed.

Elizabeth let it ring. She paced the kitchen, focusing on the crown molding of the ceiling as she waited for the answering machine to pick up. She was not fit to speak to other humans yet, and she knew it.

Finally, the generic beep of the machine sounded and a woman began to speak.

"Hello, Lady Lara," the woman's voice was strained, and she made a point to pause on the word *lady*. "This is Rose Faith Byrnes calling in regards to your rather scandalous entry in today's paper."

The older woman's voice began to rise in indignation, "Now I don't know what sort of behavior is acceptable in the United States," her voice teetered on the edge, "but we at the Dingle Ladies Society are not accustomed to one of our members engaging in acts of sexual perversion in back alleys!"

It took everything in Elizabeth's body not to pick up the phone and unleash herself on Rose.

The bloody nerve!

She placed both hands on the counter and focused on her breathing. If she picked up the phone now she would undoubtedly lay into her so fervently that she was likely to give the poor woman a heart attack.

And then there would be something else to blame Elizabeth for. She could imagine the headline, "Lady Lara Kills Kind Respectable Rose Faith in Callous Verbal Attack."

Rose continued her assault, "We will be reviewing your invitation to join our society at our next council meeting. Good day!"

Mercifully, that was the end.

Elizabeth's head was spinning. Her emotions and her brain were on overload. She needed to get out of the castle. Get out of Dingle.

"Connor!" she called out. She moved through the kitchen and up to the next floor in search of him.

"Yes, Lara?" He opened the door to his study just as she reached it.

"I need to go, I need to get out of here. Let's get on a plane or rent someplace nearby. I don't care just take me away from here."

She bowed her head feeling defeated by the world.

He took her hand and squeezed. "I'm sorry this is happening, Luv. There's nothing I would love more than to take you away from all of this, but something's just come up at the auction house in Rome. I'm afraid I have to leave right away."

She looked up at him, "Is everything OK? What happened?"

His lips set into a line, "Nothing." His jaw was strained.

Elizabeth tilted her head, "Really?" Her voice was dry.

"Well, not nothing. Just nothing I can't handle. It's fine. I'll be back before you know it, just focus on relaxing and taking some time for yourself."

She stared at him blankly. *What did that mean?* Like she was some fragile creature who just needed to take it easy and it would all be all right?

She needed him to stay and fight with her or take her away so she could get enough distance from it all to think clearly.

He read most of the thoughts as they crossed her face.

"I'm sorry," he said again, his head bowed with guilt. "But I have to go." He kissed her forehead, leaned down to grab the overnight bag at his feet, which she hadn't noticed, and walked around her.

She stood at the door to his study and listened to his footsteps travel down the staircase and through the foyer.

And then the front door opened and closed.

Elizabeth stared at the picture on her screen. She wasn't sure how long she'd been sitting there.

She was numb.

The grief she felt over losing Camille, the frustration of not having answers, the anger that had bubbled over because of the damned newspaper, because of the stuffy and judgmental Rose Faith, and even because of her absent husband, all had worked to short circuit her brain.

There was only one thing to do.

Enya.

"Play, Enya," she said out loud. Her smart speaker responded in a soothing, monotone voice, "Playing songs by Enya."

The long lyrical opening melody of "Caribbean Blue" filled the room.

She moved over to the daybed by the window and lay down, staring up at the intricate design on the ceiling, until she cleared out everything that troubled her.

Only the soothing sounds of Enya and the delicate pattern of the white ceiling existed.

After what must have been three albums and several hours, Elizabeth sat up.

Her mind was clear and her spirit was calm. Although she had no idea what was to be done about any of it, she did know two things for certain: she needed to get away to gain some distance from the situation and she didn't need a man in order to do it.

Quickly, she came up with a plan.

She moved to her computer and found her way to the holiday rental website where she had found Rhia's Irish cottage.

She used the map feature to narrow the results. The rental needed to be less than an hour away, and it needed to be secluded, preferably near a forest and a lake.

Within minutes she found what she was looking for, a three-bedroom glass lake house only forty-five minutes away.

The listing called it *The Glass Treehouse*, and described it as, "an oasis of serenity, perched amongst the trees and over-looking Lough Aisling."

She scrolled through the pictures eagerly and read the reviews. It was perfect, she booked it for a week starting today.

She glanced at her phone, it was 4:07 p.m. An hour to pack, if she was lucky she could be there by six.

For the first time in what seemed like ages, she felt in tune with her inner voices.

"Play 80s rock throughout level two," she said to the castle's smart speaker system. They'd had it installed throughout the house so they could play the same song in multiple rooms, entire floors, or even the whole house.

Bon Jovi immediately began to blare in every room on the second floor.

The music moved through her, it was hard not to dance while she packed.

Since she had just finished unpacking from her trip to California, re-packing turned out to be the easiest thing she'd done in days.

She would've been out the door within half an hour if she hadn't remembered that she would probably require sustenance while she was away. And she had no idea how long she would be away. Overnight? Just for the weekend? The entire week?

Instead of braving the local supermarket, she ordered food from her five favorite takeaway restaurants. There was pizza, pasta, Thai, Indian, French crêpes and freshly baked baguettes from the new French boulangerie which had just opened.

She went down to the wine cellar and picked out several bottles to pack.

It took her several trips to load her bag, the booze, and the food in her Tesla. It was no small feat, since the garage was actually some distance from the castle proper.

But she managed it. Declan was usually responsible for bringing the car around and loading it, but there was something wonderfully freeing about loading her own car.

Her brain stopped on the thought. *Freeing to load her own car?* She made a mental note to get a grip and buy a book that reminded her of the real problems happening in the world, but today? Today she would just be kind and allow herself to think and feel whatever the hell she wanted.

The evening had turned brisk, she wrapped a shawl around her shoulders, left a note for Connor in the kitchen, set the alarm and locked the front door.

The drive was glorious. She opened the windows and let the cool summer breeze fill her lungs and cleanse her spirit.

It was an easy drive until she reached the small winding path that led up to the Glass Treehouse. She drove slowly, taking each turn at a time, whilst stealing glances here and there of the cliffside and the lough below.

She arrived at the top and parked her car on the plateau behind the house. She grabbed her bag and went to investigate.

It looked like a cabin from where she stood, but from the pictures she knew the other side was made completely of glass.

She unlocked the door and entered into a massive open-plan kitchen, dining, and front room area. It was all set up to lead to the key feature—the gigantic glass wall which covered the entire back of the house and half the walls on either side. The corners of the room were a seamless edge so as not to obstruct the view.

Her bag dropped to the floor with a thud, her feet took

her automatically forward. Trees surrounded her on either side as she stared down at the clear waters of Lough Aisling. Something in her chest relaxed. She was a world away here.

"Wow," she said, feeling breathless.

Elizabeth settled into the plush papasan chair in the corner where the two glass walls met.

The listing hadn't lied. It really was like being perched in the trees. The tall pines were directly to her left and the small, but bright blue Lough Aisling stretched out below.

There wasn't a person or building in sight. It was exactly what she needed.

She munched happily on her pizza and drank her glass of wine.

Her phone buzzed against her body. She fished it out of her pocket to find a text from Dree.

"Babes, I was going to come over to help you drink up some of that wine cellar of yours and concoct maniacal plans of revenge on the paper, but I just got the green light for another set of secret shows in Dublin. We're heading out now to make the final arrangements."

Elizabeth answered her. "No worries, I'm not at the castle. Went to Lough Aisling to get away."

Dree responded with lightning speed. "Brilliant! I'm glad you and Connor are getting some time alone, away from all the muck."

Elizabeth didn't bother correcting her assumption about Connor.

The phone buzzed once more.

"Will probably be back tomorrow—promise those bastards will pay! They already reached out to me because they wanted an exclusive interview with Kilian. He overheard the call and basically took the phone from me and told them to go to hell and how dare they print that rubbish about you. Probably wasn't the wisest move on his part, but I couldn't help but love him for it."

Elizabeth texted a smiley face emoji blowing a kiss.

Audre returned the emoji and finished with, "We've got your back."

She pocketed her phone and looked out at the water below. The sun had begun to set, the last rays permeated the sky turning it an enchanting shade of pink.

The sky to her right had turned a dark, stormy shade of purple. Big menacing clouds were gathering in the distance.

The gentle summer breeze had begun to turn. Wind swept through the trees. The pines on her left couldn't have been more than ten feet away from the glass. She felt like she could reach out and touch the needles.

The forest around her was so thick and lush that the smell of pine filled the house. She drank it in, it worked like an elixir and reminded her of California.

Her eyes found the clouds again, the rain would soon find the lake.

She tried not to think about Camille and the fire. Tried not to think about what it might have been like. Thinking about her tugged at the scar that had formed after the grief of losing Mags.

Life was a strange business. A jumbled mess of experiences and heart-wrenching loss.

She breathed deeply, trying to center herself in her body. The temperature was comfortable, but she still found herself wrapping the shawl more tightly around her shoulders.

The rain started then, pounding on the trees, the roof, the water below. It was magnificent to witness from her perch in the trees.

The Irish rain had come to wash the day away.

She curled up into a ball and listened to it fall. The beautiful acoustic simplicity of Bob Dylan's "Shelter from the Storm," played in the back of her mind.

Elizabeth welcomed the all-consuming storm. She took a deep breath and surrendered.

The crack of thunder seemed to shake the house. Elizabeth woke with a start.

She'd fallen asleep in the papasan before the last of the daylight had gone and woke to find herself completely in the dark. She unfurled her limbs, stretching them out painfully as the lightning hit the lake.

The flash illuminated everything outside.

Another crack of thunder and then another electric display of nature.

She stood up and walked to the glass. The trees were swaying violently, they almost appeared to graze the house.

She found her phone and looked at the time. It was two in the morning.

Another flash of lightning turned the entire lough a mesmerizing shade of silver.

She'd just resolved to go to bed when she heard it.

There was a clicking sound coming from the front door.

She activated the flashlight function on her phone and kept it low to the ground as she approached the entrance.

The handle rattled for just a second.

Elizabeth stopped.

Then it happened again.

She looked around for something to use as a weapon, but found nothing. She glanced back to the kitchen, but could not see a knife block.

Carefully, she inched closer to the door and moved the peephole cover.

She looked through the glass. A flash of lightning illuminated a bob of silver hair.

It was. . . .

It couldn't be. . . .

The person turned their eyes to the peephole and looked straight at her.

Elizabeth's breath caught in her chest. She quickly

fumbled with the lock, turned the handle, and threw the door wide open.

Standing in front of her, back straight, clothes soaking wet . . . was Camille Cortez Fairhurst Hennings.

8

COMPANY

*E*lizabeth's mouth dropped open. "Wha—?"

The lady standing in front of her clucked her tongue, "Well...?"

Elizabeth's heart was pounding so hard she could hear it in her ears. "But..."

Again, the woman was impatient, "Well, aren't you going to let me in? Honestly, Elizabeth, what's gotten into you?" She rolled her eyes and her giant suitcase straight past Elizabeth and into the house.

She found the coat rack by the door and made quick business of hanging up her things.

Elizabeth stood gaping at her. She realized that she must be dreaming, waking up in the papasan was really only the beginning of the dream. The lightning, the thunder, the door, and now this woman who looked and sounded exactly like Camille were all part of an elaborate dream.

Because Camille was dead. She saw the fire. She spoke to the FBI.

Camille walked up to Elizabeth and snapped her fingers in front of her eyes, trying to get some reaction, some sign that she was mentally present.

For a moment concern furrowed her brows and darkened her eyes, followed by a look of warmth and then concern and then impatience again. She took Elizabeth's hand and gave it a squeeze.

This dream was incredibly real, she thought. It really felt like she was holding her hand. It felt like the hand she held only a week ago, soft, wrinkled, and weathered with all the wisdom of an eighty-two-year-old.

Camille waited for Elizabeth to regain her senses. But she wasn't a patient person and after a few seconds, she slapped her hand in an effort to rouse her.

It worked.

"Ouch!" Elizabeth winced.

For the first time it dawned on her that it wasn't a dream.

"Holy sh—"

"Yes, yes!" Camille said impatiently, walking over to the kitchen finding a glass and pouring herself some water.

Elizabeth inhaled all at once, gasping for air. She hadn't realized she was holding her breath. "Oh my God, are you . . .

Is it really . . . ? Oh my God!" She ran to the woman standing in her kitchen and threw her arms around her.

She felt like Camille. Elizabeth squeezed her, hard. Before she knew what was happening, she found herself choking back sobs. And then the tears came, hot and wet.

She didn't know how long they stood there and she didn't care. Her eyes stung and her head pounded with the force of her uncontrollable weeping.

"OK, OK." Camille's voice had softened. She rubbed Elizabeth's back soothingly. "You didn't really think a fire could take me out, did you?"

"No!" Elizabeth managed through mangled breaths. "Yes!" Speaking had led to a new wave of heaving. She hadn't cried this way, like a child, since she had grieved for Mags, and even then she wasn't sure she had ever cried quite in this way before.

With Mags it had been all grief, and regret. She sobbed now with grief and relief, and something else . . . a sense of having been saved, of having escaped from a terrible fate.

Whatever this miracle was, it felt like getting Mags and Camille back in a single instant.

Elizabeth pulled herself away and examined Camille's face. "You're alive! It's really you." She'd stopped sobbing, but now found herself riding some strange euphoria. A small giggle escaped her lips. Her hand went instinctively to her mouth. But then she laughed again.

Camille exhaled dramatically and rolled her eyes, releasing Elizabeth to go place herself on the couch facing the window.

Elizabeth started to laugh in earnest, they were loud, wild fits. She sounded deranged.

"Ay Dios mío, ahora qué te pasa?"

Elizabeth's ears perked up as her brain processed the Spanish, it was strangely soothing and worked to bring her back to the present.

She joined Camille on the couch.

"Well?" She wiped her face with part of her shawl. "Are you going to fill me in or are you going to wait for me to finish going through all the symptoms of shock before putting me out of my misery?"

Camille sipped her water. Her short hair had begun to drip onto her ivory silk blouse. Instead of answering Elizabeth, she reached down into her large purse and extracted a beautifully embroidered handkerchief with the initials CC in red. She took her time squeezing her short locks into the fabric.

Elizabeth waited, some part of her brain had registered she probably should have offered her a towel, but she wasn't completely over the shock and found that she could not actively move her limbs, all she could do was wait for answers.

A flash of lightning hit somewhere beyond the lake, demanding their attention. The thunder followed, making the glass rattle.

Camille cleared her throat and turned towards Elizabeth. "It was three in the morning—almost two days ago now—the FBI intercepted a transmission that indicated there would be an attempt on my life." She took another sip of her water.

"They told me they were sending agents, they were just starting to explain when I heard it."

Elizabeth leaned in, "Heard what?"

"The explosion," Camille swallowed. "From the direction of the sound, it happened in my bedroom. I should have been asleep, I would have been asleep, but I had a dream." She stared out towards the lake as another strike illuminated the water. She seemed transfixed, lost in the memory.

When she didn't continue, Elizabeth prodded, "A nightmare?"

Camille shook her head, "No, I was walking on a footpath surrounded by tall trees, in Golden Gate Park, I think, when Magdalena suddenly appeared, took my hand and told me to wake up." Her body vibrated, like a chill had just run down her spine.

Elizabeth leaned over to unfold the blanket that was casually draped over the couch and placed it over Camille.

"So I woke up, looked at the clock, registered the time— almost three in the morning. I was thirsty, I went to the kitchen, and then the phone rang. It was the FBI. They'd only begun to explain when it happened," she repeated.

"I grabbed whatever I could. Luckily the fire took a few

minutes to spread. I grabbed my largest suitcase from the hall closet, some clothes from my storage closet on the other side of the house, my laptop and hard drives from the office, and emptied both safes."

Elizabeth considered, "Whoever it was banked on you being in the bedroom. There were no other explosions? The security alarm wasn't tripped? Does the FBI know who's behind this now? Wait, how long were you in the house after the explosion? You didn't know there wasn't another bomb. What the hell were you doing spending time caring about stuff?!"

Camille held up a hand to stop her, "Let me finish," she said sternly, sitting up taller.

"Sorry." Elizabeth sat back and waited.

"I—*calmly*—left the house with my suitcase and waited in the trees opposite the driveway." She said it like it would have been more of a tragedy if she had lost her head and run out of the burning building screaming, like a normal person.

But then her shoulders drew together a degree, she leaned forward, and placed her elbows on her knees. She laced her fingers together and took a deep breath, when she spoke again her voice had gained a shaky rasp. "I watched as my entire life, everything I had worked for, everything I had built, caught fire and burned."

It was unnerving. Camille had been a presence in Elizabeth's life for as long as she could remember, and in all that time she had never seen Camille so affected by anything. A sole tear fell down her cheek. She quickly wiped it away before it found the edge of her chin. Within the same breath she sat up straighter than before and regained every ounce of her composure.

That was Camille, tough as nails. Resilient.

"I waited in the trees for a few minutes before Agent Jackson drove up the driveway. He took me to headquarters where a handful of agents and the director decided that we should use the opportunity to gain an advantage. They were no closer to identifying who was behind the attacks, so they would fake my death and wait to see who came slithering out of the woodwork.

"They kept me at headquarters for twenty-four hours before I realized that I needed to regain control of the investigation. I gave them the slip when they relocated me to a safe house outside the city. I had contacted Brian Jamison within the first few hours of the explosion—he was my back up plan, in case the feds couldn't get it together fast enough. You remember Brian?"

Elizabeth cleared her throat, "Yes, I know Brian. He was the executor of Mags' will and he helped her orchestrate the plan with the box of letters." She smiled to herself, remembering her great-aunt's insane and incredibly convoluted plan to bring Elizabeth back to life. Mags couldn't have known how it would all turn out, and yet, it had worked. She shook her head, marveling at the brilliance of it all for what seemed like the thousandth time.

Camille sat back, "That's right. I'd forgotten," she smiled.

"What did Brian do?" Elizabeth brought them back, eager to understand just how Camille had been delivered from the dead to appear at her door in Ireland.

"He chartered me a flight, and I flew here."

"But how did you get out of the country without being recognized, or it leaking to the press?"

Camille waved away Elizabeth's concerns, "A wig, big sunglasses, a trusted pilot, a fake passport."

"Fake passport?"

Camille rolled her eyes in exasperation, "Yes, yes. Anyway, I drove to your castle first, but there was no answer so I broke in and found the note you had left your husband and so here I am."

Elizabeth's mouth dropped open, "You broke into my house?" The front door was massive, the locks were impenetrable, the security alarm was state-of-the-art. Either Aidan or Henry would have been in the guardhouse keeping watch.

She tucked a strand of her silver hair behind her ear and waved Elizabeth off like it was no big deal. "Don't worry," her accent was thick, she sounded like Rita Moreno's character in *West Side Story*, or her character in Netflix's *One Day At A Time*, adding to the impression that Elizabeth should just relax, "I locked up and reset the alarm before I left."

Elizabeth was awestruck. Fake passports? Giving the FBI the slip? Breaking into a castle which was basically a fortress? But all those thoughts were drowned out when something suddenly occurred to her, "Oh God! All your pictures, your albums . . . the black and white photos of you and Mags as kids! Your parents . . . the ranch in Mexico!"

Her stomach fell to her feet, it was a sickening sensation. "Those memories, that history . . ." she was breathless, "was priceless."

Then she remembered that only half an hour ago, she'd believed that Camille had burned in that house, and her emotions turned quickly to overwhelming gratitude. She launched herself across the couch and hugged Camille tightly again. "I'm so glad you're alive." She bit back the tears.

Camille hugged her, for the first time that night, in earnest, accepting all the love and emotion that Elizabeth was offering.

The two women held each other in silence until a torrent of Irish rain began to fall, first in a relaxing wave and then with a pounding rhythm that was amplified by the tall pines which surrounded them.

Elizabeth broke away, but held onto Camille's arms, "I still have so many questions, but how about a drink first."

"Oh mija, now you're speaking my language."

Elizabeth took Camille's hand and led her to the kitchen, she wasn't letting go unless she absolutely had to. "Let's see, I brought wine, but I think I saw some hard liquor in the cabinet."

They found vodka and tequila in the cabinet next to the fridge along with an array of mixers.

The women quickly took stock and then spoke at the same time, "Margaritas?"

They looked at each other and laughed.

9

THE RAINBOW

*E*lizabeth woke early. They had stayed up for hours talking, until the pinks and purples of dawn started to permeate the sky.

She'd gone to bed exhausted, but on some strange high. Everything that had affected her so much and had led to her escaping to the glass house, no longer seemed to matter. She felt amazing.

The effect was she'd only been able to sleep for a couple of hours. She woke starving and still giddy from the night before.

She made scrambled eggs and tomatoes with the bits she'd found in the fridge.

She took her bowl and placed herself in the papasan, watching as the last of the clouds from the storm cleared, giving way to the sunshine and a brilliant rainbow which was neatly framed by the glass.

She devoured her breakfast and then grabbed her camera from her bag. She put on her shoes and slipped out the front door, framing the scene in her lens and taking a picture of the rainbow with the purple clouds, the sunshine, the lake and the trees.

She knew it was the type of picture which some would scoff at, claim it was too pedestrian, simple, while others would be left breathless, completely enchanted by its beauty.

She knew exactly what she would do with it. The print would be larger than life, wall-sized. It would find a home in her office.

She wanted to remember that feeling forever. The feeling of hope and possibility and happiness. She breathed in the air and closed her eyes willing herself to immortalize the feeling and the memory in the catalog of her thoughts.

A small breeze swept through the trees sending a concentrated dose of pine in her direction. She took it in, deep into her lungs, letting it intensify her sense of peace.

The trees were still speaking gently, swaying in the breeze, when she slipped back inside.

She found Camille already milling about the kitchen, using the French press to make coffee. "Buenos días."

Elizabeth said good morning back and hugged her fiercely, she took her time letting go.

"Goodness," Camille breathed, "I'm not used to so many hugs."

"Oh well, you better get used to it, because I'm not stopping!" Elizabeth said, like a defiant ten-year-old.

Camille chuckled, "Stubborn, just like all the Lara women."

Elizabeth made herself some Earl Grey and then joined Camille at the small table on the other side of the kitchen.

"What now?" Elizabeth sipped her tea. "How exactly are you going to, as you said, *take control of the investigation*? Especially since everyone thinks you're dead."

Camille looked out the window, "Oh, I have my ways. Don't you worry about a thing, I've got it *completely* under control."

Elizabeth almost snorted her tea, she raised an eyebrow, and stared at the woman sitting in front of her. "Cam, your house blew up, you faked your own death, the FBI will be looking for you, someone's trying to kill you, and before that someone was carrying out a series of targeted attacks on your fifty billion-dollar company, which the US government believed was part of a bigger plot to destabilize one or more of your business entities in order to further a, as yet unknown, terrorist plot," she finished, now completely out of breath.

She stopped to take in a lung-full of air. "Which part—*exactly*—is completely under your control?!"

Camille scoffed, using her hands to express how insignificant Elizabeth's concerns were to her, "You let me worry about it. I just need to lay low and figure out what's next."

Elizabeth tilted her head and drew her eyebrows together, giving her a *really?* look.

Camille rolled her eyes like an exasperated teenager, "Lizzie, you don't get to where I am without outsmarting everyone," she tapped a finger to her temple. "And it didn't hurt that I had certain . . . skills and connections which could prove to be very useful in a situation like this."

Skills and connections? She wasn't sure she wanted to know. "But—"

Camille held up her hand, "Elizabeth," she said sternly, "all I need from you is a place to stay for a while where I can gather my thoughts and put a new plan into motion. *That is all.*"

Elizabeth sighed. "Will you at least tell the FBI where you are?"

Camille shrugged. "Perhaps in a few days," she said absently, like she hadn't a care in the world.

Elizabeth couldn't help but feel that Camille was deliberately being vague about her plans and she could only guess as to why. To protect her? From what? And what the hell did she mean, *skills and connections*?

She could read the woman sitting opposite her well enough to know that she wasn't going to get all the answers she was looking for, Camille had closed herself off and given as much as she was prepared to give in that moment. Elizabeth stared at her dark tea and took another sip. "Of course you can stay with me. Or you could stay here, I rented it for the week, but . . . I could extend the lease?"

She stopped to consider. "On second thought, I think you should come home to stay with me at the castle. I can have our security team in place by the time we get back. They can be trusted. We'll need to come up with a good disguise and you should go by a different name."

"Don't worry," she said in that same exasperatingly relaxed tone, "I know I will be safe at your house." She took a sip of her coffee and smiled. "I have to say, I am also looking forward to getting a glimpse into your life here."

Elizabeth smiled back. How wonderful it would be to share it with her, it was almost as if Cam would see it for herself and for Mags somehow. Represent her family before she'd found Connor, and Ireland. She found the idea made her giddy, but then she remembered Camille's social nature and wondered if even Elizabeth and Castle Bannon could keep her out of harm's way. "Yes, but you have to stay at the castle," her voice grew grave. "Even with the disguise it's not wise for you to go into the town or to meet anyone."

Camille wiggled her eyebrows. "Oh, I'll be a good little girl. Won't be any trouble at all, you'll see," she said with a mischievous twinkle in her eye.

Elizabeth shook her head, "Uhuh, sure."

"Ah, I almost forgot." Camille rose abruptly and left the

kitchen, returning a minute later with a large envelope, which she handed to Elizabeth.

"What's this?"

"Open it, you'll see. I was pretty certain last night, but I didn't want to say anything until I checked my case, made sure that I hadn't been mistaken because of all the chaos."

Elizabeth reached in to find a stack of black and white photos. They were weathered with time, the edges frayed, but they were there in her hands.

Elizabeth looked up, confused, "I thought they were lost in the—"

Camille shook her head, "I've always kept these in the safe and as for the rest of the albums, I grabbed the oldest ones, I have them here with me. And the ones I wasn't able to collect in time are still preserved, because I had everything digitized years ago. I had copies on drives in the safe and duplicates in a safety deposit box at my bank in San Francisco."

Elizabeth stared at her, trying to process her words.

Camille's voice was steady, reassuring, "You see, nothing was lost."

"Are you serious?" Elizabeth blinked. "All of it? We have copies of everything?"

"Actually, we have most of the originals, and yes all of the copies."

She could feel her face start to break into a smile as the joy registered. Before she knew it, her smile was so big, she thought it might resemble Connor's Christmas morning smile.

She smiled so hard her face hurt.

Elizabeth loved the way Camille thought, the way she had safeguarded what was precious.

Camille stood up as Elizabeth took her time rifling through the oldest of the photographs. The beautiful black and white pictures of Mags, and her sister Aurora—Elizabeth's grandmother—and Camille. Elizabeth's family. Her people, her history.

She was giddy.

"I never asked you," Camille called over her shoulder breaking Elizabeth's reverie. She was putting something away in the kitchen, "Why are you up here by yourself? Where is this husband I've heard so much about?"

Elizabeth stopped. Remembering everything that had come before Camille had shown up on her doorstep. It all came rushing back. But her joy was too strong in that moment, it kept her successfully rooted to the present.

Not wanting to relive it, she settled on a vague truth, "I just needed to clear my head . . . *and* . . . I was grieving." She tried not to think too hard about the explanation, her anger over the "article" was still there, albeit a mere shadow of what it had been before Camille's resurrection.

Camille nodded. She opened her mouth to say something and then thought better of it. She settled on a question. "Did you want to stay up here?"

Elizabeth placed the photographs carefully back in the envelope and handed them to Camille for safekeeping. She walked to the glass wall to look at Lough Aisling below.

It had turned into a bright sunny day with a California blue sky, setting off the Ireland green all around them. There was nothing else to do at the glass house. She'd gotten more than she ever could've hoped for in just a single night.

She turned back, "No, let's go home. I want to show you my life here. Show you our Irish castle."

"Well, mija, it's quite a house," Camille breathed.

"It is, isn't it." Elizabeth nodded in agreement. They'd just finished the tour. It had taken nearly forty-five minutes. They hadn't even touched the grounds.

Elizabeth returned Camille to one of the guest suites on the third floor where they had left her luggage. "I'll let you get settled, I'm just going to go into town to see what kind of disguises I can rustle up for you. Do you want a wig? Or should we dye your hair?"

Camille wheeled her giant suitcase to its place by the window before turning back, "Oh I'm not going to miss the opportunity to go into town with you. See your new home. Plus," she checked her hair in the mirror, "I will *not* have you choosing my look for me!"

"But Camille, what if you're recognized?" Elizabeth blinked rapidly, she hadn't anticipated this argument, "I mean you're not as famous as Oprah, but you're pretty well known, even internationally. And you're all over the news just now. The fire was a big deal."

Camille was still looking at herself in the mirror. She held up a hand, "I'll wear a big hat and sunglasses. Don't worry."

Elizabeth protested, "I really don't think—"

"Ehhh! I'm coming with you, you just try and stop me." She gave her a look that said *go ahead, try it, I dare you.* It was effective, even through the mirror.

Elizabeth sighed. "You're exasperating, you know that?"

Camille waved a hand and laughed, "Tell me something I don't know."

She stared at her urban auntie, trying to convince her with her eyes.

Camille's lips set in a line, she turned from the mirror to face Elizabeth.

The two women stared at each other.

After a minute, Elizabeth rolled her eyes and gave up. "Fine. We're leaving in five minutes, but I'm finding something very un-Camille-like for you to wear and I don't want any arguments!" She turned on her heel, not waiting for a response.

Camille smiled as Elizabeth left the room.

. . .

Twenty minutes later, they pulled into a spot on the small main street. The colorful village was buzzing with energy.

Elizabeth glanced at Camille for the tenth time, praying that she looked different enough.

She wore a wide-brimmed hat and oversized sunglasses. They covered her head well, but weren't so glamorous that they'd draw attention. Elizabeth had made her tuck her hair into the hat and put on a peasant top with wide-legged ivory pants.

Camille was known for her dark, but bold power suits, usually worn with a touch, or a large serving, of flare on the side.

She always looked like a fierce CEO.

Elizabeth hoped the clothing was enough of a departure from her regular image that she'd go undetected until they could source a more permanent disguise.

Camille was enchanted by the black, old-world street lamps and brightly colored buildings. The streets were filled with people now, some going about their business, others stopping here and there to take a picture. She smiled in approval, "How charming!"

They turned off the main street and headed to Sally's Boutique, the best place to get upmarket wigs and other bold statement pieces.

The shop was painted a vibrant shade of light blue. Delicate gold Celtic patterns were painted on the glass in ornate swirls.

Elizabeth reached for the door handle, but before her fingers closed on the brass knob, she turned to her companion and lowered her voice, "Please *try* to blend in and not draw attention to yourself. I *need* you to stay safe," she pleaded.

Camille opened her mouth, no doubt to give Elizabeth another version of "Don't worry," in that same exasperatingly relaxed tone, but then she closed it again without comment. She nodded instead.

Elizabeth gave her a small smile, "Thank you," she whispered.

The little bell over the door gave a sharp ring as they entered.

The walls were filled on either side with glamorous wigs made of real hair. In the middle, there were racks of shirts, trousers, dresses, and scarves.

There were bright pinks and bold patterns. Yellows and greens. There were capes and catsuits, and clothing spanning the last six decades.

It was the kind of store where a bold fashionista might go to get statement pieces, or an eccentric would go to pick up a regular wardrobe, or where more mainstream dressers could get an outfit for a costume party. Or, where famous lady billionaires currently presumed dead, could go to find a disguise to keep them hidden from assassins, the press, and the FBI.

"Hallo, Lady Lara!" Sally herself said from behind the counter.

She smoothed her sparkly blue-and-white striped blouse and touched the edge of her short curls. "How can I help you today?"

Camille went silently to the racks, and began pulling pieces, taking only a second to decide before either placing them back on the rack or into the large basket she'd grabbed from the entrance.

The quick screeching of the hangers on the steel rods worked in contrast to the soothing Andean pan flutes playing through the store speakers.

Elizabeth smiled kindly, "Hi Sally, this is my friend . . . uhhh . . ." she stopped cold. After all the care she'd put into a temporary disguise, she'd, somehow, completely forgotten a new name.

"I'm Cam," Camille said brusquely, shooting a hand up into the air so Sally could see her arm from behind the rows of clothing.

Elizabeth turned bright red. *Shit.*

Camille hadn't even tried. Elizabeth smiled again and quickly turned the attention toward the proprietor herself, asking about the business and about her daughter.

Sally cooperated with the change in conversation eagerly. Talking animatedly about the busload of tourists that had come through the day before and the influx of new customers that had followed the Summer Festival.

But she was most excited to report that her daughter, Ava, was moving back from Dublin, and would, in fact, be in Dingle later that same day.

Sally was bouncing with the thought.

"That's wonderful," Elizabeth shared in her excitement, it was difficult not to, Sally's smile was so big she looked like she'd just won the lottery. "And is she looking forward to coming home?"

Elizabeth had never met Ava, but if she was anything like the kind, joyous woman standing in front of her, she was sure she'd be someone worth knowing.

"Yes, I believe she is. She'd been unhappy with her job and busy city life for some time, you know she's almost thirty-five now? I wager a change of pace will do her good."

The bell at the door rang again, signaling a new customer.

"Well I look forward to meeting her." Elizabeth began to excuse herself.

Sally bowed her head, "Thank you, Lady Lara."

"Please, Sally, call me Elizabeth." She reached out and squeezed her arm affectionately.

Sally pressed her lips together and tried to suppress a shy smile. She nodded and turned bright pink, clearly pleased with Elizabeth's request.

Just then, the person who had walked into the store made herself known. It was Patty O'Shea, a round woman not much taller than Mona, who was known for being kind and well-meaning as much as she was known for being inadvertently unkind and a gossip.

"Oh it was so terrible, Lady Lara," Patty launched herself straight into it, "to see that picture in the paper. Simply awful! If it had been me, I would have just died! I'll tell you I had a right good shock when I saw that picture of you and Lord Bannon, I nearly choked on my morning tea. I tell you, I did. My husband came in from the next room to check on me! And he never does that, can you imagine?"

The blood rose to Elizabeth's face, hot and wild. She tried to breathe slowly as Patty continued her well-meaning assault, completely oblivious to the distress of the person in front of her.

She was so blindsided by Patty's cluelessness that she stood rooted to the spot for several minutes. She forced herself to nod every few sentences, not trusting herself to open her mouth.

At some point she had a vague notion that Patty had moved on to more pleasant topics, like the wonderful food stalls at the Summer Festival and the various events still to look forward to throughout the summer, but Elizabeth couldn't hear any of it.

She'd successfully placed the picture and the media nightmare behind her, pretty much as soon as Camille had walked through the door of the glass house. All of her other troubles seemed small and manageable . . . more than manageable, *insignificant.*

But here was this woman bringing it all into the present and reminding her that the media shit storm that had driven her to leave Dingle in the first place, hadn't even begun to blow over.

Elizabeth was so distracted by the encounter that she didn't notice Camille ask Sally for several wigs and check out with a whole new wardrobe.

Camille walked by Elizabeth and squeezed her arm, not stopping to acknowledge Patty or to speak at all. The bell rang again as she exited the store.

Camille's touch and the sound of the bell roused Elizabeth out of her fugue state long enough for her to regain herself. "It was lovely to see you Patty, my best to your family." Elizabeth gave her a forced toothy smile.

Patty smiled in earnest, clueless as ever.

"Goodbye Sally, thank you!" Elizabeth called over her shoulder as she exited the shop.

Outside on the street, the cool morning air went a long way to help soothe her. Without a word she took most of Camille's bags and started walking.

Camille followed Elizabeth's lead only speaking again when they were in the car. "Who was that woman and what was she talking about?"

"Nothing, she was no one. I don't want to talk about it." Elizabeth said through gritted teeth.

Camille tilted her head and examined Elizabeth. "You should have slapped her."

Elizabeth choked back a laugh. "Oh yeah, I'm sure that would have gone over well."

Cam shrugged. "It's not supposed to go over well, but you're right I wouldn't have slapped her either," she paused, "but I would have thought about it."

Elizabeth couldn't help but laugh, which she was sure was Camille's aim to begin with. She shook her head and started the car.

"Is there a grocery store nearby? I'd like to pick up a few things."

Elizabeth was nearly back to herself, "Sure, what do you need?"

"Oh, I feel like baking," Camille answered pleasantly.

"You bake?"

"Yes. Why are you so surprised?"

"I don't know, I've never seen you cook and you always have chefs around."

"I cook! I just relied on chefs for most of my meals and when I had company, because I didn't have time then. But I still baked."

"You did?"

"Yes! Who do you think made all of those cookies and cakes you had when you came over? The lemon cake we had last week at my house . . . and the cookies?"

"*You* made those? Seriously?" She turned to study Camille's face. "They were so good!"

But then Elizabeth's thoughts turned back to the shop.

"Wait, I was going to pay at Sally's. You shouldn't use a card! Wait, how do you even have a credit card if you're dead?"

"I don't! I used cash."

"But . . . didn't they make you show ID at the airport when you changed the money?"

Camille looked over at her, "My dear," she began, "I'm a billionaire. We billionaires tend to keep stacks of cash nearby. I had plenty stashed in my safe, in multiple currencies, of course." She said it like it was the most obvious thing in the world.

Elizabeth nodded, "Of course you did." She started the car, resigned to the very real possibility that she was just beginning to know the real Camille.

10

BAKING & LIFE

The twenty-foot high leaded windows in the solarium bathed the room in afternoon light. Elizabeth sat in the love seat opposite the bay window, looking out at the gleaming water of the pool.

Focusing on the water helped still her, she sat for some time, transfixed.

Her phone buzzed against her thigh, snapping her out of her meditative state. She retrieved it from the side pocket of her leggings. A text from Connor:

Thinking of you. I'm sorry I had to leave. Shouldn't be more than a few days. I love you, Lara. -Connor

He'd only been gone a day, but how much had happened.

She remembered her anger, remembered how he'd left her to deal with the picture in the paper. How he hadn't even bothered to explain, to tell her what had happened at the

Roman auction house. What, exactly, was demanding so much of his time and attention?

What had been so important that he had to leave when she needed him the most?

None of it mattered now. She had Camille back. Elizabeth smiled to herself as she thought of her husband coming home to find the woman of the hour not only alive, but safely installed in one of their guest suites.

She was just about to text *I love you back*, when someone knocked on the door.

Elizabeth turned her head towards the entrance of the solarium, "Come in."

Their head of security, Aidan Parker, entered. She'd called him before they'd left the glass house.

He was a tall man with brown hair and handsome features. If he hadn't become a soldier, he could have had a career as an actor. He walked towards her, back ramrod straight, with all the confidence and seriousness of a soldier. "Good evening, Lady Lara."

Elizabeth opened her mouth to ask him to call her by her first name for the thousandth, but thought better of it. She'd been correcting him for years. If it hadn't stuck by now. . . . "Hi, Parker," she said instead.

"We've secured the perimeter. There will be a five-man team stationed outside at all times. Two at the front, two at the rear and a roving patrol. We've checked all the cameras and motion sensors. Everything is in order. I'll continue to monitor the situation and adjust our numbers if necessary. You can count on us to keep you and Ms. Cortez safe."

"Thank you, Parker, we appreciate that. And the others? Do they know the truth about Camille?"

"No, I thought it best to contain that information. All the team knows is that there is a heightened threat against the family."

"Not even Henry?" Elizabeth asked. Henry Davis was their other round-the-clock security guard who worked under Aidan.

"No, with your permission I'd like to keep Ms. Cortez' true identity secret."

She examined his face. She thought she caught something in his eye. Suspicion? Surely it was something else entirely. Elizabeth nodded slowly, "Whatever you think. I'll defer to your expertise."

He thanked her and walked to the door.

Elizabeth looked up sensing he needed to say something else. "Yes?"

He hesitated. "Lady Lara, I feel confident that we can keep you, your guest and the castle secure, but are you certain you don't want me to call Declan and have him return early?"

Declan had called the day of the Summer Festival and expressed his interest in staying on for an additional two-week course in . . . Elizabeth couldn't remember what. "No, thank you. I'm sure we'll be fine. Let Declan have his fun."

"Of course." He bowed slightly, but then stayed rooted in place.

Elizabeth looked up again, raising her eyebrows, "Yes?"

"Wouldn't it . . ." he began, sounding uncharacteristically flustered, "be prudent to call Lord Bannon and inform him of the situation? I'm certain he would choose to come home so that there would be a man in the house."

The blood rose to Elizabeth's face for the second time that day. Instinctively, she stood up so he would understand the severity of her words.

"Parker," she started slowly, deliberately, with an edge she made no attempt to conceal, "I've been held at gunpoint, drugged *twice*, and kidnapped. I can handle myself. And my guest, Ms. Cortez? She may be wise in years, but she has more than five decades of martial arts experience and I'd wager she could take any one of your men, including yourself."

It was his turn to feel the blood rise to his face. He now looked as flustered as he'd sounded a moment ago.

But Elizabeth wasn't finished. "We don't need a man in this house. And I'll thank you to remember that. The estate is large and the grounds vast, I trust you and your team to keep it and us secure, but I'll have no sexist bullshit here."

His face changed again, this time with a look of contrition. He stared straight into her eyes, "My apologies. It will not happen again, you have my word," he said with a sincerity she felt instantly.

Elizabeth was satisfied, she let out a breath, and the tension in her shoulders. "Thank you. And thank you for your efforts in keeping this family safe," she said kindly, her voice filled with gratitude.

She hoped he could feel her renewed warmth.

He'd turned rigid during her monologue, but now his features softened and his body relaxed. "Of course." He gave her a small smile and excused himself from the room.

The solarium grew silent as his footsteps faded. Her eyes returned to the pool and the shimmering water, after only a few seconds she realized that the exchange had made her desperately thirsty.

She went to the kitchen for a glass of water and then noticed the time, it had been a couple of hours since she'd seen Camille. She had just resolved to go check on her when her guest waltzed into the kitchen as if on cue.

"Ta daaa!" she announced. "What do you think?" She twirled in place.

Somehow she'd managed to turn her signature silver bob into a vibrant blue. She wore a form-fitting black jumpsuit with a plunging neckline and mesh sleeves.

She also looked thirty years younger, which, Elizabeth realized was not entirely due to her change in hairstyle and wardrobe.

She moved closer. More than half the wrinkles on her face were gone.

"Well? What do you think?"

"I think . . . you look fabulous!" Her hand reached out automatically, to touch Camille's face. "How did you—"

Camille was beaming, "They're these wonderful little contraptions." She reached her temples, below her hairline and peeled something off. "See it pulls the skin taught."

She removed it completely to demonstrate.

"Wow."

"Isn't that something? I'd heard about them years ago, but never got to try them, so when I saw them at Sally's, I thought, well I'm dead, why the hell not? Aren't they something? Look, I have another one that pulls my jawline and neck."

Elizabeth's eyes followed Camille's fingers, then they settled back on the vibrant blue. "Where did you get hair dye? What happened to the wigs?"

"Oh Sally had quite a selection of hair dyes too, I picked up a few. I'll still try the wigs, but I know myself, I won't be able to wear a wig all the time. It will drive me crazy. And I see these women in their sixties, seventies, and eighties and I was always curious about having blue or pink or purple hair so again—"

"Why not." Elizabeth finished for her.

"Exactly! I think I'm going to like being dead. It's so freeing!" She fixed the device at her temples back into place. "Good disguise, right?"

Elizabeth nodded in agreement. "I can't disagree. You

look great and definitely not like Camille Cortez Fairhurst Hennings."

Camille gave her a hard look.

"I mean, you always looked beautiful as yourself. It's just now you look nothing like yourself, which was, in fact, the point of the disguise." Elizabeth gave her a sheepish grin. "You know what I mean!" She reached out and squeezed Camille's arm.

"Oh calm yourself, my love. I know what you mean."

They both laughed.

"Now, where can I get an apron so I can start baking."

Elizabeth showed her the cupboard. Camille chose both a chef's coat and an apron.

An hour later, the kitchen was filled with the smell of two cakes and a dozen cookies coming together. Camille had made full use of the large gourmet kitchen and the three ovens.

Elizabeth sat at the kitchen table absently scrolling through her Instagram feed, while Camille happily finished baking.

She had offered to help, but Camille had shooed her away. Every once in a while Elizabeth glanced up and watched Camille work. She'd never seen this side before.

The act of baking and mixing and cracking eggs and melting

butter and throwing ingredients together seemed to propel her into a Zen-like state. Camille was radiating a stillness, a sort of peace, which Elizabeth had never sensed from her before.

When the baked goods were safely installed in their respective ovens, she turned her attention to dinner. "I'm going to make the kielbasa sausages with a veggie stir fry."

Elizabeth stood up, "Sounds great. Wine?"

"Yes, please."

"What's this?" Camille was looking down into the open recycling bin tucked into the space next to the refrigerator.

"I don't know." Elizabeth walked over to see what she was looking at. The newspaper with the damn picture on the cover and the libelous article was sitting on top.

"Oh, that," she said dryly. Going to the drawer to retrieve the wine opener. She put more force into cutting through the foil on the bottle than was strictly necessary. "That's what passes for journalism apparently," she said through gritted teeth.

Elizabeth looked over, Camille was reading.

"Huh." Camille finished.

Elizabeth watched as Cam's eyes settled back onto the picture.

She gave a low whistle. "That's some husband, caliente!" she let out a soft chuckle, but then took in Elizabeth's silence. "The picture really bothers you."

Elizabeth unclenched her jaw to answer, "Of course it does, look at it. But I think the article is actually worse. They make me out to be some Jezebel who seduced him. It's not some nice moment between a husband and a wife—which, of course, *Connor* instigated. It's some tawdry thing, and apparently it's all my fault. I'm so tired of these double standards and sexism everywhere I look!"

"Oh mija, you're preaching to the choir. The media is mostly filled with a bunch of assholes, you can't take it personally."

"Yes I can. I'm not one to sit down and shut up when something is unfair."

"Well to each their own. I found that standing up to the media in any way shape or form only seemed to hurt my business. And all I cared about was my business. Building it, maintaining it. I had a different set of priorities, but you've always been a champion for what's right."

Elizabeth scrunched her eyes together, "I don't know about that. I was a pretty big asshole there myself for a while. Represented whoever our client was in a divorce . . . although, I guess I did manage to pawn the really morally questionable clients off to others, because I didn't want to have to champion evil people."

Camille shrugged. "At heart, I'm sure you were a champion even during your ruthless lawyer years."

Elizabeth considered that.

"What does Connor say?"

She huffed in frustration, "That it will just blow over soon."

"Well if this bothers you so much, why isn't he here?" Camille struck a nerve.

"There's something happening at his auction house in Rome. I don't know it's been taking up a lot of his time. I'm guessing whatever it is, has been happening for a few weeks now since something was up before I left for California."

"You don't seem to know much at all." Camille zeroed in and struck the same nerve.

Elizabeth winced.

Camille wasn't deterred. "Is he usually vague about his business?"

"No."

"And you trust him generally?"

"Yes, of course."

"Well then I'm sure he has a good reason for not sharing his business troubles with you."

Elizabeth considered. It had been strange that he didn't specify the reason why he had to go. He just said that he had to and apologized for leaving, but why hadn't he told her what was wrong?

She shook her head, "I don't know why he didn't tell me. Maybe he thought I was dealing with a lot and he didn't want me to worry, I don't know." She straightened, "I trust my husband," she said more firmly.

"Don't get me wrong, I was upset that he was leaving in the first place. Leaving me to deal with this media shit storm and angry that he wasn't as incensed as I was, but . . . I don't know." Elizabeth set her glass of wine down and placed her elbows on the kitchen island, burying her face in her hands. "I don't know what to do."

"About Connor?"

"No, about that," she motioned towards the recycling indicating the paper. "Or . . ." Her mind returned to the offer she had received. The offer she hadn't thought of in days.

"Cam, you know those inner voices that everyone has, the ones that tell you what's right and what's wrong for you?"

"Like a conscience you mean?"

"No, well yes, but no I mean more like those inner voices that tell you which path to take. They sort of whisper and if you listen, they always steer you in the right direction. They sort of make it impossible to go wrong in life, but you have to be able to hear them."

"Oh sure. It's kind of like your gut, but it's also intuition, you mean like that?"

"Yes."

"Oh I definitely relied on my inner voices to build my company. There are things I just knew. I knew when I first started that if I just put my head down and went after this idea I would make it big. And then I knew when the time came to diversify. Knew when to go into real estate. There was no one telling me to do it, it wasn't a trend then . . . it was just . . . my path."

"Yes, exactly."

She stared down into the rich red color of her wine,

taking the stem between her thumb and forefinger and turning it in a circle.

Camille set her glass down on the island. "Is there a reason you asked?"

Elizabeth nodded, still looking into her wine, "These last five years have been amazing, so much more than I could've dreamed of for myself . . . but when I first came to Ireland I was so disconnected from those voices—it's what fundamentally went wrong during my lost decade as a lawyer—I couldn't hear them, and when I came here to grieve Mags, I was forced to be still for the first time in years.

"And I had Mags' box of letters to kick me into high gear. The grief, the letters . . . *this* place, all of it worked to finally reconnect me. And reconnecting with those inner voices was honestly the greatest accomplishment of my life.

"But over the years, with the traveling, and the photography exhibitions, and finally just living this full life, I don't know, at some point, I just stopped being able to hear them, you know? And I guess I asked you, because . . . I'm so afraid."

Camille was surprised by the torrent that flowed out of Elizabeth. "What are you afraid of, Lizzie?"

"I'm so afraid that somehow I'll get lost again . . . or maybe it's that I'm afraid I'm already lost. I had no idea back then, during that lost decade. Mags knew it, but I didn't." She shook her head, some remnants of the shame she'd felt then, at not having listened to her great-aunt when she'd been alive, rose to the surface.

"I've just been so desperate lately to reconnect with those voices. I thought going to California and packing up Mags' things, being on my own for a bit, that maybe I'd be able to hear them again. And I really needed to hear them, especially since I have a choice to make and I really need to know what I should do."

Camille was alarmed. "Are you OK? What do you need to decide?"

"I'm fine. It's nothing bad. It's just that, again I'm worried that I'm already lost." She took a sip of her wine and let the flavors invigorate her mouth. She stared into her glass, realizing that she'd never even said the next part out loud. It was a huge honor and no one knew about it.

Until now.

Elizabeth let herself feel happy for a moment—without all the complicated feelings she'd attached to it from the start. It was a nice change.

She sat up a little straighter and looked at Camille, "I've received an offer, an invitation really, from the Met in New York. They offer it once every two years to a photographer of note, it's a *big deal* to be asked. If I accept, I'll have a show at the Met and need to move to New York for a year to be their artist in residence."

11

THE HOUSEGUESTS

"*L*izzie, that's amazing! Congratulations, mija!" Camille said in a rush. She was on her feet now, propelled by her excitement.

"Why aren't you celebrating? I don't understand what's to think about? This is your dilemma?"

"Thank you," Elizabeth smiled, again allowing herself to just feel the joy of it, even if only for a moment longer.

"Yes, I know it's a big deal . . . a highly coveted honor. But, I don't know if it's an honor I want," she said simply.

"It isn't?" Camille was confused.

"It's an entire year in New York, and I'm done with the days where I choose to climb a ladder, just because it's a ladder I can climb. I'm afraid this would be just that, conquering another ladder, and that's not why I started taking pictures again. I picked up a camera again because I wanted to, I just wanted to—there was no other reason. It was liberating."

"It's OK to enjoy something, to do it completely for pleasure, and still be acknowledged for being good at what you do," Camille observed, studying her carefully.

"I know . . . and it has been wonderful getting all of this acclaim and all of these opportunities, I'm just worried that—"

"That saying yes will lead to your getting lost again," Camille finished.

"Yes, or mean that I'm already lost."

Camille didn't immediately respond. She let the silence grow between them.

Elizabeth kept thinking out loud, "Don't get me wrong, I'm happy that I was chosen, but I just don't know if I should do it and I don't hear anything from inside. And honestly I'm not going to do something if I don't think it's right for me."

"Well, do you think it's wrong for you?"

"See, that's what I don't know. I feel happy, I feel honored, but beyond that I don't know anything. Returning to photography was this amazing period in my life that went right alongside coming to Ireland and Mags' box of letters and opening myself up to Connor and opening myself up to life again.

"I started doing it for just the pure joy of it and then I got that photographer of the year award by sheer dumb luck. And the next thing I know I'm traveling the world, getting to have these amazing experiences, documenting them all and then being tapped to exhibit everywhere.

"I definitely think that was all meant to be, and I was living my best life and I *was* following the voices then, but at some point . . . and I don't know when exactly it happened, I stopped being able to hear them. At some point I stopped being directly connected to the Universe. And I don't want to repeat the mistakes of my past."

"Is that what you were doing at the house in the woods?"

"Something like that? I wanted to get as far away from . . . ," she motioned towards the recycling again, "and I needed to grieve and process losing you, but yeah I suppose that was partially the point. To hear myself again and to feel confident —to know what to do."

Elizabeth stood up and started pacing, "Like that article and picture, the old me would've known exactly what to do and I don't mean old lawyer me, I mean me who I was five years ago, four years ago, three years ago.

"I would have just instinctively known what the best thing was to do. But in my current reality, I *don't* know. I'm just angry and overwhelmed and keep falling into a tailspin."

"Mija, you really need to change your perspective on the article. Because that picture is hot, and your husband is a total fox."

Elizabeth raised an eyebrow, "Fox?"

Camille narrowed her eyes, "Stay with me," she scolded. "And the people who know you don't give a damn. And the married people who know how difficult marriage is and how easy it is to lose that chemistry and that spark, will envy you, or maybe even congratulate you for still being so into each other after what? Four years of marriage?"

Elizabeth nodded.

"I mean, I remember *my* marriages." She held up a hand in a *just a moment* gesture.

Camille disappeared and then returned with a small photo album. "I don't think I've ever shown you these." She flipped to a page near the beginning, "This was Daniel Straton, my first husband."

She examined the picture of a young Camille in a 50s style white dress standing next to a man with light brown hair in a blue suit. "What happened?"

"Well, we were married in 1957—I was stupid young—only twenty-two, it was just before I started my company."

"When did you get divorced?"

Camille nodded, "1957," she laughed. "We were only married for three months. It was a learning experience, let's just leave it at that." She pursed her lips, thinking, a small mischievous smile appeared for a moment and then was gone.

She flipped to a page in the middle, "This was Noah

Fairhurst, my second husband and Isabelle's father." She turned the page again to a photo of a baby girl with a ribbon on her head. Camille brushed the picture lightly with her finger.

"That was a good marriage until my company took off and I didn't have time to be a proper wife or mother. That marriage lasted from 1961 to 1966. Isabelle was four when we got divorced. They had a lovely relationship the two of them. Unfortunately, he died just a couple of years after the divorce."

Elizabeth watched Camille's face as some unknown emotion colored her features. "I'm sorry."

Cam shrugged, "Así es la vida." She flipped through several pages of Isabelle at various stages of childhood.

After briefly stopping at some pictures of Elizabeth and Mags, Camille flipped to the end, "And this was my third husband, Stephen Hennings. He was a lovely man. We were married for ten years until he died of a heart attack twelve years ago. Do you remember him?"

Elizabeth tried, "Vaguely? I think I only met him once or twice, he was never around."

"Well you must have been, what, eighteen when we married? You were off and busy at Yale by that point and then you went immediately into law school—"

"And then my lost decade." Elizabeth finished.

Camille nodded. "He was also a busy man, he had his

own company to run, which is probably why your paths never crossed when you came by the house."

Elizabeth looked at the photo of Camille with the younger man.

"I was sixty when we married, he forty-five," she smiled mischievously. She flipped the page. There was a picture with the same man and a child. "That's Josh, his son from a previous relationship. I was Stephen's first wife, his previous girlfriend was fifteen years younger than him, so our marriage caused quite the stir in his circle. Men don't typically go from a hot trophy girlfriend fifteen years their junior to a hot trophy wife fifteen years their elder!" She laughed, remembering and delighting in the scandal.

Elizabeth was surprised. "Did he leave his girlfriend for you?"

Camille was taken aback, "Oh goodness, no! They'd broken up years before he ever met me, and anyway she'd been exposed as a gold digger at some point. He kept things civil for the child's sake, but that was it."

They looked through several more pages of pictures, "Oh look how young we were!" She pointed to a picture of her and Mags together. She sighed and closed the book.

"I guess you are a bit of a marriage expert," Elizabeth chuckled.

"And don't you forget it. No, it wasn't always easy, but I think I did get it right with my last one, with Stephen. His son was a little shit, but he didn't live with us and that was hardly my fault, but yes, my business and my last marriage those are my only real accomplishments in life."

"Oh please!"

"No, really. Business and my third marriage. I was a disaster of a mother." She shook her head.

"Oh come on, I'm sure that's not true."

"No, really. You never really knew my daughter. She wasn't around by the time you were born."

Elizabeth had some vague recollection of Isabelle. A young woman with flowing brown hair. She remembered her coming by the house a few times. She and Camille always seemed to fight, but Elizabeth couldn't be sure, she had been so young then.

"I loved my daughter, but I was not taught to be a mother. Mine was not loving. I actually received more love and attention from your great-grandfather, Alejandro. He was a really good man and I was lucky to have grown up," she stopped considering her words, "as part of that family. The Laras. But," she took a sip of her wine. "Some people shouldn't be mothers. And I was one of them."

"I've never really heard you speak of your daughter. What happened?" Elizabeth ventured hesitantly.

"We . . . had a falling out," her voice shook.

"Well," Elizabeth paused, not sure she should ask again, "what happened?"

Camille read her face. "I know what you must be thinking." She took in a deep breath, "Let's just say the falling out was severe. My career put her in mortal danger and she spent the rest of her life cutting all ties and burying any connection between us. She even had her birth certificate changed."

Elizabeth's mouth fell open. Her curiosity was overflowing, but she correctly sensed that Camille wouldn't give her more even if she asked. "I'm sorry," she said, trying to be sympathetic instead of curious. "You know what happened with my mother, of course."

Camille nodded and looked down. "Poor Carolina."

"But I was lucky too. Mags was the best. And I was lucky to have you as well. You were always like my aunt and another powerful mother figure." Elizabeth reached out and squeezed her hand.

Camille let her.

"Anyway, that very long tangent down memory lane and talking about my marriages was supposed to help give you some perspective on the article. Marriage is a long road, the thing in the paper is a bump in the road and if you change your perspective on it, you'll see that, to those who have brains and aren't judgmental asshats, you actually come off rather well."

Elizabeth let that thought marinate.

Camille squeezed her hand, "Keep trying, Lizzie. You'll find your place here, you'll reconnect with your voices. I'm sure of it."

Elizabeth smiled wistfully, "I wish I could just hear them already!"

"Well maybe you need some more out-of-the-box thinking. Have you tried meditation?"

Elizabeth nodded, "I've tried yoga, meditation, walking. Maybe I just need to go off into the woods for a month by myself, become a wild wolf woman and then I will hear them again."

"Is that what worked last time?"

"No."

"Well then, what did?"

Elizabeth considered. "I guess there was the month I just stayed in the cottage across the lough. Kind of had this embarrassing meltdown at the Cliffs of Moher and Connor brought me home, and then I just slept and I grieved and I cried and I read books and it rained. But then it stopped raining, and I rejoined the world again. I ate chocolate and opened myself up to Connor, I danced. I took photographs."

"They were all things you wanted to do?"

Elizabeth nodded.

"They were all things that involved you opening yourself up to the world?"

Again Elizabeth nodded.

"Well, what do you want to do right now?"

Elizabeth's lips turned up into an impish grin, "Eat some of the cookies you just made?"

"OK, that's a good start. What about tomorrow?"

Elizabeth pursed her lips, "Tomorrow's the full moon. I just read that it's a supermoon and will appear four times bigger than usual. I'd like to do something with the moon. My go-to is to photograph it, but I don't think I want to do that."

Camille's face slowly split into a smile, "I've got an interesting idea, it's a little out there, a bit crazy. Are you open to trying something new?"

Elizabeth's eyes grew wide. "Sure," she hesitated. What, *exactly*, did Camille classify as crazy?

"Have you ever heard of a moon circle?"

She shook her head, but she was suddenly at attention.

"It's a type of women's circle that comes together at the full moon. And there's guided meditation and other things. From what I understand it's a sort of celebration of the divine feminine. A celebration of sisterhood. At least that's what I've read."

"A moon circle?"

Camille nodded, "A moon circle."

Elizabeth was intrigued, her brain was buzzing with the possibility.

Camille could see the idea taking root in Elizabeth's brain. "Now, if you'll excuse me I need to finish dinner." She walked back to the stove.

Elizabeth nodded absently and went back to the kitchen table to look at her tablet.

A quick Google search later, the idea of a moon circle took hold. All she needed was a group of women. They could have it at the castle, perhaps on the great lawn past the pool and near the grotto.

It *was* a crazy idea, but something inside her perked up. She looked over at Camille, "If I was able to put this thing together by tomorrow, and we had it here, do you think you would come?"

"Sure, why not? After all, I'm dead and I'd love to support you. Women need other women . . . and maybe part of finding your place here is finding your support system."

Elizabeth walked over to the stove and put her arm over Camille. "How'd you get so wise?"

"Decades of practice." Camille kissed her cheek.

Elizabeth gave her another affectionate squeeze before walking back to the table, thinking about how glad she was to have her at the castle. A side benefit to the moon circle would be to keep Camille at home. She was a social creature by nature and would have trouble staying put for long.

If she brought women over and had this moon party maybe it would help keep her in one place, help keep her safe.

She quickly made a mental list, they would need at least eight women. Cam, Dree if she was around, Kaitlin Morgan, maybe Mona, and she could ask Bree.

She had no idea if it would work, but she thought it was worth trying. She took out her phone and was about to text Dree when the doorbell demanded her attention.

She set her phone down and went to investigate.

Dree's timing was impeccable. She didn't wait for a hello she just threw herself at Elizabeth and hugged her tightly, "Are you OK?"

Elizabeth hugged her back, "Yes, I'm fine thanks for asking."

Kilian came in behind her.

Audre explained, "I've just come to check on you and have a visit. And Kilian wanted to—"

"Drop off a thumb drive with some new things I've been working on, do you mind havin' a listen?"

"No, not at all. Come in, come in. Do you guys want some wine?"

"It's a yes for me, but Kilian can't stay," Audre answered.

Elizabeth turned to Kilian.

"Yeah, sorry. I have plans with some of my old mates from school. I'll just come in for a quick minute."

They moved through the foyer and found the kitchen. Camille was standing over the large six-burner stove stirring the vegetables.

"That smells amazing!" Audre moved closer to Camille.

"Oh, right." Elizabeth moved to stand next to Camille. "Guys, this is my friend Cam from the states."

Camille shook their hands, but she lingered on Kilian. She gave him a proper once over with her eyes.

He turned bright red. "Well, here's the flash drive. There's no rush I just thought it would be easier to drop it off versus emailing. Sorry to say hi and run, but I've really got to go meet the lads."

"Are you sure you can't stay for dinner?" Camille asked flirtatiously.

"No, I'm sorry. It smells amazing, I wish I could, but I promised them." He turned to Audre, "Dree can I talk to you for a second?" he motioned.

Audre and Kilian walked to the entrance of the kitchen and whispered something, bringing their heads closer together for a few seconds before Kilian turned to excuse himself, "It was lovely to meet you, Cam. Liz, don't listen to those maggots at the paper. And don't worry we have your back."

He walked over and gave her one of his bear hugs.

"Thanks," she said into his bicep.

He excused himself and was gone a minute later.

Camille let out a low whistle, and turned to Dree, "Your honey is one damn good looking man."

Audre turned an imperceptibly faint shade of pink, "Oh he's not my man. We're just . . . I mean I'm his—we're just really good friends. I'm his manager and business partner."

Camille stared at Audre, examining her and holding her in her gaze for an uncomfortable moment. "You mean you and him aren't?"

Audre shook her head.

"Why not? Is there something wrong with you?"

"No," Audre said, uncertainty colored her voice.

"Cam!" Elizabeth protested.

"No there's nothing wrong with me, thank you. What if he's just not my type?" she answered more confidently.

"Oh, I see." Understanding dawned on Camille's face. "You like the ladies. Well that's wonderful." She returned to stirring the veg.

"No, I don't." Audre stopped. "I mean, well there was that one time at Uni, but no, I generally prefer men."

Camille turned around again, "But you don't like *that* man?"

"No I like him very much we're just not romantically involved."

Again, Camille started more slowly, her accent was thick, "Then what's wrong with you? That's as fine a man as can be found anywhere. What? You don't like to be happy?"

"Cam!" Elizabeth stood up.

"Just to be clear, I'm not saying you need a man to be happy," she stopped, a sparkle of mischief colored her eyes, "it's just that they sure can be fun. But. . . ." Camille shrugged and held up her hands in defeat, turning back to the veg.

Audre's face went from embarrassment, to shock, to something else Elizabeth couldn't decipher. She moved closer to Camille. "Wait a minute, you look familiar."

Elizabeth was on high alert. She hadn't planned on revealing Camille to anyone except Connor and the security team.

Camille stopped stirring the vegetables and turned

towards Dree, back straight, face grave. She crossed her arms and waited.

"Oh my God! You're—" Dree went white.

Elizabeth walked over to stand between them.

"But—" Audre Bright looked like she might fall over.

"Breathe, Dree."

"How—" her eyebrows scrunched together, he mouth wide open.

"Audre," Elizabeth said calmly, "this is Camille."

Audre extended her hand in a slow, robotic kind of way. Camille extended hers quickly and shook firmly.

Audre's lips had finally started to regain movement, "Camille. Fairhurst. Hennings," she said in awe.

"Camille *Cortez* Fairhurst Hennings," Cam corrected.

"Wow, it is such a pleasure to meet you. Wait—" She turned to Elizabeth, all the confusion was back in an instant. She shook her head and waited for an explanation.

Elizabeth opened her mouth to answer, but she didn't know where to begin and she didn't know how much she should reveal.

"Babes, come on. You've got a badass lady billionaire standing in your kitchen . . . She's making dinner like that's the most normal thing in the world." She turned back to Camille, "I've always looked up to you by the way. I think you are such an inspiration to strong women everywhere. Thank you."

Audre took Camille's hand once again and shook it more fervently.

Camille extracted herself, but was pleased. "Thank you. Lizzie, do you want to explain, because my dinner is burning."

Elizabeth took Audre's hand and led her to the table. She poured her a glass of wine and gave her the short version.

"Wow," Audre said, sitting back in her chair just as Elizabeth finished. "It's like a movie."

Elizabeth grew serious. "Dree you can't tell anyone, OK? Seriously. The FBI doesn't even know where she is. Only I know and Aidan our head of security here at the castle."

"You mean Connor doesn't know?"

"No, not yet," she said more harshly than she had intended, "he'll find out when he gets home." She tried to change the subject. "Hey, how long are you going to be in Ireland? And where are you staying again?"

"I'm not sure yet. Anywhere from four to six weeks. It all depends on the Dublin shows and then the big stadium concert. Why?"

"Well if you're popping into Dublin and other parts of Ireland here and there why stay at a hotel? Why don't you stay here? We have plenty of room and it would be nice to have you around while you're in the country."

"Oh, I don't know Babes. I don't want you to get sick of me, I can be a lot."

"I can see that," Camille said dryly, now emptying the contents of the pan into a large white serving dish.

Elizabeth shook her head and rolled her eyes before turning to Audre. "Don't listen to her. And you are never a lot, you are just Audre. I know you and I still love you."

"Hmmm . . . I don't know. Are you sure?"

Camille interjected, "Listen to the woman. She doesn't want to stay here. You can't force her," she said a little too innocently.

"Don't be silly," she ignored Cam. "You're my best friend and I never get to see you for very long so why not make the most out of the time you're here?"

"All right," Audre's face broke into a smile as she came around to the idea. "I *have* always wanted to live in a castle. I accept."

Elizabeth laughed. "Great!" She squeezed Audre's shoulder before moving to the cupboard to retrieve a set of plates. She placed them on the kitchen island and then remembered, "Dree . . .?"

"Yes, Babes?" Audre said, not looking up from her phone, already engrossed in canceling her hotel reservation and making arrangements to collect her things.

"How do you feel about moon circles?"

Audre looked up immediately, "Well they're bloody brilliant, aren't they! Oh God, I love them!" She stood and joined the other ladies at the kitchen counter.

"I did one last summer just outside of London because I

really wanted to try it and because I was feeling a little meh about life.

"And it completely opened me up and freed so much headspace. I was just lighter and more open to the world, to the possibilities I tell you, I was."

Then she lowered her voice conspiratorially, "I actually had the best sex of my life the very next day. Ah-mazing." She slapped the counter with a *how do you like that* motion.

Camille narrowed her eyes, and looked at Elizabeth, "Hmmm . . . you know . . . I'm beginning to like her."

Audre registered the comment with a huge smile before continuing, "And then at the end of the week I got a raise I'd been wanting, which turned out to be neither here nor there because I quit at the end of that month to go manage Kil."

Her energy was contagious. Audre was vibrating.

"Wow," Elizabeth said breathless. "Now I'm really intrigued."

But Audre wasn't finished, she grabbed her arm in mock alarm as she remembered something, "You know, I think it was actually the thing that opened me up and made me follow my intuition when I heard Kilian's song later that month. It was like . . . I just knew I could launch him into stardom.

"And I was light and limber," she started to move her body in unpredictable ways to demonstrate, like she was grooving to some music only she could hear, "and just feelin' the Universe, you know?" She laughed, her whole body practically shaking with the force of it.

"OK, I'm sold," Elizabeth slapped the counter herself. "Are you up for one tomorrow night right here?"

Audre's eyes grew so large, Elizabeth thought they were going to pop out of her face. She clasped her hands together under her chin and bounced in placed. A sound not unlike "squeee," left her lips.

12

THE MOON CIRCLE

*T*he night was deliciously warm.

The sky was clear, and the moon cast its silvery goodness down on the great lawn of Castle Bannon.

Audre had taken it upon herself to organize everything, especially after she'd understood Elizabeth's reasons for bringing the circle together in the first place. She was a big proponent of her best friend reconnecting with her inner voices, and so, Audre was adamant that Elizabeth should sit back, relax, and just enjoy the experience.

She also insisted on leading the circle, and, owing to the fact that Dree was the only person with any actual moon circle experience, and the fact that it obviously gave her so much pleasure to organize the whole thing, Elizabeth was happy to surrender.

Everything was setup on the great lawn beyond the pool just before the grotto.

They had turned on all the lights of the estate. The twinkle lights which surrounded the pool, the lights in the trees, the uplighters that framed the manicured trees and bushes around the lawn.

But Audre had wanted even more ambiance.

"Dree, don't you think this is going to be overkill?" Elizabeth had asked when Audre came home with boxes and boxes of extra twinkle lights.

"Shhh!" was all the response she was going to get.

Audre threaded more lights through the ivy that climbed up the grotto and then arranged some in neat rows across the lawn.

There were hundreds of lights, possibly thousands, strewn across the green grass. In the middle she had defined the circle itself with a long, single string of lights, and tall white pillar candles.

Two tables had been brought outside to hold the accessories of the night. One table held ten yoga mats, and ten yoga bolster cushions as well as several blankets in case the night turned cool.

The second table held a dozen tea lights, a dozen leather bound journals, sparkly pens, and a dozen black and purple permanent markers.

There was a deck of tarot cards and a series of inspirational quotations laid out face down on the table.

The ladies began to arrive at nine. The summer nights were long in June and Audre had wanted the circle to begin and end when the sky was as black as possible and the moon a giant silvery orb overhead.

Elizabeth, Audre, and Cam, were joined by Connor's longtime friend and one of Elizabeth's closest Irish friends, Bree Wilde.

Then there was the effervescent Mona who, although she had no real idea of what the night would entail, had been extremely pleased to be asked. Elizabeth had encouraged her to bring a couple of friends and she had been happy to oblige.

She had brought her longtime friend Cailin Dean, who had once danced with Mona and Rhia, Connor's mother, in a professional dance troupe when they were in their twenties. Cailin was much taller than Mona, with long willowy limbs. Elizabeth imagined what she must have looked like at twenty, and the delicately elegant dancer she would have been on stage. The perfect ballerina.

Then there was Mona's other friend, Alice Stewart, she had shrewd eyes and looked skeptical, but had been prevailed upon by Mona to attend.

And finally Kaitlin Morgan. She was Kaitlin Massey when she had first met Elizabeth all those years ago, but was now Morgan after marrying Connor's friend and former business associate, Shaun Morgan.

It had been Shaun who'd failed to inform Connor that

he'd rented out Rhia's cottage five years ago, thereby facilitating Elizabeth's and Connor's first naked encounter.

She smiled at the memory.

They stood together in their group of eight, thinking they were complete in their party, until the doorbell rang once more.

Audre and Elizabeth exchanged quizzical looks.

Kaitlin turned bright red, and remembered, "Oh, I'm so sorry. I completely forgot. I ran into an old friend this morning just after receiving your invitation and I was so excited that I invited her to come along." Kaitlin smiled shyly, clearly embarrassed. "I hope it's OK," she added quickly.

Elizabeth put her at ease and reminded her that she had, in fact, mentioned that she could bring a friend if she wanted.

But Kaitlin was still as red as a Ferrari.

"Seriously, Kait it's fine. More than fine." Elizabeth tried to ease her anxiety.

Audre went to answer the door and a second later she returned with their ninth woman.

Kaitlin greeted her at the entrance to the living area, "Everyone, this is my good friend from school, Ava O'Reilly. She's just moved back, what was it? Yesterday?" She looked over at the woman. "Anyway, she's just come back and I thought it would be nice for her to meet some new people."

Elizabeth welcomed her. "It's nice to meet you. O'Reilly .. . you wouldn't be Sally O'Reilly's daughter? Because I was in there yesterday and she was so excited for you to come home."

Ava tucked her straight vibrant red hair behind her ear, her dark green eyes perked up, "Indeed I am. Oh no, was she going on about me?" Her eyebrows furrowed together, "I hope she didn't talk your ear off."

"No, not at all. We're happy to have you."

Ava smiled graciously, and nodded. Elizabeth introduced all of the women to each other, and introduced Camille as "Cam," an old family friend from the states.

"OK, ladies," Audre began, "I hope you're ready. Now if you'll just follow me." She led everyone out through the castle foyer, the grand lounge, and the solarium to give them the most impressive view of the backyard.

Audre beamed as the women took in the grounds completely covered in fairy lights and vibrant colored uplighters.

There were more than a few "Wows!" and "Jaysus, Mary, and Josephs!" which gratified Audre to no end.

Elizabeth dropped near the back of the group intentionally, hoping to make Ava feel welcome.

Her mother, Sally, had always been kind to her and she wanted to repay the favor. "So how is it being back?"

Ava smoothed her boho chic flowy blouse as she walked. She cleared her throat, "It's been nice. I mean I'm a little overwhelmed, Ma is so excited, she talked my ear off all last night, and she's already started to make plans. I don't think she ever thought I would come back to live in Dingle."

"Why not?" Elizabeth asked bluntly before she could stop herself.

"Oh, I was always the dreamer, the one to want to go far away to Uni, to work, everything, all my dreams were always out there," she used her hands to motion. "But, life has a funny way of changing you."

She sounded sad.

"Are you OK?" Elizabeth asked gently.

"Oh, yes. You know, the usual, burnout, sexist pricks everywhere you look, a bad breakup."

Elizabeth gave her a sympathetic look. "I'm sorry about the breakup."

She shrugged, "He wasn't right for me. I always knew he wasn't right for me . . . and yet . . . I don't know. I don't know why I didn't leave sooner. It wasn't bad or anything. We just didn't fit. Sorry I'm probably not making any sense, here I am going on and you've only just met me. Don't listen to my sad story. It's really not sad, but like with every breakup, if there was any love at all, you feel it."

Elizabeth nodded. "What's the story with the sexist pricks?" Elizabeth asked, trying to get her mind off of her former relationship, as they went by the last of the trees surrounding the pool and made their way towards the grotto.

"Oh you know, work stuff. I'm a journalist, guess I just got passed up for a promotion one too many times."

Elizabeth's ears perked up, "And are you still going to pursue journalism here?"

"Yes, in fact, I had just accepted a position at the Dingle Daily, when I bumped into Kaitlin this morning and she told me about your gathering."

Elizabeth was instantly on edge. Her recent experiences had taught her to put a wall up with reporters, to guard herself against Ava O'Reilly. But Ava herself didn't feel like a threat. She felt like good people.

Elizabeth was still trying to reconcile her feelings when they reached the circle. Luckily, she was spared from giving Ava a response.

Audre motioned all of the women to the tables. "All right you lot, please grab a yoga mat and a yoga bolster roller cushion and set them up in a circle on the inside of the twinkle lights that you see here. Try to make them equidistant from each other so we have a nice round circle, OK?"

The ladies did as they were told. Elizabeth chose a purple yoga mat and a dark green bolster cushion.

Nine mats were arranged in a circle. Audre went around fixing them to make it as perfect as possible.

"OK, now please come to the table and pick up a tea light candle, a leather-bound journal, a pen, then take a tarot card," she quickly spread out the tarot deck so all of the cards in the deck were accessible. They were all face down.

"Take a card, but don't look at it and then also take one of these cards," she picked up a white index card, "but don't look at it either until I tell you. And then finally make sure to take a black or purple Sharpie."

The women did as they were told and settled onto the yoga mats placing the items they had just procured on the grass in front of their mats.

Audre had planned the evening perfectly; the moon was bright and beautiful overhead. It waited in the sky and watched over them, blessing them with its light.

"Please get comfortable. Find whatever position on the mat feels good to you. You can lie down, you can use the bolster under your head or under your knees, or not at all. As you might have guessed, I will be running this soirée. I ask for complete silence. I will now be lowering my voice, as I guide you through an initial meditation."

Elizabeth's mat was placed between Audre and Camille.

Everyone was seated except for Audre. She reached for a white pillar candle from the table, lit it, and placed it in the center of their circle.

She stood in front of it, at the heart of the circle, like a high priestess. "We are here together this night, to give thanks for the blood that flows through our veins, for the breath that flows through our lungs, for the life force that runs through each of us. We are here under the full moon, bonded together in sisterhood. We open ourselves up to the Universe, to the magic and possibilities of this life. We do this through love, through gratitude, and through our joint power as women. Please repeat after me."

Audre spoke slowly, deliberately. "We are here together under the full moon."

The women's voices came together in unison.

"We are here to regain our power. We are here to celebrate life. We are here to bond together in solidarity."

The group repeated her words.

"We are open to any and all revelations that should transpire. We give ourselves over to the divine feminine and the Universe."

The women followed.

"Now close your eyes," Audre instructed. "And lie down, get comfortable, this will be a nice long guided meditation."

Next to her, Camille moved the bolster under her knees while Audre stood and moved around the circle as she prepared to begin the meditation.

Elizabeth followed Camille's example and put the bolster under her knees. She closed her eyes and breathed into the mat.

"Close your eyes. Take a deep breath in, hold for five seconds, and release. And again."

Elizabeth felt herself sinking further and further into the mat.

"Allow yourself to feel heavy. To feel grounded, connected to the earth. You are one with everything and everyone around you. All part of the same cosmic energy. The same divine love. Take a deep breath in, hold for five, and release. Allow the concerns of the world to float away.

Imagine writing them all down, one by one and sticking them in a balloon. In a moment, you will let the balloon float away. It will move past the stratosphere away from you, never to be seen again."

Elizabeth remembered the horrible picture, the hurtful words. She remembered Connor leaving, his bag packed at his feet, just as she'd asked for help. She thought of the offer and New York and the choices she had to make. She thought of Camille, and her life still in danger.

"Take another deep breath, this time hold for ten seconds, if you can, and release as slowly as you can manage. See the red balloon filled with all of your problems and worries and concerns. See it float away, watch it until you can see it no more. It has now disappeared and it has taken all of your cares with it."

Thirty minutes later, Audre brought them out of their deep meditative states.

Still lying flat on the mat, Elizabeth wiped the tears from her eyes with the back of her hand before opening them. She sat up slowly and noticed that several of the other women had also shed tears. They looked around at each other bleary-eyed, but awake.

They all sat up slowly, their bodies coming back to life. Kaitlin sighed and moved her shoulders in a circle. Cailin stretched her arms overhead. Ava wiped the tears from her eyes and crossed her legs.

Mona's cheeks were flushed, she hugged her knees to her chest.

Bree massaged her neck, stroked her arms, and even moved her hands over her breasts, as if she were reacquainting herself with her body.

It appeared that only Alice and Cam hadn't shed any tears. Camille looked around, she was perplexed by all the crying, but even she looked a thousand times more relaxed than before.

No one spoke, they were all still very much at peace. Now accustomed to Audre's voice guiding them through the meditation.

"Now please pick up your pen and your journal." Audre continued in that same relaxing tone. "Begin by writing five things that you're grateful for. Then five things that you want for yourself tomorrow. And finally write down three things that you want for yourself this year.

"We'll take ten minutes to do this, if you finish quickly please free write for the remainder of the time. You can write anything. Some people choose to write about what they felt during the meditation, others want to expound on their desires, you can just doodle if you like.

"No one else will be reading these journals. It can be complete nonsense, you can be as vulnerable or as nonsensical as you like. This is just about you, your words, your mind. Begin."

"OK, we've reached the point in our moon circle where we each share something. It can be what you felt during the meditation, you can talk about what you just wrote, you can talk about the pain and anxiety and problems that you've been dealing with.

"You can share anything that you like. This is a safe place. We are all sisters here. There is nothing that you cannot say. Who would like to begin?"

Bree cleared her throat, "I'd like to," her voice was slightly hoarse from not speaking, she cleared it again, "I'd like to have really amazing sex within the month."

Everyone laughed.

Bree smiled deliciously and kept going, "I'd like to have really amazing sex, and I'd like to find someone to share my life with." She grew serious. "You'd think that being bisexual I'd have more choices," she looked down, "and I've been with a lot of amazing people. But, I don't know, maybe I'm just broken. Maybe I don't know how to be happy.

"I never really fancied myself the marrying kind. But I guess now that I'm in my forties, something's changed. I'd like to find a woman or a man," she stopped, she swallowed hard, her voice strained, "to share my life with. Yeah that, that's it."

The women smiled at her and gave her reassuring nods.

Bree smiled back, she sat up a little straighter, such was the effect of saying things out loud and being heard.

"I'd like to share something," Mona began, clearing her throat nervously. "I've been married for more than forty years, but I feel," she began to cry, "I feel so lonely. It's like my Richard, he doesn't see me. And sometimes, I don't know who I am anymore. I've been Richard's wife for most of my life and Sam and Mollie's mother, and I have my career."

She looked over at Elizabeth and still managed a smile as the tears streamed down her face, "But, I can't remember the last time I felt like me. The me I was born as. All the little bits and bobs that make me who I am." She looked down at her hands.

"And I feel . . . *trapped*. I love my Richard, I do, but sometimes I feel like I made a mistake. Not in marrying him, but in letting go of the things that were important to me. Like dancin'.

"I saw one of those dancin' shows on TV last week and I told him that maybe I should start up again. I wasn't serious, ya know how you go on, but he said," she stopped, and wiped the tears from her face, "he said that it would be bleedin' ridiculous. Ridiculous for me to start dancin' again. And I don't think he meant it to be mean, but it really stung, ya know? I don't know what to do. I just can't go on like this."

Camille reached out to grasp Mona's hand. Mona took it gratefully.

Many of the women had already begun to cry again, but no one more than Kaitlin. "Shaun and I," she swallowed, "we've been trying to have a wee baby for years now. I wanted one as soon as we were married, but . . . the good Lord hasn't seen it fit to bless us. And I've always wanted to be a mother. I keep a good face on, for Shaun, but I'm really just—" she started to cry uncontrollably, "I'm just," she choked, "*heartbroken!*"

Ava leaned over and wrapped Kaitlin in her arms, holding her until she stopped crying.

The women all watched, and sent their love, and waited for Kaitlin to resurface from her pain.

Cam went next, "I won't cry," she said in a steady voice, her accent thick, putting up her pointer finger, "and it's not because I'm always calm or apathetic, or that I don't feel things or care."

She took a breath, "It's that I wasn't taught to cry. Emotions were to be bottled up or harnessed towards improving yourself. But that's not to say that I don't feel deeply, that I don't have regrets, that I don't have a painful past." She looked down at her hands.

"I loved my daughter, I regret the mother I was to her, but I don't know that I could have done it any differently—even knowing what I know now.

"And I know this is not something you're supposed to say . . . but, sometimes, I regret becoming a mother. I regret not questioning whether or not I *should* be a mother. Back then, it wasn't a question, it's just what you did."

She leaned back on her hands and looked up at the moon, "And I regret that I did not fix things with my daughter while she was still alive. But . . . ," she exhaled loudly, "I hope that I find another way to make amends."

Elizabeth wanted to reach over and hold Camille's hand, but Camille was still gazing up at the moon, her eyes fixed on one place. She seemed entranced.

Ava spoke next. "I would just like to be happy. I guess I'm at a bit of a crossroads. So much of what I chose for my life hasn't really panned out. Moving back home is a new start for me and I guess I'm just . . . *hopeful*?

"I'm hopeful that things in my life will start to come together, that I will find fulfillment in my work. I feel lighter after the meditation, thank you," she said to Audre.

"Yeah, I guess that's all I want to say. I have the pain from my past, but sitting here with all of you, I mainly just feel hopeful for the future. I feel lucky to be here, *thank you.*"

The women nodded, many smiled, and said, "Welcome home."

Audre went next, "I'm very grateful. My life has always been fairly put together. I've always had a good job, I've always been confident, lucky with men, and I've always had a spectacular sense of style," she said in a light tone, always hamming it up.

Everyone laughed.

"But I don't think I've ever been this . . . *happy* in my life. It's been an amazing year for me. I'm doing things I never dreamed of—and I dreamed some pretty wicked dreams."

Everyone chuckled.

"I'm grateful and I'm hopeful for what's to come . . . *but* . . . there is this part of me, the part of me that's still a little girl, still waiting for the rug to be pulled out from underneath her, like when my dad left.

"I think that was the last time I was this happy—all the way back to when I was eight. When my parents were together. And I guess getting to this level of happiness again as an adult, part of me is terrified and part of me wants to open up, feel every moment and enjoy. I want to let certain people in. I want to be able to let go and trust."

Elizabeth looked over at her. Audre's face had grown somber, deeply sad, but then she regained herself, "I'm hopeful, yes, I'm hopeful, that perhaps, after some more time, after getting used to this level of happiness again, that I'll be able to open myself up to the other parts of life. The other parts of me which perhaps I've kept closed and hidden away." She gave the group a small smile.

Elizabeth squeezed Audre's hand and smiled. It was a gift and a privilege to know and understand her best friend a bit better. She hoped Dree would let herself be happy. Open herself up and give life with Kilian a chance.

Audre's ambivalence towards her boyfriend, Julian, seemed to make a lot more sense now.

Elizabeth was certain that he was an emotional place-holder. It was a relationship of convenience that kept Audre safe, protected. Safe from Kilian.

Poor Julian. And then a moment later, *poor Kilian.* Finally, she made it back around, *poor Audre!*

Cailin and Alice were quiet, each lost in their own thoughts. Both unsure of what to say. Audre assured them that they didn't have to share anything at all.

They both looked deeply relieved to be let off the hook. Cailin thanked them for having her and even Alice expressed her gratitude for the experience.

Only Elizabeth remained. "First of all, I'd like to thank all of you for coming. There's been a lot happening in my life recently, some of it might seem obvious."

A few people nodded knowingly.

"I'm so happy to be home in Ireland, I am, but it seems that coming home permanently has led to things I couldn't foresee. I just feel this weight," her eyes began to water, she stopped and swallowed, willing the tears not to brim over, "this weight to be perfect.

"To be what the community wants me to be and I know I can't live up to that. For a long time, I lived a life that didn't make me happy, that was built on expectations, perfection, and a certain façade. And I swore I would never do that again.

"That's how I know that I can't be what they want me to

be. So there's that. And then there's why I wanted to hold this moon circle.

"I think many of you have heard me speak about my inner voices. Some people call it intuition, or a gut feeling, or your guardian angels, I don't know. I just know that throughout my life when I have paid close attention and been able to hear those voices guiding me, that's when I've been rock solid. Completely myself. On the path I was supposed to be on. In tune with life, in tune with everything around me, in tune with the Universe.

"And somewhere along the way during these past five amazing years I stopped being able to hear them. And I just want to hear them again. I missed out on a lot the last time I got lost and it was a big deal finding myself here at Rhia's cottage all those years ago. And I'm just, I'm so afraid to get lost again."

She wiped the tears as they streamed down her face.

"Anyway, thank you all, and especially Audre. I felt more calm and more grounded during the meditation than I have felt all year long.

"Hearing your stories and the battles you're all facing, it makes me feel like I'm not alone. And even though we're all struggling with different situations, I feel like we're all a part of the same divine fabric, the same stardust. All connected. Thank you." Elizabeth bowed her head.

The women all expressed their appreciation in different

ways, looking around the circle and smiling, and bowing their heads, and clasping their hands in thanks.

Each of them looked younger, lighter, and more at peace.

"All right ladies," Audre began, "thank you for sharing. Please remember that everything that was said here was said in confidence and is to stay within the circle. Now please light your tea candles." She passed the lighter around.

"And now turn your tarot card over and then your white card. I'm passing around three books, they're all the same. They will tell you about the tarot card you've chosen. This will give you an insight into your current life, where you are right now, and help guide you to where you want to be. And the other white card is a quote that will hopefully resonate with you or at least inspire you."

Elizabeth turned her tarot card over. She studied the beautiful colors and intricate design, tracing her finger along the edges. She leafed through the pages of the book to find her answers.

Then she turned the white card over and found her quote. It spoke to her. She closed her eyes and repeated it silently over and over, willing it to imprint itself on her brain.

"OK, everyone," Audre broke through her thoughts, "please sit on your yoga bolster and either cross your legs or stretch them out in front of you, whatever feels comfortable.

"Now close your eyes and think of a word, a single word, that you feel right now. That you're taking with you. A word that if you were to see it again and again, it would inspire you, it would give you hope.

"It would remind you of the things you've learned tonight and the feelings you are coming away with. It can be anything, it just has to be one word—two max," Dree amended.

"When you're ready, take your permanent marker and write the word somewhere on your body. It can be anywhere as long as you will be able to see it and be reminded."

Elizabeth closed her eyes, the word that floated to the surface was . . . *freedom*. She wrote it in small, delicate letters on the underside of her arm, above her left wrist.

"Now open your eyes. Take your tea light in the palm of your hand and repeat after me. Under the moon, we are one. Under the moon, we are loved. We take the light of the moon into our bodies, we give thanks for the earth and the sky above. We celebrate the divine above and the divine within us. We send our love out into the world and we leave this circle as sisters."

They repeated it.

"Now hold a single wish for yourself in your mind. When you're ready, blow out your candle."

The women blew out the candles one by one. They took a collective breath together and looked around them. Everyone looked lighter, everyone looked happier, everyone looked renewed.

Audre lifted the white pillar candle in the middle of the

circle and blew it out. "Ladies, I hope you're feeling light and limber and alive. We have some food and refreshments back at the castle for your enjoyment. Don't worry there's wine, *lots* of wine."

The Dingle Daily News
Lady Lara Resident Hippie Hosts Mad Moon Circle
By Reuben Hurley

The Dingle Daily has obtained exclusive information that our resident California Lady, has brought the women of fair Ireland to Castle Bannon for a witchy moon circle.

Reports say that she was to host the event at her home last night during the full moon. The Dingle Daily, took to the streets to find out the community reaction.

Certain townsfolk were confused, like Bill Callahan, "What's a moon circle? Is she a witch?" While others like, Tom Rattigan were amused by the idea. "If she wants to have a circle, let her have a circle. It's all a laugh. People need to lighten up."

Some residents were rightfully concerned that Lady Lara was introducing an unwanted occult element to our corner of the country.

Respected long-time resident and head of the Dingle Ladies Society, Rose Faith Byrnes said she, "Was shocked by these recent developments. The news that Ms. Lara could bring such a dark and potentially sinister gathering to our community is simply unprecedented. We at the Ladies Society, are disheartened and truly shaken by Ms. Lara's choices."

Although reactions to the circle varied, everyone we spoke to had questions about what actually takes place at a women's moon circle.

According to the interwebs, a women's moon circle is a gathering of women at the full moon. There are spiritual elements, and each circle varies, but there is one tenant that all circles seem to abide by: no menfolk allowed.

13

THE RECLUSE

*E*lizabeth woke the following day feeling new.

They had stayed up into the early hours of the morning talking about life, about love, about their hopes and dreams. They'd left most of their pain in the circle—only their good spirits remained. The tone and direction of the conversations reflected this, there was scarcely an exchange that wasn't either hilarious or uplifting.

Everyone let their hair down, even Camille. Whether it was the wine or the vulnerability, no one knew, but the women were all keen to laugh and know each other better.

They gathered in the grand lounge, the room which had been renovated the least because its opulence reminded Elizabeth of the Great Lounge at The Ahwahnee Hotel in Yosemite.

They sat on the couches and on the floor. Talking one-on-one and talking all together in a group. There was so much laughter that Elizabeth's face was sore from smiling.

The birds chirped merrily outside the window of the master bedroom, bringing her back to the morning, and back to how good she felt.

She showered and dressed for the day, stopping briefly in front of the bathroom mirror, looking into her own eyes, trying to divine that which eluded her still.

She looked like herself, a few more lines, a bit more wisdom, but beneath it all the fear that had plagued her, the fear that she was lost, bubbled up somewhere inside of her.

She felt good, she was happy, but she would not be truly at peace until she felt fully connected to herself.

The moon circle had been a step in the right direction, but there would be more to her path.

The phone on her bedside table buzzed.

A text from Connor:

Are you OK, Luv? What exactly happened last night? What is the DD going on about now? I'm sorry I can't protect you from this. Call me I'd love to hear your voice and to hear how you're doing. Just let me know you're OK.

A sinking feeling began to take her. What was he talking about? But she didn't get a chance to respond.

Her phone buzzed several more times in a row.

Dree: Babes, don't give it another thought. Seriously, hold on to the feelings you had last night. Screw them!

I wonder who told them? It better not be Ava. Didn't she say she was starting there soon? I didn't have her pegged for one of those rat bastards, but I've been wrong before. I've gone into town to run some errands, I'll be back by lunch. XX

And they kept on coming.

Bree: The bloody nerve of 'em! Feck the lot of 'em.

Elizabeth left the bedroom and ran downstairs to the kitchen.

Camille was sitting at the table with a coffee in one hand and a tablet in the other. "Buenos días," she said.

"Buenos días" Elizabeth replied. "Have you seen—"

"It's on the counter." She motioned in the direction of the fridge. "I left it there so you could easily throw it in the recycling bin where it belongs."

Elizabeth saw the paper folded over on the counter.

The headline made her fear the worst. The text itself was pretty insubstantial.

It couldn't even be called an article. There was nothing to suggest that the paper had any inside knowledge at all. Their attack on her did not affect her in the same way as the picture of her and Connor. But it still stung.

She wondered what she had done to deserve such vitriol. But she knew the answer. *Nothing.* She was just a plaything to them. She would never be able to do right in their eyes. They would always sensationalize her words and actions.

She threw the paper in the recycling bin, agreeing with Camille about where it belonged.

Camille took a sip of her coffee, "Well . . . at least they have command of alliteration," she said lightly.

Elizabeth made herself a cup of tea and joined her at the table. "Are you trying to cheer me up by being funny?"

"Now don't go accusing me of any such thing."

She wasn't quite sure how to feel. She was angry and frustrated, but not overly concerned. Their words couldn't touch her like before.

Her phone buzzed again.

She didn't immediately recognize the number, but then she remembered that she and Ava had exchanged mobiles sometime between their third and fourth glasses of wine. She hadn't yet added Ava's name to her contact list.

Elizabeth read the message quickly.

"What is it?" Camille asked.

"It's from Ava. She says:

Liz, I'm so sorry. I didn't say anything about last night to anyone.

Alfie and Reuben were standing a few feet away when Kaitlin and I bumped into each other and she invited me to the circle.

I can only guess that they overheard us.

I just needed you to know that it wasn't me. I had no idea the paper was coming after you like this, Ma has caught me up on what they've been doing. Deplorable.

Hope you won't hold it against all journalists. Thanks again for being so welcoming last night.

"Of course it wasn't Ava. Did you ever think it was?" Camille asked.

"No, I didn't get that sense from her. For a second, I thought I should be more guarded, but I felt comfortable with her. Still, it's good of her to reach out and give it to me straight. And her guess about Alfie and Reuben overhearing the conversation is probably accurate since there aren't any actual details in the stupid thing."

"You seem OK about it," Camille observed.

Elizabeth took a deep breath, "Well, I'm not as good as I was when I woke up this morning with the sun shining and the birds chirping, and feeling great because of last night, but . . . I'm better than I thought I would be.

"Maybe by next week I will be completely immune to seeing my name thrown into the mud by these asshats. Maybe I should do something outrageous like go into town and have lunch! Tomorrow's headline can be: Lady Lara Eats Avocado Toast and Destroys the Planet."

"That's the spirit." Camille returned to reading her tablet.

Elizabeth stood up, "I feel like a walk. Care to join me?"

"No, thank you. I've already walked five miles on the treadmill, done an hour of kickboxing cardio, and half an hour of Tai Chi. I want to relax for a couple of hours before lunch."

Elizabeth suppressed a smile. "Of course you did." She tried not to laugh. Even dead, Camille was still outworking everyone.

She squeezed Cam's shoulder as she went. "OK, see you in a bit."

The trees welcomed her as she took her favorite path through the forest. Her fingers grazed the bark of her favorites, a few Pines and Oaks, a couple of Dogwoods.

She took the time to thank them for their existence as she filled her lungs with the fresh pine air.

The trees could take practically anything away, make her feel at peace. Make her feel at home.

The Japanese had a term for it, *shinrin-yoku* or *forest bathing*. It was based in the science of nature and was the simple art of being calm and quiet amongst the trees.

The sun shone brightly, setting off the greens all around her.

It was a beautiful day.

She listened to the birds, as they surrounded her. They whistled and chirped and sang their songs. They flapped their wings and flew from tree to tree. An entire society of creatures coexisting harmoniously with each other.

The breeze kicked up, swirling around her, wafting hints of jasmine into the air.

She walked without thought, completely lost in the magic of the trees, the perfection of nature itself.

It was a blissful sort of surrender.

She walked until she found a familiar clearing. The big

rock she'd climbed the day Camille had "died" stood in the middle. How different it looked today. Its rough surface, bathed in sunlight, looked inviting.

She climbed the rock and sat cross-legged at the top. She tried to meditate, but found her mind wandering.

After a few minutes she realized that the entire walk had been one long meditation and now that she had forced herself to sit and try, she couldn't. Such was life.

She straightened her legs and leaned back on her hands staring up at the sky. The breeze had transformed into a light wind that moved the puffy white clouds quickly across the sky.

She lost herself in the shapes and figures in the clouds.

After a few minutes, her eyes came back down to earth when she heard movement in the trees.

And like before, the same man who had found her on the rock that fateful day, came into the clearing.

"Hello," Elizabeth was eager to make his acquaintance. She had thought of him several times in the week that had passed. She had wanted to thank him for his kindness in watching over her that day.

He came closer before speaking, "Good day to you. You seem well." He observed.

"I am, thank you. And thank you for last week. For . . . leaving me alone, and then watching out for me."

He held up his hands, "T'was nothing really. It would've

been a sin to leave a distraught person alone in the woods. I'm glad to see you're on the mend."

"I'm Elizabeth Lara. My husband and I live at Castle Bannon," she said abruptly in response.

He smiled. "Yes, I know Lady Lara. It's a small town."

"Yes, apparently it is." She looked down at her hands. "Just don't believe everything you read," Elizabeth offered.

"Oh I never do." He nodded, wisely. "I find there's quite a lot of rubbish in the papers today."

She looked at him. Examining his thin face. He looked like a kindred spirit.

"I'd say that's a fair assessment," Elizabeth agreed. "I'm sorry I didn't catch your name."

"I am Ben Harrison Malone, pleased to meet you. My house is on the land parcel next to yours. I believe I'm your nearest neighbor. Near being a relative term in this case." His eyes crinkled with a smile.

His energy reminded her of Matthieu Fleury, her great-uncle.

She liked him instantly.

She climbed down off of the rock so she could speak to him more easily.

"Ben . . . may I call you, Ben?"

He nodded simply.

"May I walk with you for a spell?" she asked.

"I'd be glad of the company." He grabbed his hat with his

thumb and forefinger and tipped it in the way older men sometimes did.

They walked for a few minutes in comfortable silence.

"Ben, how long have you lived in Dingle?"

"It seems like my whole life. I was born here, went away for university, worked a few decades in London, then came back with my wife almost thirty years ago."

"What's your wife's name?"

"Her name was Marie." He walked with his hands clasped behind his back.

Elizabeth looked down, "I'm sorry."

Ben considered before speaking, "Thank you. She passed some time ago, but I suppose I never got over it. Does anyone ever get over the loss of a spouse?" He asked rhetorically.

Elizabeth thought about what it would feel like to lose Connor. They'd only been married a handful of years, but the thought was devastating. She couldn't imagine what it would be like to lose him after thirty years together. Or forty years.

A shiver ran down her spine. She shook her head, willing the thought to leave her alone and never come back.

"Ben, do you mind my asking how you spend your time these days?"

Ben stopped and turned to look at her, "No, I don't mind. But is there a specific reason you'd like to know?"

She shook her head, "No, I'm just curious. Just letting my

mind wander to wherever it wants to go. I'm sorry. If I'm bothering you, please just say so."

"No," he started walking again, "it's not a bother. It's just peculiar is all. Folks don't ask me questions like that anymore. I'm a bit of a recluse you see, so whenever I go into town people don't tend to speak to me.

"And if they do it's more along the lines of the polite how are you doing? And they're satisfied when I say fine, thank you. That's as far as conversations tend to go with me. I was never very social and then when Marie died, well, I suppose I stopped bothering to try."

Elizabeth didn't know what to say.

"The answer to your earlier question is I walk, I read, stay home, I paint. Every once in a while, when my business manager comes by, I have to listen to earnings reports and quarterly statements and whatever nonsense I'm supposed to be informed about. My family owns several of the businesses in town and in other parts of Ireland."

She let that sit for a second. And then without thinking, "Are you lonely? I'm sorry, I don't know why that just came out."

He chuckled, "They sure don't make them like you around here. Don't be sorry, you're the first person I've really spoken to in years. If you can imagine that. And I find I enjoy your openness.

"Loneliness is a state of mind and most of the time I'm surrounded by life. In the books that I read, and the memories I hold in here," he tapped a finger to his temple. "And in the trees and wildlife I encounter every day on my walks. But sometimes, yes, I suppose."

He stopped walking again, turning towards her. "Now let me ask you a question, if you don't mind. What changed from last week to this?"

She considered how to answer without lying. "I was grieving. Someone very close to me died. It was a shock."

"I'm sorry to hear that. What helped you since then?"

Elizabeth thought carefully, again not wanting to lie, but needing to protect Camille. "I think that maybe, people are never really gone. It's difficult because we miss them and they're not physically with us but . . ." she trailed off not wanting to continue, because she wasn't sure she could explain the rest without feeling uncomfortably dishonest.

And she didn't want to feel that way with this kind human.

She tried to answer his question more specifically, "I've also taken care to only do things that I wanted to do these last few days, and that's helped."

He didn't immediately respond.

The sound of their feet on the path filled her ears.

He glanced in her direction, a look of curiosity written on his face. "What were you doing before?"

She considered. "Some things I wanted to do, I guess. Some things I had to do. I'm trying to do exactly what I want every moment of every day right now. I'm hoping it will lead to . . . *enlightenment.*"

"How intriguing. And what, pray tell, do you want to do today?" He asked, genuinely interested.

Elizabeth allowed her mind to wander for a minute, "I think," she smiled, realizing exactly how she wanted to spend her afternoon. "I think I want to see a man about a dolphin."

Ben grinned, a hint of mischief in his eyes. "How splendid. Well, Elizabeth, it's been lovely speaking to you. I'll take my leave now, it's time to return to my house and I like to take the long way back. Have a wonderful day."

He held out a hand. She shook it gratefully.

"Thank you, Ben. I hope to see you again soon."

"Likewise."

He turned and took another path, barely visible to the naked eye. Known only to those whose feet already knew the way.

Elizabeth felt enlivened by the conversation. By meeting a relative stranger in the woods and potentially having made a friend.

She turned back, walking briskly towards the castle. She was eager to set her afternoon plans in motion. She hoped her favorite rock star was free to take her to see her favorite dolphin.

14

SWIMMING WITH DOLPHINS

The sun stayed out for the rest of the day, making the vibrant colors of the beautiful Irish village come alive.

Audre, Camille, and Elizabeth approached Kilian's boat, *The Starship*.

They found him tiding the main deck.

He wore only a pair of khaki shorts. His bare chest glistened in the sun, his curls flew wildly all around him with the ocean winds.

"Permission to come aboard, Captain," Elizabeth called up.

He straightened, looking in their direction, "Permission granted," he said still tying the rope around his arm. He set the rope aside and put out his hand, helping the ladies onto the deck one by one.

Camille went first.

"Hello," Camille took off her sunglasses and took her time examining Kilian, not bothering to disguise what she was doing.

Kilian's whole body seemed to turn red.

"Hello again," he said politely, bashfully.

Camille would not be deterred, "So shy, my goodness. They tell me you are a rock star. Surely you are used to women admiring your body?"

"I'm afraid not, I mostly try not to think about it," he admitted, still a bright tomato.

"And it's that humility," Audre began as Kilian took her hand to help her onto the boat, "that makes you irresistible . . . to your fans," she quickly corrected, an imperceptible blush touched her cheeks.

Kilian didn't release her hand when she reached the deck. He smiled down at her as she looked out towards the water. He was looking at Audre like she was the moon and the stars.

Elizabeth shook her head, "Yes, you're absolutely irresistible, Kilian. Now a little help here please?" Her voice snapped him out of his Audre reverie.

"Sorry, where is my head," he extended his hand to bring her on board.

Audre looked down and quickly walked away to stand by Camille who had moved to the bow to enjoy the view of the water.

"Thanks for doing this," Elizabeth said to Kilian.

"Oh no worries. I'm honestly glad you asked. I had an entire day free for the first time in forever. Didn't know what to do with myself and I'll always jump at the chance to bring Elizabeth Lara a little joy."

"Awww, thanks Kil. I heart you too."

She took his arm, they walked slowly towards the others at the bow. "It's Dree's first time on *The Starship*, right?" she asked him.

"Yes, it is," he answered without having to think.

"Well then," Elizabeth prodded, "maybe you should give her a tour?" She relished any opportunity to throw her friends together in a non-professional capacity.

Camille and Audre turned to face them as they approached.

Kilian smiled broadly, "Right, then. Who'd like a tour?"

"Sure," Audre accepted.

Camille opened her mouth, but Elizabeth successfully gave her the eyes, signaling that she should decline.

It worked.

"Oh, you know," Camille chuckled. "Seen one boat, seen them all. It's lovely, thank you, but I think I'll just enjoy the view."

Kilian nodded, taking Audre away on the tour.

Elizabeth placed herself next to Camille and linked her arm through hers.

"You know, a quick tour of a boat won't bring those two

together." Camille watched them go. "They've spent most of the year together constantly. It'll take something bigger to breach her defenses."

"I dunno, remember what she said about the last moon circle she attended in England? Maybe the one from last night will open her up enough that she'll finally be open to him?"

Camille raised an eyebrow and tilted her head. "But didn't you tell me that she already had a boyfriend?"

Elizabeth had completely forgotten about Julian. "She said she does. I asked her about it last week and she said that they were doing fine, but she didn't sound too excited. And she never mentions him."

The more she thought about it, the more certain she became that her conjecture last night had been right.

Camille considered. "Perhaps there's more to that story than we know."

"Perhaps." Elizabeth watched her friends as they walked, comfortable in each other's space, closer than good friends, but not as close as lovers.

How she hoped they would find a way.

They found Fungie within minutes of setting out. Kilian took the boat far enough away from the harbor that they could have a measure of privacy.

Elizabeth jumped in right away. Fungie greeted her with

a steady torrent of squeaks. She put her palm out in front of her.

He swam towards her until his nose touched her hand. She swam in a circle and he followed, never losing contact with her.

It had become her standard greeting for him.

She and Connor swam with Fungie often. As often as they could manage. But each time was a new thrill. Elizabeth turned into a little girl and for a few hours lived only to have fun and play.

It was never lost on her how wonderfully magical her life had become.

From courtrooms and depositions and hateful angry spouses, to a beautiful creative life, with a beautiful husband, and a dolphin to call her friend.

She played with Fungie on her own for several minutes before she returned to the boat and encouraged Audre to join her. She got in reluctantly, but only after Camille.

It had surprised Elizabeth since she hadn't thought Cam would want to splash in the water. Ever the unpredictable one, Camille got on the ladder leading to the water, stopped halfway down and then launched herself into a cannonball, splashing wildly into the ocean.

Audre was roused and clearly not about to let an octogenarian out adventure her.

She climbed down the ladder at a more measured pace, before finally letting go and getting into the cool water.

Fungie took to both Camille and Audre. Although Audre continued to hesitate.

"He's not going to bite you, Dree." Elizabeth had tried to assure her.

"I know," she started to shiver, her accent was thick. She sounded like Mel B again.

Kilian stood on the top railing, not even bothering to climb down the ladder. Completely unhindered by the height, he flung himself off the boat and plunged into the cold water, screaming, "Yahoo!" as he went.

The four of them swam merrily with Fungie for the better part of an hour. Elizabeth showed them some of her favorite hand signals. The dolphin happily obliged, performing trick after trick for an eager audience who smiled and laughed and whistled in appreciation.

Camille got out first.

Kilian and Dree were swimming towards the boat when Kilian used his hands to send a small tidal wave of water in Audre's direction.

"Oh no you didn't." She splashed him back.

Before anyone knew it, they were engaged in a vigorous water fight.

They laughed and howled and shrieked.

Elizabeth watched as Audre closed the distance, putting her hands on Kilian's shoulders and trying to submerge his head below the water.

He tried to swim away, but when that didn't work, he

wrapped his arms around her waist and held her in place, lifting half of her torso above the water.

The mood changed in an instant.

They suddenly stopped laughing.

He gazed up at Audre with a look so intense, it sent shivers down Elizabeth's spine.

Everyone should experience a look like that. It was a look of love, of adoration, of devotion.

Elizabeth felt a pang of something in her heart. All at once she ached for Connor.

Audre's face stilled, her eyes trained on Kilian's. Her breathing became shallow. And for a moment Elizabeth thought her friends had finally found each other.

Just then, Fungie launched himself out of the water, flipped twice in the air and came back down with a large splash, gaining everyone's attention.

The spell had been broken. Audre moved her arms and Kilian released her.

Fungie swam to Elizabeth, nuzzling her affectionately. "Oh, buddy," she whispered close to his head. "I love you so much, but that was absolutely *terrible* timing," she shook her head and frowned.

Fungie squeaked joyously and bopped his head. She stroked his melon and then wrapped her arms around him.

. . .

After *The Starship* docked back in the harbor, the foursome walked to the evening food trucks that lined the street nearest the water. They chose the French truck, "Escar-to-Go".

It was an evening of dessert crêpes with various toppings all around.

Elizabeth went with her favorite: Nutella and strawberries with powdered sugar. Kilian and Audre had the same, while Camille chose caramel and banana.

"This is grand," Kilian mused. "I haven't had a day like this in an age."

Elizabeth looked at him. "But you like what you do, right?"

"Oh yeah, without a doubt. I love to make music and I love to perform. Would be nice to have a few more days like this, though."

Audre raised an eyebrow, "Are you trying to tell me something? Am I working you too hard?" She poked at his ribs.

"No, but I wouldn't be mad at you if you decided to put a couple of months in the annual schedule for an Irish summer. Make it a regular thing?"

Audre pursed her lips, trying not to smile. "I'll consider it."

"And how do you like your new accommodations?" Kilian prodded, pointing his question at Audre.

"Oh, you know," Audre began in a cheeky tone, "it'll do."

"I'm glad we meet your approval," Elizabeth laughed. "So what's next on your world tour."

Kilian took a bite of his dinner. "Oh, let's not ruin this fine Irish evening by talking shop."

Audre gave him a sharp look, "Ruin? Do you not like being a rock star?" she teased.

Camille looked from one to the other, "You know," she looked at Kilian and then at Audre, her accent was especially thick, "it's really not good to suppress your emotions. It *ages* you. And those who think they have time, that life will wait for you to do this or that before you can be happy? *Are. Wrong.*"

She stood up and placed her plate in the appropriate bin before continuing. "Life doesn't wait for anyone, it all just moves on without you."

She scrunched her napkin into a ball and tossed it into the recycling bin from where she stood. "Now, if you'll excuse me, I'm going to take a stroll through the town. Lizzie, I'll call you when I'm done. See where you are."

And with that, Camille walked briskly away from them.

Elizabeth wasn't quick enough to join her. She would've preferred to go with her and leave Kilian and Audre to talk.

But the moment had passed.

The threesome spoke animatedly about this and that, before Elizabeth remembered she hadn't responded to Connor's morning text.

She found her moment, leaving her friends alone and

walked to the water's edge. She took out her cell phone and dialed Connor.

The phone rang several times, before going to his voicemail.

She heard the beep, opened her mouth to speak, but found she didn't know what to say.

He'd only been gone for a short time. But life was moving on without him. She didn't know where to begin and she couldn't explain it over the phone.

She settled on, "It's me, I'm fine. I love you. See you when you get back."

She hung up the phone and willed her husband to come back.

She missed her best friend. There was so much to tell him and as happy as she had come to be through last night's endeavors and today's adventures, it seemed incomplete because she hadn't been able to share it with him.

She pocketed her phone and turned back to her friends.

Audre was busy on her phone and Kilian had shoved his hands in the pockets of his hoodie.

Something had clearly happened between them. And it wasn't good.

Elizabeth sighed. They'd only be in Ireland for the summer. She wondered what she would have to do to bring them together.

Would it even be possible?

Maybe they would never find their way and Audre would

remain closed off and Kilian's love for her would remain unrequited.

She thought of Kilian's latest song, the beautifully sad lyrical melody and the heart-wrenching lyrics they had written together.

She said a little prayer and hoped that her friends would not suffer the same fate.

15

THE GOOD FIGHT

*E*lizabeth stretched her arms and straightened her legs all the way to her toes. It had been a delicious sleep. A restful sleep, no dreams that she could remember.

The sort of dead to the world sleep that could reset your mind and your body.

For the first time since she could remember, she wasn't holding any tension anywhere in her body. It was the type of deep physical Zen which only came after a very long sleep or a very satisfying night of lovemaking.

She reached for her phone on the bedside table. It was 12:17 in the afternoon. She'd been asleep for eleven hours.

Her messaging app showed a notification. There was only one from Dree:

Hi Babes, Kil and I are taking Cam on a day trip out. You were still asleep, and we didn't want to wake you. Have a great day! Will probably be back late. xx

She put her phone down, slid back into bed and looked up at the intricate ceiling. She focused on her breathing, feeling the sensation of her chest rising and falling. The patterns in the ceiling swirled together, it was beautifully delicate. She continued in this way for an endless period of time, just breathing.

It was a simple luxury, to be able to stay in bed and be still. To be able to do nothing. It was exactly what she wanted to do.

Suddenly, an idea came to her. She sat bolt upright.

It hit her like lightning, the self-assurance, the certainty, the peace that came with knowing exactly what was right. She got out of bed, giddy as a schoolgirl.

She quickly changed and got ready for the day before heading to her office to get stuck in.

"*Thank you,*" she said to herself, blissfully grateful that she'd been given a glimpse, a window into her voices.

She sat down at her computer and set things in motion.

An hour later she was finished. She re-read the eight-hundred word piece she had just written. Proofing it for the tenth time. Every period in its place.

It was exactly what she wanted to say.

She took a deep breath, trying to contain her excitement. It was time to fight back, time to write her own rules.

She did a quick internet search and found what she was looking for. She dialed the number and waited.

"This is the Dingle Daily, how may I help you?" a soft female voice answered.

Elizabeth cleared her throat, "Yes, this is Elizabeth Lara. I would like to speak to the editor please."

"One moment."

A few seconds later a man with a throaty voice and a thick Irish accent answered, "This is Barnaby O'Hanlon, Editor-in-Chief, how may I help you Lady Lara?"

"Yes, hello. I'm calling to inquire about your submission guidelines for opinion pieces."

"I beg your pardon? I'm not sure I understand. *Opinion pieces?*"

Elizabeth hadn't anticipated this response. "Yes. Your Op-ed section? Every newspaper tends to have one," she said slowly, hoping he would catch up.

"Oh, right you are. Unfortunately, you see, the DD is a small paper and we are in fact missing several of the sections that you might find in a larger metropolitan paper. We don't have an opinion section. I'm sorry. Is there anything else I can do for you?"

He was curt. But not just a regular kind of curt. A smug asshole kind of curt.

She thought for a moment, something about what he had just said, didn't sound right. She could have sworn she remembered reading a few opinion pieces over the years.

She considered, "I've written a piece, Mr. O'Hanlon. It's a piece that is in direct response to the articles written in your paper about me, my behavior, and the alleged negative influence that, by your measure, I have seemingly used to corrupt the people of *our* fine city."

She emphasized *our*, clearly placing herself as one of them, instead of an outsider. "It also ruminates on the problem of double standards towards women. Considering the current political climate around the world, I believe it is a timely piece and I humbly ask that your paper print it."

She was met with silence. He cleared his throat, "Ms. Lara," he emphasized the *Ms.*, "this is a newspaper. We write about the news, and relevant stories that affect our community. I'm afraid as I've already stated, we do not accept opinion pieces. I'm sorry," his voice crescendoed, as haughty as ever, "but we cannot make exceptions even for the wife of Lord Bannon."

The fire returned to Elizabeth's face, she took a measured breath, careful not to be heard over the phone, "Is there nothing I can do to persuade you? Perhaps I could just send it to you and then you could decide?"

She was really trying.

She had grown more merciful since leaving the law. She

was giving him a lifeline, giving him an opportunity to do the right thing, *before* she annihilated him.

The last thing she wanted was to go to war with anyone, least of which an entire paper, and one which had been the voice of the community for over one-hundred years.

But if that's what he chose, and that's what it came to, then there would be no other choice. She would find a way to take the fight to him.

She waited, giving him a few more seconds to come to his senses and be reasonable.

"I'm sorry, but that's my final decision. Good day Ms. Lara."

Elizabeth sat back in her chair, gripping the phone to her ear. "Don't give it a second thought, Mr. O'Hanlon." Her voice was a fictitious sort of sweet and cold as ice. "You've made your choice," she said slowly, deliberately. "Good day to you . . . and . . . *good luck.*"

He hesitated, she thought she could hear a gulp on the other line, "Thank you?" uncertainty colored his voice.

Elizabeth hung up and set her phone down on her desk. She leaned back in her chair and closed her eyes, taking big deep breaths, to steady herself and not let the anger overtake the certainty she'd had minutes ago.

And just like that, the answers came once again.

She had hoped to play nice, hoped to fight back, using the paper and hopefully bringing some enlightenment, some fairness to its pages, but it hadn't worked.

Still, she would not be deterred. The way presented itself almost immediately.

There was just one final piece to verify before putting her plan into action. She went down to the kitchen to make herself a cup of tea and to find the paper in the recycling bin. She found it right on top.

She set it down on the floor and quickly rifled through its pages, sure enough she had been right.

She found what she was looking for, an opinion piece by a man named Bill Callahan, complaining about overtourism. He thought that people should care more about preserving the town and their way of life than making a quick buck off the busloads of tourists.

It was a classic opinion piece.

It was true that the paper didn't appear to have a separate op-ed section, but she remembered reading other opinion pieces in the past. They put them in the back under no separate category.

Barnaby O'Hanlon was a liar and a sexist prick.

But she was no damsel in distress, this was a fight that O'Hanlon would be sorry he'd ever started.

For she was uniquely qualified to correct this particular injustice. And she had a responsibility to set certain wrongs, right.

It was time to fight back.

She took her tea to the office and immediately started planning her strategy.

At first, she considered sending it to one of the larger papers in Dublin. Also, she was sure that Audre would make the introductions to the London papers if she asked and there were Elizabeth's own connections at *The New York Times*, the *San Francisco Chronicle*, and the *Los Angeles Times*.

If her situation with Camille had been different, that's exactly what she would've done.

She would have sent the article to all the major papers, using her contacts and friends to get it printed. *Everywhere.*

Then she'd watch as an international media shit storm rained down on Barnaby O'Hanlon.

But, she had to consider Cam. The last thing either of them needed was for the international media to descend on Dingle and for anyone to come asking questions while Camille was staying with her. A more measured approach would be required.

She did a quick search and bought a domain name: www.aladysvoice.com.

She went to work immediately, scouring YouTube for answers, and teaching herself how to build a website. She would never again be silenced by a man.

It was time to show the people of Dingle what they could expect from her. She would tell them exactly what kind of lady she would be.

. . .

Elizabeth worked through the rest of the day and evening, she had tunnel vision. She was on a mission, and she wouldn't stop until she saw it through.

She built the site and revised her piece to include the conversation with Barnaby. To call him out on his decision not to print her words.

She'd also broadened the scope of the article, emphasizing a woman's right to be and do whatever she likes, *at any age*. The days of respecting the patriarchy, of living anything but an authentic life were long gone.

She hoped it succeeded in turning her anger and frustration with the paper into something positive that had the potential to spark a real movement in the local community. That was her hope, but she knew that hopes and wishes didn't always match reality.

It was the best she could do, what she needed to do . . . and that would have to be enough, for now.

She took a deep breath and hit the publish button. A buffering circle appeared in the middle of her screen and then a few seconds later the website was live.

She exhaled all at once, completely exhausted from the day's efforts.

Her brain had been in control for most of the day, but now her body was screaming at her, willing her to reconnect with it. Her stomach growled loudly, painfully.

She hadn't eaten anything, an unfortunate byproduct of being in the zone.

The light on her phone was flashing, signaling a notification. She checked her messages, finding one from Audre from the hour before. It reiterated that they wouldn't be back until late, whatever that meant—it was almost eleven at night already.

Not expecting her guests back until after midnight, Elizabeth went downstairs to rummage through the fridge. She found many of the take-out options she had ordered for her week at the glass house. Most of it hadn't been touched since Camille had unexpectedly turned into their resident chef.

It had surprised her how much enjoyment Cam took from cooking, it was almost like a daily meditation.

She opened each container, reacquainting herself with the contents. The Indian food looked good, but the pizza was amazing if she re-heated it in the oven.

She had just settled on the Indian food, when she heard it. She put the container down on the island and walked out into the foyer.

It was silent.

Had she imagined it?

But then she heard footsteps and someone fiddling with the door. Quickly, she took out her phone and checked the security schedule.

All five members of the security team were supposed to be in place or at least at the guardhouse watching the security feed.

She opened the app that connected her to all the security

cameras on the property. She clicked on the front door view, but could not see anything because it was obscured by something she couldn't make out.

She walked to the large pot by the door where they kept their umbrellas. She took out a long sturdy one and gripped it like a baseball bat.

Mentally she considered her options, she was barefoot, and it would take some time to make her way through the castle and out to the back door, and then she would be in the pitch black running with no shoes.

Using the umbrella in a surprise attack, was her best option.

She gripped the umbrella more tightly as the adrenaline surged. She took a deep breath.

And then the door was swinging open, but the security alarm wasn't going off.

She saw a bouquet of balloons first, which was confusing to her adrenaline addled and mostly starved brain.

Before she could process what she was seeing, the person moved the balloons to his other hand, revealing his face.

It was Connor.

He set his overnight bag down on the floor.

Life had moved so quickly in recent days—he'd been gone for all of it, it hadn't even occurred to her that it might be her husband.

"Elizabeth? What the hell are you doing?" He looked at her.

She tilted her head in confusion.

"Jaysus, are you all right? Why are you gripping an umbrella like that? Has somethin' happened?" He closed the door behind him.

He didn't stop to let her answer his barrage of questions. "I saw the security detail. Why do we have so many of them on duty just now?"

Elizabeth's mind and body were still coming down from the adrenaline rush of preparing to physically fight.

Uncertainty colored his features. "I brought you these," he picked up his bag and walked towards her with the balloons.

Balloons? How strange.

She was still incapable of speaking.

He shrugged, "I thought they would cheer you up. I don't know, it was silly, I guess."

The balloons were met with silence.

He shifted his weight. "What? You think they're bleedin' awful, don't you? I knew I should have gone with the roses, but I thought they would be too cliché," he scolded himself.

Elizabeth opened her mouth to answer, but then the door swung open again.

They both turned to look.

Camille walked through the door pleased as punch, with not a care in the world.

"Good evening, my loves." She waltzed past them. "Connor, it's nice to meet you finally. I'm off to bed. Good night children," she called behind her.

Connor saw her face and recognized her instantly. He let go of the balloons and dropped his bag simultaneously. "Jaysus, Mary, and Joseph!"

16

THE TALK

The door opened a third time. It was Audre.

Dree saw Connor's white face, "What's the matter, Connor? You look like you've seen a ghost."

She gave him a cheeky smile before heading off to bed, "See you tomorrow."

Connor turned back to Elizabeth, "It seems I've missed quite a lot."

Elizabeth crossed her arms, "Yes, you have."

"Care to fill me in?"

"Happily," she said flatly.

She thought to go to the kitchen, and fix herself a plate, but found that all the commotion had scared away her hunger, temporarily. "Let's go for a walk. I need some fresh air, just let me get my shoes on and a sweater."

He nodded, "That's fine. I'll run my bag up to our room."

He walked halfway up the stairs before turning around, "It is still *our* room, right?"

"Yes!" Elizabeth answered. "Camille and Audre are in a couple of the suites on the third floor, in the other wing."

"OK, just checking." He threw her a cheeky smile hoping to lighten the mood.

The night had turned cool, Elizabeth wrapped her long cardigan around herself tightly.

Connor had turned on the lights, so they could fully appreciate the grounds. They walked in silence to the bench near the grotto.

Elizabeth sat with her arms and legs crossed. She found she was annoyed with her husband. She hadn't realized the full extent of it because she had been busy.

But now with him sitting there opposite her, she found she wasn't eager to share. "How'd your business go?"

He looked away, "It's fine. Everything is fine." His jaw set in line.

Typical Connor.

"Oh, really. Is it?" Elizabeth continued in the same flat tone.

"Are you going to fill me in on what's been happening here?" he changed the subject.

"Well, the short version is that someone blew up Camille's house, but she escaped and then the FBI decided to fake her death in the hopes of acquiring some new leads in the investigation they were running before the bomb."

"Investigation?"

"Yes," she nodded. She figured that attorney-client privilege needed to be waved to an extent in order to keep Cam safe.

"Cam's business has been under attack for the last few months. The FBI thinks it's part of some larger nefarious plot having to do with terrorists trying to destabilize some of her key businesses.

"So anyway, they faked her death, and took her into protective custody. And then, a couple of days in, when they were transferring her to a safe house, Camille decided to take things into her own hands."

Elizabeth shrugged and shook her head. Typical Camille. "So she, as she put it, *gave them the slip*, secretly chartered a flight here, broke into our house, found the note I had left you, drove up to the house on Lough Aisling I'd rented, and found me there a few days ago.

"She's been staying here ever since. And Audre moved in shortly after that. She knows who Camille really is, but she doesn't know the rest of the business and FBI particulars.

"The only people who know Camille's true identity and that the FBI faked her death, are me, you, Audre, and Aidan. Kilian's been hanging out with us a lot lately, I'm surprised he hasn't mentioned anything."

"No, he wouldn't. He's not great with faces," Connor explained.

Elizabeth nodded, now understanding.

"I've introduced her to a few people. She didn't take kindly to the idea of a fake name, so we've just been calling her Cam. That pretty much sums it up."

She sat back and breathed. Filling him in was exhausting.

He was silent for more than a minute.

"But you're happy about it?" he asked.

"About Cam? Yes, of course! It feels amazing to have her back, and frankly, this whole thing has brought us closer. It feels really good to have her around."

"Why didn't you tell me when you called?" there was an edge of resentment in his voice.

"Connor, this isn't something you talk about over the phone. We have no idea what kind of threat Camille is under. We have to keep the truth about her contained."

He took a moment to process everything. "Does the FBI know where she is?"

"Nope." She rolled her eyes, frustrated. "She says she'll tell them 'when she's ready.'"

Elizabeth looked down at her hands. "She's the smartest person I know, and she's very strategic. I think she has a plan and she knows what she's doing. But, either way, she's staying here, and she's like family so we're going to keep her safe."

"Of course," he said. "We'll do whatever she wants, whatever you want." His voice softened.

"How did the lustrous Audre Bright come to stay with us?"

Elizabeth gave him the short version.

He reached over and took her hand. "I'm sorry I wasn't here." He was contrite.

She softened, "Yeah, I really needed you. Needed my husband, my best friend."

He let go of her hand and sat forward, placing his elbows on his knees and his face in his hands. He huffed. "I'm sorry," his voice was mumbled.

Elizabeth thought about what to say next, "Don't be sorry, tell me why you had to go. Over the years I've accepted that you are sometimes more vague than I'd like, but this time you literally gave me no explanation."

She lowered her voice, "What's going on, Connor? Why aren't you talking to me?"

He sighed, "Lara, it's fine. I'm fine. Business is fine."

He was a broken record.

"OK, well, when you put it like that. Great, I'm convinced," she said sarcastically, throwing her hands up.

"Elizabeth, I'm tired. Can we please talk about this tomorrow?"

She examined his face, he looked exhausted. She wanted to soften, willed herself to bridge the gap between them, but there was no excuse for his lack of communication.

What could possibly justify the way he was treating her?

"I'm going to bed, I love you." He stood up, not waiting for an answer.

He took one of her hands in his and squeezed it, trying to reassure her before he left.

He considered leaning down to kiss her. But he correctly deduced that she had closed herself off to him.

"I love you," he said again, before turning to walk back to the house.

Elizabeth watched him go, his silhouette was framed by the twinkle lights in the trees.

She was worried.

In the four years that they'd been married, they'd never really had a major fight. Tifts, yes. Fights, no. But then again, he'd never been this tight-lipped about any aspect of his life with her before.

She had some vague notion, some vague thought, about the reason marriages implode.

She worried that this is how it would start. This is how they would start to drift apart from each other.

She walked back to the house, her stomach began to grumble, reminding her that she still hadn't eaten. She made her way to the kitchen to fix herself a plate.

She tried to distract herself from her growing marriage concerns. She reread her blog piece and then sent a text to the women's moon circle group that Audre had created for them to all stay in touch. It read:

Ladies, I recently decided to create my own website. I

published a piece that I hope you will all read. Please feel free to share it. Let me know what you think. xx Elizabeth

She went upstairs and crawled into their bed. She cuddled up next to Connor, wrapping her arms around him and burying her face in his back.

He stirred slightly and grabbed her hand, bringing it up and nestling it in his chest.

"I love you," he said groggily.

"I love you back," she whispered before drifting off to sleep.

17

THE WOMEN OF IRELAND

By midmorning Elizabeth had heard from nearly all of the women in the circle. They sent enthusiastic messages about the piece and promised to share it widely.

The website she had created only yesterday must have worked because it already had more than a thousand hits.

She sat back in her chair.

Right, what now?

She had done what she wanted to do, what she needed to do, she had gotten her side out there and the community seemed to be listening, or at least they were curious enough to go and read it.

She walked to the window and looked out at the pool and great lawn. Camille was strolling beyond the trees, near the ancient Oak which had stood in the same place, for hundreds of years.

Cam took a seat on the swing set up on one of its branches. She had a cell phone to her ear. And she kept looking around her. Elizabeth examined her backyard. There wasn't a single person in sight.

Was she looking for someone? Or was she making sure she wasn't being overheard?

Camille, what are you planning?

Elizabeth thought it was high time she took another run at her, to see if she was ready to share with the class.

Elizabeth passed Connor's office on her way downstairs. The door was closed, but she could hear him arguing with someone over the phone.

His voice was raised. She thought about knocking to check on him, but then thought better of it.

He would fill her in when he felt like it. She took a deep, frustrated breath, resisting the urge to force him to tell her.

She refocused on her mission and walked out to the backyard, taking care to walk along the edge of the landscaping, where she could take cover amongst the trees.

"Hallo, Lady Lara," said a man from behind her.

She jumped. "Hi there, Henry. How are you?" she asked, breathless.

Henry Davis was their other full-time security guard. The tall man with a strong physique and the beginnings of a middle-aged man tummy smiled at her pleasantly. "I'm doing all right. Can I help you with something?"

"No, no, thank you. I'm just having a walk under the trees," she said awkwardly, quickly changing the subject. "And how is your daughter Aimee? What is she five now? Did she like the paint set we bought for her birthday?"

Henry flinched, or at least that's what Elizabeth thought it was.

"Henry, is everything OK? With Aimee?" Elizabeth tried to read his face.

He looked conflicted. He had started to open his mouth, when he heard something in his earpiece. He pressed a finger to his ear and listened before speaking into his wrist. "Understood, on my way."

He looked at her apologetically. "I'm sorry Lady Lara, I'm expected back at the guardhouse." He bowed his head in a leaving gesture and then he remembered, "Aimee loved the paint set. Uses it every day, she does. Gonna have to run out and get her another soon." He nodded and smiled before making his exit.

Elizabeth returned to her own mission.

The tree line went all around the estate. She arched her neck to see if Camille was still on the phone at the Oak tree. She was.

Elizabeth was careful to keep her in her sights, she was still talking animatedly on the phone. If only she could get closer.

She would have to crouch behind a line of hedges in order to get as close as possible. She ducked down, losing sight of Camille for a few seconds as she maneuvered herself into place.

She peeked out along the side of the hedge nearest the Oak tree swing, but Camille wasn't there.

"What are you doing, Lizzie?" a voice said from behind her.

Elizabeth jumped again.

Camille was standing behind her arms crossed, eyebrows raised.

Elizabeth smoothed her shirt and stood up, back straight, trying to salvage some of her dignity. "I was eavesdropping," she admitted. "Well, trying to anyway."

"And why were you doing that?"

"Because you were clearly talking to someone, maybe talking about your strategy, your plan? I doubt you were calling the FBI to tell them where you are. Were you calling the FBI?"

"No," she said simply.

"Cam, I know you have a plan. You're the smartest person I know. A master strategist, but I can help."

"I know that. But I have my own way of doing things, Lizzie. And I prefer not to explain what I'm thinking until it becomes absolutely necessary."

"Any idea when it will become absolutely necessary?"

Camille's eyes twinkled with mischief. "Oh I have something brewing which I hope will yield some interesting information."

"That's all I'm going to get, isn't it?" Elizabeth said blankly.

Camille gave her a cheeky smile. She looked very pleased with herself.

And that was all she was going to get.

"Well if you're not going to tell me, how about we go into town for lunch?"

Camille was surprised. "Are you sure you want to go into town? It seems to me you've been avoiding it since I got here."

"Maybe. Well not so much avoiding as having no inclination to venture forth and potentially get accosted by well-meaning people."

"Ahhh," Camille said.

"But I feel good today."

"Does it have anything to do with the fact that your website has gotten more than a thousand hits in less than twelve hours?"

"Maybe. Who knows how people will respond, but at least I got my side out there. Hopefully gave people some food for thought. And now I would like to go into town and have some lunch on this fine summer day, would you care to join me?"

"Oh all right." Camille hooked her arm through Elizabeth's. "Maybe we could try that new Mexican food truck we saw at the harbor the other day."

"Ehhh," Elizabeth began.

"What? Is it bad?"

"I honestly don't know, but I have found that most Mexican restaurants I've tried in Europe tend to let me down."

"De verdad? Yeah, I can see that. When you grow up having tacos and quesadillas in the Mission, nothing can compare."

"Exactly," Elizabeth agreed.

The town was abuzz with a frenzied sort of energy, especially for a Monday.

There were dozens of women out on the sidewalks talking with each other. The female proprietors of the businesses on the little main street and customers alike were all talking excitedly about something.

The women stopped talking abruptly as Elizabeth and Cam approached. It was bizarre. They smiled at Elizabeth. Gave her strange approving nods.

Elizabeth tried to smile back in acknowledgment.

What the hell was going on?

And then they saw it. Posted on nearly every lamppost and every building, was Elizabeth's opinion piece.

"What the—," she said under her breath.

Camille turned to Elizabeth, "Did you hire someone to do this?"

Elizabeth shook her head completely baffled. She couldn't explain it.

Many of the women standing in groups and talking were holding copies of Elizabeth's piece.

The women continued to smile at them and say hello in a friendly manner, but it was starting to feel creepy. Like they all knew something she didn't.

She tried to be positive. "Well that's a good sign," she said to Camille. "At least it doesn't look like I've pissed anyone off."

Camille laughed, "Well sure, not the women."

They turned the corner and nearly bumped straight into Mona.

That afternoon she had an extra bounce in her step. Her face was flushed, and she wore a smile so wide, she looked like a small round Cheshire cat.

Her energy was off the walls. Wild, manic. It wasn't a bad energy, it was more of a high on life, can't stand still, I'm so excited, kind of energy.

"Oh Elizabeth, Cam! How lovely to see you today," she said, her voice every bit as excited as the rest of her.

She handed them one of the papers from the orange stack in her arms.

It read, "Women's Dance Troupe Ages 50+" in bold letters, with an elegant border tying the flyer together.

They looked up at her.

"My daughter helped me with it this morning." She let out a little giggle. "I was so inspired that I made up my mind right then and there. I am putting together a dance troupe for women over fifty!"

She barely stopped to take a breath, "I have it all sorted, we're going to perform at the first music and dance night of the summer. In five days time!" She giggled again.

"Mona, that's amazing! But . . . what inspired you?"

Mona's eyes grew wide, like she couldn't fathom what Elizabeth was talking about. "Why the words. *Your words,* Elizabeth. I read them and I just realized how much of my life I had been livin' because I thought I couldn't do this, or that, and I wasn't supposed to want these things. And then I read what you wrote and it hit me all at once. Isn't that grand?!"

Elizabeth was dumbstruck, "*Really*? It had that big of an effect on you?"

Mona nodded, eyes still wide.

Camille asked, "Who's in it, your dance troupe?"

"Oh, I don't know yet. I just came up with the idea, but I feel like if I don't do this now, I might as well keel over right here! We're meeting in a couple of hours. Cam, do you dance? You look like you could be a dancer, you should join us."

Camille hesitated, "Thank you, Mona," she said graciously. "I'll think about it."

Mona was the type of woman that even Camille couldn't help but like instantly. Her warmth, her kindness, her excitement were all contagious—and even Camille Cortez Fairhurst Hennings was not immune.

Elizabeth processed everything Mona had just said, "Wait, you're putting the group together today? Then performing in five days?" She raised her eyebrows.

"Yes!" Mona was emphatic. Elizabeth had never seen her so determined, so commanding.

"Mona, are you OK?" Elizabeth ventured. Mona was practically vibrating in place. "Does Richard know?"

Mona nodded, "Yes, I told him first thing this morning. The useless wanker—he's not a useless wanker—" she corrected, her voice softening, "he really is a lovely man once you get to know him." And then her voice took on the same harsh tone she'd started the sentence with, "But today? Today he's a useless wanker. He mumbled something which I'm sure wasn't very nice, and left the house!"

"Oh no, are you all right?"

"Never. Better!" she said with that same wild manic energy.

Camille and Elizabeth exchanged a look.

"I'm telling you Elizabeth, I've had a fire lit under me. And I'm not going to let it be snuffed out again! If anyone has a problem with that, feck 'em! Feck the lot of 'em!"

"OK!" Elizabeth and Camille nodded together. "Well then I'm very happy for you. Lots of luck!"

"Thank you, Elizabeth. And thank you for posting those wonderful words. It's exactly what this world needs, I tell you, it is."

"Thank—" Elizabeth started.

"Oh there's Abigail Geran! I seem to remember she was quite limber in her days. Hallo, hallo there!" She called to the woman she'd pointed out and walked away from them abruptly.

Both women were left feeling utterly confused, and inexplicably excited. Such was the wake of the indomitable spirit of Mona Porter.

They had just about made it to the restaurant, when another woman approached them. She looked vaguely familiar to Elizabeth, but she didn't believe they'd ever met.

"Ms. Lara," the woman wearing a flowery dress and carefully coiffed shoulder length hair began, her voice stern, "I am Rose Faith Byrnes. We've spoken on the phone."

Elizabeth had a sinking feeling. *Wonderful.*

"Oh, yes, hello. Pleased to meet you in person," Elizabeth said in a measured tone.

Rose Faith pressed her lips together before speaking, "I suppose you're happy about this circus."

Elizabeth had no idea what she was talking about. "To which circus are you referring?"

"This! The flyers, the women rising up as if we needed to declare our independence!" She motioned to the street they were about to turn onto.

There were more women standing on the sidewalk in groups talking excitedly, just like on the main street.

Rose narrowed her eyes, and gave her a withering stare.

Elizabeth took a deep breath and prepared herself.

Rose continued, "The women of Ireland have always been *fiercely* independent!"

Elizabeth waited, but there didn't appear to be more. "That may be, but movements and societies tend to stagnate. I'm sure you are aware of the serious injustice and sexist practice of the local paper where I, myself was targeted unfairly."

Rose straightened and crossed her arms.

"I was labeled a Jezebel for simply showing my love for my husband. When, in truth, *he* was showing me!" Elizabeth stood up a little straighter, determined to make this woman understand, exactly who she was. And exactly who she refused to be.

"You see he simply couldn't wait to get his hands on me," she said it slowly, watching Rose's features change, watching the blood rush to her face. "He ushered *me* away from the crowds, but I was the one labeled."

Rose's face changed infinitesimally, her lips relaxed a degree, her brow furrowed.

Elizabeth continued, "I was the one labeled. I was the one responsible. I seduced *him*. There wasn't a single piece of blame or outrage placed on my husband because he's a man. And the paper is run by a man and other men like him, who seek to throw women to the wolves in spite of the truth."

Rose's demeanor was visibly changing. Elizabeth couldn't tell if it was because her words were having an effect on her, changing her opinion, or because Rose Faith Byrnes was not accustomed to being spoken to so directly.

"In their latest piece, *in which you are quoted*," she kept her voice calm, but deadly. "I was practically labeled a witch for inviting my own friends to my own house, and *meditating*."

She let that one sink in.

Rose turned almost purple.

"Is it fair that there are no classes for mature adult women who want to dance? Why is that? According to the flyer in your hand there seems to be ample interest. There are a dozen more examples which I could list off the top of my head where society's patriarchal expectations of women are doing real harm and caging women through the guise of propriety, morality, and gender norms.

"Women should be able to be bold, to be sexual, to dance, to drink, to be vulgar—or proper—as long as they don't pass judgment on others . . . basically, I believe that if we're not harming anyone, we should be able to do exactly as we like."

She took a deep breath, "I'm sure a wise woman like yourself isn't blind to the double standards, the injustice, and the sexism that women face in every aspect of our daily lives.

The real question is why aren't you doing anything about it now? Why have you limited your efforts to balls and fundraisers and flower planting?"

Rose opened her mouth, but nothing came out.

She took a frustrated breath before turning on her heel and disappearing down the next street.

Camille put an arm around Elizabeth, unable to contain her amusement. "That was, as they say here, *bloody brilliant!* I'm so proud of you," she laughed.

It felt good to tell the truth. To call people out, to stand up.

"Come on," she put an arm around Camille, "let's go have lunch."

She was making her own rules now.

18

MERRY MCGEE'S

The soft warm lights of the old-world lampposts made it appear that the sidewalk and street were glistening.

It had rained all day and only stopped the hour before. The streets were still wet, the dirt and grime had been washed away.

They were headed to Merry McGee's, which was hosting a women's only night.

The last couple of days had been a whirlwind. Women had come together from across all generations, united by the conversation.

The conversation that Elizabeth had started.

They now questioned everything. Their eyes had been opened. They could now see how much of their lives were wrapped up in expectations and dictated by antiquated views.

The topics #dinglewomensmovenemt and #aladysvoice had started to trend in Ireland.

Visitors to Elizabeth's website now topped fifty thousand.

Mona had rallied nearly sixty women to show up for her dance troupe meeting on Monday, but only eight were left after she explained that there had been a cancellation in the evening's entertainment for the first music and dance night of the summer and that they would be filling the slot, performing in front of most of the town.

The eight women, including Camille, much to Elizabeth's surprise, had been practicing for several hours each day since then.

They rounded the corner and turned onto the street which housed Merry McGee's.

A group of men with pints of Guinness in their hands stood outside Dodger's a couple of doors down. They were busy people watching and talking amongst themselves.

"What the devil is going on?" One of the men looked around and noticed all of the women filing into Merry's.

"Where have you been man? Didn't ya know the ladies are rising up?!"

"Rising up? From what?"

"Oh, who knows. They've got it in their heads that they need to be rising up from somethin'."

"But why are they all goin' in?"

"Meredith's hosting something. It's *women's only*."

"Women's only? Who's ever heard of a pub havin' a women's only night?"

The other man shrugged, "It's a new day, Danny."

"Maybe we should go have a look and see what's goin' on?" the man named Charlie answered.

A third man shook his head, "No, she's hired a big lass to stand at the door. She's not letting any men in. Chris O'Connell already tried."

"Is that right?"

"It is indeed." He finished the rest of his Guinness. "Well, looks like it's time for another."

Elizabeth looked down and tried to suppress a smile as she passed them.

The men clapped each other on the back and headed into the Dodger pub for another pint.

There were dozens of tables placed evenly throughout Merry McGee's. With the bar on the far side and a small ten-inch raised stage next to it.

It was a sight.

The voices hit you first. Young women, wise women, girls who had just come of age, all coming together and chatting animatedly about the last couple of days.

A lone female fiddler stood on the stage, playing an Irish tune and adding to the atmosphere.

There wasn't a man in sight.

They found a table near the bar. After settling in, Audre and Camille rose to get drinks for the group.

Elizabeth caught Meredith McGee's attention, "Meredith, do you think it would be all right if I took some pictures?"

"It's fine by me. Hang on," she made her way to the middle of the room and whistled. Everyone stopped. "Are there any objections to Lady Lara takin' some pictures?"

Elizabeth surveyed the room quickly, everyone seemed to be smiling and nodding their agreement, but she was careful to take notice of those women who weren't as vocal or excited to give their consent. She clocked only one or two of them and made a mental note not to approach them throughout the night.

The rest of the women seemed eager to oblige. Some smoothed their hair while still others did nothing to change themselves, only taking a drink and laughing heartily.

Meredith returned to Elizabeth. "Go on then, Lady Elizabeth. Do you think these will go up on your website?"

"Honestly, I don't know. I didn't know what to expect from tonight, I brought my camera just in case."

"Have you already got your drinks then?" she said just as Audre and Camille returned with pints of Guinness for the table.

Elizabeth nodded, "It seems we have, thank you Meredith."

It was an hour of listening to different women, listening

to them talk about their lives, and how they felt the community around them had been set up to fail them as they evolved into the women they were supposed to be.

Elizabeth alternated her time between sitting and drinking with Audre, Camille, and later Mona, Cailin, and Ava, and walking around to take pictures of the women as they found their voices, and found solidarity with each other.

As the night went on, more women filed in, until the place was standing room only.

Women's only night was a hit.

It seemed natural that women of all ages would want a place to gather, and be, and talk.

What a thing it would be to create a women's center where all the ladies could gather on a regular basis. But that was a thought for another day. She filed it away for later.

At about 11:30, a woman in her forties walked to the middle of the room. With a high-pitched whistle, she got everyone's attention. "So then, Meredith, what are we meant to do? Are we here to put something together?"

Meredith came out from behind the bar, "You can if you like. I just thought it would be a right good thing to bring all the ladies together. Have somewhere we can socialize away from the men for a night, but what you do or don't do, is up to you."

Someone else stood up and called out, "Well I for one would like to do something. Lady Lara is right, we aren't really free to be who we want to be. For whatever reason the town has been built-up, with the men more in mind than anything."

All eyes turned to Elizabeth. She stood up, completely unsure of what she would say until she actually opened her mouth, "I'm so pleased that you read my words and that they touched you. I don't know exactly what the answers are, as much as I love the town and all of you, I'm still new.

"And I don't want to pretend I know what's best for anyone here. I wrote what I wrote because I had to. I couldn't keep silent, keep taking the injustice. But, I'm sorry, I don't know what the next step is. I don't have all the answers."

She sat down again.

"But you're right, Lady Lara," a woman with a squeaky voice called from somewhere near the back. "When was the last time the paper covered anything related to women? It's always about the rugger and the football and which bigwig man is retiring."

"Old Barnaby, he's the one who should be retiring!" someone else called out.

"Here, here," dozens of women called out and whistled.

Meredith McGee joined in, "Aye, he's been the editor for an age and I don't think our town is the better for it."

More women nodded and vocalized their agreement.

Elizabeth felt that she needed to step up and make sure the night didn't turn into a *we hate Barnaby* party, "I'd just like to make something clear, I'm not here to get anyone fired. But I am here to stand up. Stand up against the patriarchal voices who would silence us. And stand up for what is right. I'd like to ask all of you, what are some other opportunities, or classes, or just anything that you all wish you had access to here in town?"

A woman in her fifties stood up, "I've always wanted to learn to dance." She turned bright red and quickly sat back down again.

"Me too," someone else said from the corner.

"Why aren't there any classes for adult women?" Mona spoke out. "Not for women in their twenties or thirties or sixties or seventies! There's just classes for the wee ones, for the weans, it's like we only matter when we're girls."

Half the room erupted in applause, the other half hit their tables heartily with an open palm.

Mona beamed.

A woman with short white hair that curled elegantly against her scalp stood up, "There is a senior society," she pointed out.

The person next to her answered, "Yes, but they only go on day trips to places we've seen a million times or arrange golf trips and knitting circles. Which is wonderful if you love golf or knitting, but there isn't much left for the rest of us."

The woman with the short curly hair responded, "I *love* the knitting circle."

Her friend replied, "That's peachy, but is that all you want to do, Nora? There's nothing else you want to learn before we're all dead and buried?!"

The woman looked at her friend, considering. "Well . . . I've always wanted to learn how to," her soft voice stopped, pausing for effect whether she'd intended it or not, the other women around her leaned in and waited. Women from around the room craned their necks, trying to see the woman called Nora and hear about what she wanted to learn. Nora took a deep breath, "I've always wanted to learn how to . . . paint a naked man."

Audre leaned into their table, "I've got to be honest. I did *not* see that coming!"

The lively conversations continued well into the night. It was one in the morning before their group piled out of Merry McGee's, just as merry as could be.

Ava, Audre, Camille and Elizabeth, laughed and howled as they walked down the street.

Elizabeth turned to Ava, "And you have absolutely no idea, how this all started? How my opinion piece was printed and plastered all over town?"

Ava didn't turn to look at her, "I have no idea," she said, much to innocently, before winking mischievously.

They had just reached the end of the little street, where Elizabeth and her houseguests would turn to walk the ten-minute shortcut back to the castle, when they heard a pair of girls turn onto the street from the harbor.

They walked arm in arm, giggling about the night's

happenings. They nodded and smiled, acknowledging the women across the street. Elizabeth's group returned the gesture.

Ava turned to make her exit, "Well ladies, it's been a proper craic, it has, I hope—"

But a high-pitched shriek filled the street.

The women turned to look. Across the way a tall man in dark clothes, wearing a mask that covered half of his face had just knocked the two girls down and ripped their bags from their shoulders.

Elizabeth didn't think, she handed her camera off to Audre and ran across the street.

The two girls were clutching each other, still in shock.

The man had taken off as soon as he'd gotten what he'd come for. He was already halfway down the block.

As quickly as Elizabeth had run across the street, Ava had taken out her phone and was recording the entire incident.

The rest of the women had crossed over to help the girls.

Elizabeth reached into Audre's bag and found what she was looking for. She grasped Audre's small reusable water bottle, which fit in the palm of her hand, and took off running at full speed. She managed to close half the distance before she planted her feet, aimed and threw the bottle, hitting the man in the back.

He was knocked to the ground by the force of it.

Elizabeth quickly closed the remaining distance and grabbed him by his black sweater. He flung his arm backwards to hit her or shake her off, but Elizabeth grabbed it instead and twisted, using his own momentum to throw him down onto the sidewalk.

She placed her knee in his lower back, and used her weight to pin him.

Her friends caught up to them. He was now surrounded. Elizabeth stood up, turned him around, and removed the mask.

To her shock he was just a kid, maybe seventeen.

Elizabeth was so surprised, he managed to shake her off completely, but not before she yanked the girls' bags out of his grasp. He shoved his way out of the circle that had surrounded him and took off running.

Ava held out a hand, helping Elizabeth up. "Don't worry, the Garda will catch up to him, I'll see to it." She winked.

Elizabeth handed the bags back to the girls, checking to make sure that they were OK. They were both fine, at most they'd suffered scrapes to their palms and knees from being knocked down, but Elizabeth could see the real toll written on their faces.

A few minutes before they had been young women, in their late teens or early twenties, secure in the knowledge that their world was safe.

That they were safe.

Elizabeth wondered if they would ever feel that way again.

The Dingle Daily News
Lady Lara Leaps into Action to Save the Day
By Ava O'Reilly

[A picture of Elizabeth kneeling on a man's back, holding him in place, filled the front page.]

Two young women were attacked in the early hours of Thursday morning. Chloe Weir and Mia McElligott, were on their way home from a party at a flat near the harbour when a man dressed in all dark clothing and a mask, shoved them to the ground and took their bags.

A group of women on their way home from Merry McGee's witnessed the incident. Among them was Dingle's own, Lady Elizabeth Lara, who, upon ensuring the young women's safety, leapt into action to catch the troubled youth.

Lady Elizabeth successfully apprehended and identified the young man, whose name we are not releasing because he is not yet of age.

Thanks to Lady Lara, Chloe and Mia, were protected and their bags returned.

The young man in question is now in the custody of the Garda and is expected to serve community service as well as attend a court-mandated class on violence against women.

When asked about the incident, locals across the board praised Lady Lara for her quick thinking and physical prowess. "She a superhero, she is," said pub owner Meredith McGee.

Chloe's grandmother and local seamstress, Nora Weir said, "I think the papers have been just terrible to Lady Lara. She's an unconventional lady to be sure, but thank the Lord she is who she is! I shudder to think about what could have happened to my Chloe if she hadn't been close at hand."

Local business owner, Fitz O'Leary, added that, "Dingle is lucky to have a lady like Elizabeth Lara."

[A picture of Elizabeth returning the bags to the shaken young women appeared beneath the article.]

19

MONA SENIOR DANCER

"*A*re they next?" Audre leaned over to ask Elizabeth.

"I don't know," she whispered back.

Ava leaned across Elizabeth to whisper to Audre, "I think they're on after the Irish dancing school," she motioned with her head to indicate the next dance group.

Audre's mouth dropped open, "They're making them go on after *those* girls?"

The three women looked to the side of the stage, where the young teenagers were in the final stages of primping and prepping for their performance. Their curls were perfect, their hair extensions in place, and their makeup made them look like beautiful vibrant flowers.

Audre, Ava, and Elizabeth all exchanged a worried look.

The first music and dance night of the summer was well

underway at the same outdoor bandstand where Kilian had played the week before.

There wasn't an empty seat in the house, and on top of that there were hundreds of people standing or perched on picnic blankets around the main seating area.

While the crowd wasn't as large as the Summer Festival, there were at least five hundred people there watching the performers.

They'd already seen a few bands, and a couple of dance acts, mostly kids and young twenty-somethings in small groups or duos.

Elizabeth's phone buzzed, she took it out of her pocket to silence it, but not before she read the preview of Connor's text. It read simply, "I'm sorry."

She put the phone on silent and put it back in her pocket. She took a deep breath, trying not to be sucked back into their most recent fight.

Connor had spent the last couple of days at Castle Bannon, but he wasn't really there at all. He was in his office all day long and well into the evening, always talking on the phone, or busy working on who knows what.

Elizabeth had tried, but she had run out of patience.

At lunch, she had popped into his office and asked him to come with them to watch Mona and Camille in their debut performance.

He had said, "Yes, of course. I'll be there." He'd even flashed her a wide smile, and for a moment, she saw the

Connor she knew and loved. But by that evening, he came to find her and reneged on his promise. "I just can't, Luv. I'm sorry. I have an unexpected conference call."

She hadn't said anything, just stared daggers at him.

"What do you want from me, I have to work!" he'd protested.

"Do you? Do you *really*? Because this is the first thing Mona has done for herself in decades. She's really excited, and she has spent most of her life taking care of you in one form or another, and she's definitely taken care of me. That woman deserves our support. How can you even think about not being there tonight?"

He had fallen silent, but in the end, he hadn't changed his mind.

She shook her head, "Who are you? It's Friday night, show up! Show up for Mona," she had scolded to no avail.

Camille had already left to get ready with the rest of the women, but Audre had been nearby and had heard it all. She'd been trying to cheer her up all night.

"Now for our next performers," Evan Morris came to the stage, "please welcome Dingle's Irish School for Irish Dancing!"

The pretty girls walked on stage and took their places. A quick tempo Irish song came on and the girls began their routine.

They kept their backs ramrod straight, their arms at their sides, they kicked their legs up high.

They were perfect.

As delightful as they were, all Elizabeth could think about was the fact that Mona and Camille were next.

She looked around at the crowd, hoping they would be welcoming, hoping that Mona's dance troupe was good.

The song ended and it was time.

Evan Morris walked on stage once again, "OK, now for something new and completely different. These ladies have been practicing all week for you, they've just come together, and are ready to perform for you all. In their debut performance, please welcome, the newly formed dance troupe, *Over Fifty!*"

The eight women walked on stage, wearing black tops, and calf-length pink poodle skirts.

A classic 60s songs started blaring through the speakers. They'd modified and remixed the tempo to suit their needs, and so their performance began.

The eight women including Mona, Camille, Cailin, and Meredith came to life. The first part included a section where they partnered off to do a short swing routine. Much to Elizabeth's relief, the women were good. She marveled at some of the moves they were pulling off together.

The crowd loved it.

Then they transitioned into several different styles for a solo segment, where each woman was able to exhibit a different dance.

Camille danced a sultry salsa, that had the crowd

whooping and hollering. Meredith did a ballroom jive, with impressive, quick footwork. Cailin did several pirouette turns in a row that dazzled.

Elizabeth didn't know the other four women in the group, but they each took their turns, one an advanced swing routine that delighted, two women coming together to do some Fosse inspired jazz, and the last woman doing a lyrical set.

But the entire performance ended with Mona. She'd somehow managed to regain some of her acrobatic skills. Her little round body stunned as she whipped through the air. Doing cartwheels, and front handsprings, and front tucks. Her last sequence started with a front flip and finished in the splits.

The crowd was in awe. They yelled and whistled and cheered.

The music ended and the women held onto their smiles, breathing through their teeth as they accepted the ferocious wave of applause.

Elizabeth stood up and clapped so hard her hands hurt. "Brava!" she yelled. She looked over to the side of the stage and noticed Richard, Mona's husband, clapping just as fiercely. A proud smile on his face.

Many people had started to stand as well, until the entire audience was on their feet for them.

Many phones were out, taking pictures and recording the

performance. Elizabeth turned around, the sea of flashes was blinding.

She had a feeling that the whole town would be talking about that dance for a long time to come.

The backroom of O'Leary's was reasonably packed.

"OK, ready?" Audre turned to Elizabeth handing her a shot of whiskey.

"No, I'm not, but let's do this," Elizabeth said.

Audre was really trying to bolster Elizabeth's spirits.

Mona and Camille's performance had been a highlight of the night, but Elizabeth found herself trying not to think about Connor and the state of their marriage every few seconds.

Audre could tell that her plan to distract Elizabeth wasn't working.

"Men," Audre began, "who needs them!"

Elizabeth looked at Audre, "Don't tell me you're having man trouble as well?"

Audre was tipsy enough that she was in a sharing mood, "Liz, Babes, do you want to know a secret?"

Elizabeth leaned in, "Sure."

Audre mouthed something to her, it was lower than a whisper.

Elizabeth tried to read her lips, but couldn't. She scrunched her eyes together. "What?"

Audre tried again, "There is *no man*."

"What do you mean?"

Audre took the next shot, "There is no man," she repeated, in a more normal voice. "Julian and I broke up ages ago, just after the last time you met him."

What? Her forehead was starting to hurt from having her eyebrows drawn together so intensely.

She needed a moment to process.

So that was it.

Elizabeth looked at her friend, trying to gauge her. "Are you serious? Why have you been lying?" she tried to be gentle, but her confusion, the liquor, and the noisy pub made it impossible.

She reached out to squeeze Dree's hand affectionately, hoping to make up for it.

Neither of them spoke.

Elizabeth knew Audre was protecting herself from getting hurt, trying to stay away from Kilian . . . but pretending to be with someone else?

Audre shrugged her shoulders and raised her eyebrows, finally speaking, "It was just eas—"

Someone tapped a microphone to test if it was on. Everyone stopped talking, and looked to the small stage, including Elizabeth and Audre.

Kilian had suddenly appeared, guitar in hand, with a couple of traditional Irish musicians to back him up.

Audre looked at Elizabeth, clearly surprised by his

surprise show.

The animated chatter started immediately. Everyone was excited.

"Glad to be back here at O'Leary's. This is where I played nearly every week for several years. Thank you Fitz, for putting up with me," he called out towards the bar.

Fitz answered from the other room, "Glad to have you, lad! Come back to sing again whenever you like. I'll even pay what I did before!"

Kilian chuckled and everyone laughed with him.

"I don't take Guinness as payment anymore, Fitz. I've moved up in the world!"

The entire pub laughed.

"All right, let's get this party started." Kilian launched into a traditional Irish jig.

People started whooping and hollering and clapping to the song.

Elizabeth leaned into Audre, "You didn't know he was going to do this?"

She just shook her head, her eyes trained on Kilian.

Elizabeth felt someone touch her arm, she turned to find Connor standing there in casual blue jeans and a tight-fitting black T-shirt.

For a moment Elizabeth forgot that they were fighting.

His biceps stretched the fabric of his shirt, part of the green Celtic Cross tattoo showed beneath the sleeve. Even in the dim light, she could see the muscles of his chest contracting as he moved. His blue eyes shimmered with the reflection of the pub lights.

Her husband looked delicious. She'd had enough liquor to allow her eyes to openly appreciate him.

Or perhaps Camille was rubbing off on her.

He leaned in to whisper at her ear, "Can we talk?"

Elizabeth didn't want to fight. She was done fighting. She couldn't take anymore tonight.

His lips grazed her earlobe sending a shiver down her spine. He was close enough that part of his body was touching hers. She tried to remember why she was mad.

And then she did.

All of it came rushing back.

She shook her head, "No, I'm with my girl tonight." She threw an arm around Audre.

Connor looked taken aback, surprised by her refusal to speak to him. He took a step backwards, examined her face, what he saw there, she could only guess.

Without another word, he walked away to stand on the other side of the room.

Several people had noticed the cold exchange between them, including Kilian, who was still strumming away on his guitar, playing the fast jig and singing.

The cheering and clapping and dancing seemed very far away. She and Audre held each other, neither capable of speaking.

"Lovely, that was a good one." Kilian spoke into the

microphone at the end of the song. "Now I'd like to do something a little different. Would you all please make some space here in the middle of the floor." He motioned with his hands.

People squeezed together against the bar and the walls, and moved some of the tables closer until a small dance floor was created, just as he'd asked.

"Thank you. Now I'm going to play a song, another jig, but this time I'd like to invite two people to come up and have a dance."

Kilian was looking in Elizabeth and Audre's direction. She suddenly had a sinking sensation, and a sense of déjà vu.

Elizabeth made eye contact with Kilian. She shook her head willing him to understand, to stand down.

He just winked.

"No," she mouthed silently.

But he didn't listen, "Please give a great big welcome, to our own Elizabeth Lara and Connor Bannon!"

The crowd clapped and cheered.

Elizabeth kept shaking her head. She looked around the room and found Connor looking at her. Trying to read her.

He started to move closer, eyes fixed on her face.

"No, oh come on Kilian," she called out to the stage, "I'm sure everyone would like to hear some more music from you, without our dancing."

The people in the bar all around disagreed. They egged her on, and cheered for her to have a dance with her husband.

It was a conspiracy.

Elizabeth left her barstool, begrudgingly.

Connor was there, close at hand. He leaned in to whisper, "I'm sorry, I was an eejit."

"You've been saying that a lot lately," she snapped through gritted teeth and a fake smile.

He made the most out of the short walk to the floor, "I made it in time to see them dance, it was a craic," he said with some urgency.

"I don't believe you," she whispered back, trying to keep a smile on her face so no one would suspect that they were fighting.

He looked like she'd just slapped him, "What—," for a moment he looked hurt, but then remembered that all eyes were on them. "Do you not trust me anymore, Lara?"

Elizabeth bit her lip, "I don't know what I believe, you've been different . . . and kind of an asshole. And you won't tell me why you need to work so hard. You do remember we're pretty well-off, right? What? Is it the estate, is the castle in jeopardy?"

They were talking more quickly now, aware that they would be made to dance in just a few seconds.

"No, nothing like that," he spat back. Like the idea was ridiculous.

But the fast Irish jig started then. And they were forced to come together, Connor's arm around her waist, Elizabeth's hand on his shoulder. They began to move, jumping around the dance floor together. Connor brought her closer to him, so he could whisper in her ear. "No, nothing like that," he said again.

"Well then, what?" She raised her voice so he could hear her.

But he changed the subject, he looked her straight in the eyes, "I watched them dance. Mona did a cartwheel and then she miraculously did the splits—my eyes 'bout popped out of their sockets, I couldn't believe it."

Elizabeth rolled her eyes, "You could've overheard someone talking."

He rolled his eyes back and sighed. "You stood up and clapped. You yelled, *Brava!*"

"Fine, maybe you were there," she conceded.

But they didn't get a chance to say anything else, because Kilian had taken it upon himself to speed up the tempo. It was all they could do to stay on the beat, dancing all around the small space.

Connor deftly maneuvered the tables and the people, as Kilian made the tempo faster and faster.

They were both forced to focus on the exertion of the dance. Or risk tripping over each other and someone else.

Before long the pace had them both panting, Elizabeth relaxed a degree as she surrendered to the music. Allowed the song to fill her, and then they were really moving.

The people in the pub, clapped and cheered for them.

Before long, Elizabeth was laughing.

As soon as Elizabeth began to laugh, Connor relaxed. He held his wife close to his body as they finished out the song.

The last few notes hung in the air and everyone clapped.

Elizabeth remembered herself, breaking away from Connor as soon as the music finished.

Kilian came back onto the microphone, "Now I'm responsible for this holy union. I was the one who first put them together for a dance. It was all my doin'!"

Everyone laughed.

"Mate," he said to Connor, "you never thanked me properly for that!"

Connor did a little bow, and thanked his best friend.

That got an even bigger laugh.

Everyone at O'Leary's was in good spirits, it seemed. Everyone except Elizabeth.

By midday on Saturday, a video of Mona and Camille's dance performance had gone viral. It was all anyone could talk about. The video had been viewed more than a million times.

By Sunday evening, views were up to ten million and several international news outlets had contacted Mona, asking for an exclusive interview. Their group, Over Fifty, had even received several invitations to perform across Ireland and Europe.

Mona was on cloud nine.

20

REVELATIONS

The effect of being in a week-long fight with Connor, was taking its toll on Elizabeth.

"I am heading to the pub to meet Kilian," he had come into the solarium to tell her.

She had been sitting and watching the lights of the backyard for an hour, mindlessly mesmerized, thinking about the Met's offer.

Maybe she should go to New York.

She willed herself to get lost in something, something other than the communication problems she was having with her husband.

Her eyes were still trained on the lights outside, as she processed what he had just said. "I think that's a great idea," she said in a flat tone, not looking at him. "You've not spent any real time with Kilian. Hope you guys have fun."

Connor lingered a minute before sighing and walking out.

By 10:00 p.m. that night, Elizabeth found she was tired enough to go to sleep. But she wouldn't spend the night in their master bedroom, she would sleep in her office.

She mustered enough energy to get up and leave the solarium. It was time to say good night and unplug from the world.

She found Audre working in her guest suite, researching something for Kilian's end of summer concert at Croke Park. She said good night and then went downstairs to say good night to Camille.

She found her in the living room reading on her tablet and drinking a glass of wine. "Night," she said back.

Elizabeth had just started to head up the stairs to her office when the front door unlocked and the alarm was disabled.

Elizabeth turned, her heart skipped a beat, she hoped it was Connor. She couldn't take much more, not talking was eating her alive.

But it was just Aidan coming in to give her the weekly report.

She'd forgotten.

"Everything is in order, Lady Lara," Aidan said. "The night team should be en route to relieve the day shift now. Henry and I will watch the perimeter until they arrive."

"Thank you, Aidan. We'll see you tomorrow," she said, her voice sounded every bit as tired as she felt.

He nodded and excused himself.

Elizabeth turned off the main lights in the foyer and the kitchen separately, instead of using the main light switch that worked on all the lights on the ground floor so Camille could keep reading. She popped into the living room one last time, and found Camille getting up from the couch.

"I think I'll follow your example, get to bed early tonight. It's been such an eventful weekend," Camille smiled.

It made Elizabeth smile. Over Fifty's dance success had been the only silver lining of the last few days. It had been nothing short of delightful to watch Mona finally get her due and Camille have fun.

The women turned off the last of the lights and headed up the stairs. They met Audre on the second floor landing, she was just coming to find them.

"What? I thought you were kidding when you said good night. You're going to bed at ten?!" Audre was stunned.

Elizabeth shrugged.

"Awww, Babes, you look so sad."

Elizabeth opened her mouth to protest, but she couldn't. She *was* sad.

Elizabeth looked out through the tall windows on the second floor, she noticed the light, and realized she hadn't turned off the twinkle lights in the backyard. "Oh, I forgot the outside lights." Elizabeth turned around and headed back downstairs.

Camille started to walk down the stairs with her, "And I forgot my tablet in the living room."

Audre bounced down the stairs to catch up, "Are you sure you have to go to bed?"

"I don't have to," Elizabeth answered, "but I really don't want to be awake right now."

Audre examined her face. "OK, Babes, you go to bed. I'm going to get a glass of wine."

The three women headed down the stairs to complete each of their respective tasks.

Elizabeth walked to the back of the house, to the solarium where they kept one of the main switches to the estate lights. She looked out at the stunning display for a few more seconds, relishing in its beauty, before flipping the switch.

She was making her way back through the house, when she heard it.

Something fell over in the kitchen, *hard.*

Elizabeth ran towards the noise and seconds later found Audre lying on the floor next to the kitchen island. She had a small cut on her forehead and a bump that was already starting to rise. "Oh my God, Dree?"

She quickly checked her pulse and made sure she was breathing, but then she stilled.

The hair on the back of her neck stood up. She was

instantly on high alert. She knew then, instinctively, that Audre had not merely fainted and hit her head, someone had attacked her.

Audre's injury didn't seem life-threatening, so Elizabeth refocused her attention on the bigger picture.

She quickly stood up and turned off the lights in the kitchen. Listening for any movement, trying to sense whoever was there.

She heard the faintest of movement, coming from the other entrance to the kitchen. Her eyes had adjusted to the dark, it was Cam.

Camille raised a finger to her lips and signaled that someone was upstairs.

Elizabeth quickly retrieved her phone from her pocket and checked the security cameras.

She flipped through each view quickly. Outside one of the front cameras she saw Aidan lying face down on the ground.

Oh God.

She kept flipping until she found one of the cameras at the side of the estate, nearest the guardhouse. Someone else was lying on the ground, it looked like Henry.

She kept flipping through, until she came to the back door by the solarium. A man she didn't recognize was opening the door. There was a gun in his hand.

Shit.

She walked across the kitchen quietly, joining Camille.

"I was in the living room when I heard her fall," Camille whispered. "I hadn't turned on the lights in there, so I don't think he knew I was down here, then I heard someone on the staircase."

Elizabeth brought her up to speed, that there was another intruder coming in from the back.

Elizabeth tried to call the Garda, but found she could get no signal. Only the Wi-Fi was working, and then suddenly it failed as well.

Oh no.

"What do we do?" she asked Camille.

"We could try running out the front, and get away from whatever signal scrambler they're using. But then we can't leave Audre."

"No, we can't leave her," Elizabeth agreed.

"Well then, we'll just have to take them out." Camille looked straight into Elizabeth's eyes, "Are you up for it?"

Elizabeth's adrenaline had long since kicked in. She nodded.

"How quiet do you think you can be on the stairs?" Camille asked her.

Elizabeth shrugged, "I don't know, you?"

Camille nodded, "I can do it. I'll take the one upstairs, you take care of the man who just came in through the back."

Elizabeth nodded in agreement. She took Camille's hand and squeezed, "Be careful."

"Oh, honey, I'm done being careful. It's time to find some answers." she said, a smile on her lips. "Let's do this."

They split up.

Elizabeth watched Camille ascend the stairs, quiet as a mouse.

And then she herself made her way from the kitchen to the back of the house, careful to move from position to position, to remain hidden.

She found a spot, just outside of the grand lounge. She hid in an alcove and waited. The intruder would have to pass her in order to access the rest of the castle.

She waited in the alcove for a minute, trying to keep her breathing steady. By that point, her senses were razor-sharp. She waited and listened.

Finally, she heard someone walking very carefully in her direction. Elizabeth didn't dare peek out from behind the alcove, she relied on her hearing to judge how close he was.

She was flat against the side of the alcove wall, if he passed it and didn't look back, he wouldn't even see her. From the sound of his footsteps, the man was only a couple paces away.

If she jumped out now and attacked him, she would definitely have the element of surprise, *but*, she would be in a better physical position, if he walked by the alcove and she took him from behind.

Her brain raced to process the possibilities.

She decided to come at him from behind, but it was a gamble.

He'd have to walk by her hiding place.

He was there now.

Elizabeth caught her first glimpse of him. He was at least six-foot-two, wore all black, and held a gun with a silencer pointed downwards at the space in front of him.

He just needed to keep walking, he was only two steps away now from giving her the perfect position.

But he must've caught something in his periphery, because everything changed in an instant.

His body had begun to turn and Elizabeth was forced to take her shot.

She lunged at him from behind extending her leg out and kicking his wrist, sending the gun flying out of his hand and down the corridor.

The man threw out his arm in a punch that didn't land. Elizabeth deftly avoided the hit, grabbed his arm and kicked him in one of the pressure points of his upper arm.

She turned her hips and used the entire force of her body to deliver a swift knee to the groin.

He doubled over. She put her forefinger and middle finger together and made them ramrod straight. She made a quick jabbing movement at his eyes, temporarily blinding him.

The man clutched his face and fell all the way to the

ground while Elizabeth ran down the corridor to retrieve his gun.

She went back to the man who'd just broken into her house, and slammed the butt of his own gun into his head. He stopped moving instantly.

She hoped she had hit him hard enough to keep him down for the count, because she didn't have anything else to restrain him with. And she needed to go find Camille.

She made her way back to the front of the house, careful not to make any noise. She was just about to start climbing the stairs when someone came tumbling down from the third floor to the second.

The large man came crashing down onto the landing. Elizabeth was just about to close the distance between them when Camille slid down the banister, landing like a cat in front of the man on the floor.

He made a move to get up, but she didn't let him. With a swift axe kick to his face, Camille knocked him out cold.

"You OK?" she whispered to Camille.

Camille looked fine, more than fine. She looked invigorated, like she had enjoyed the brief fight she'd had with the large man, who Elizabeth estimated was even taller than her own opponent.

"Oh yeah," Camille smiled. "Never better."

And in that moment, Elizabeth was sure that was true.

"Oh mommy dearest . . . !" A man's voice yelled up from the first floor, echoing throughout the castle.

It was a cold, deranged sounding voice. Like something out of *The Shining*.

Suddenly all of the lights on the first floor turned on. Someone had accessed the master switch by the door.

The women squinted, trying to adjust to the light.

They thought there had only been two men.

They were wrong.

Camille narrowed her eyes, trying to place what she had just heard.

"Who is it?" Elizabeth whispered to Camille.

But Camille was busy putting the pieces together.

A man of average height and build with light brown hair stepped out into view. He was holding a petrified Audre from behind, one arm around her neck, the other holding a gun with a silencer to her temple.

"Drop the gun," he said to Elizabeth.

She dropped it a few feet away from her on the landing.

Camille shook her head, "I knew it."

"Are you surprised?" The man asked.

"Me, no. I suspected the attacks on the company were more personally motivated. That's why I left protective custody. I knew they were barking up the wrong tree, but typical government men, they didn't listen."

The man started to examine Elizabeth, "So this is the famous Elizabeth Lara," he said to her.

Elizabeth was quickly trying to think through the situation, her stomach was in knots as she watched Audre's whole body shake.

"You know," the man kept talking, "I'd always hear her talk about you when I'd visit my father and my stepmother at the house."

His eyes grew wide, deranged. "The great Elizabeth Lara. She talked about you like you were superhuman. Brilliant, fierce, ah-mazing."

He walked closer to them, dragging Audre with him.

Elizabeth could see his features more clearly now, he resembled his father.

Camille put her hands on her hips. "Let her go, Josh. Your problem is with me."

He tilted his head and looked at Cam again, "So you're not surprised?"

Camille sighed. "No and yes. I suspected you were behind it, but I honestly didn't think you had the balls to pull something like this off."

"Typical Camille, arrogant until the end," he spat.

"Well, I certainly didn't think you were smart enough, or *dumb* enough, to try to take on a secure place like this. How'd you do it?"

Elizabeth looked over at Camille. What was her strategy? Keep him talking?

"It only took about a day of watching this place ... and a little digging to find a guard in need of some cash. Turns out your man Henry was willing to sell you out. Something about his daughter?" He smiled viciously. "I don't know, I don't care." He waved the gun around for a moment. "Of course he thought we were only going to steal a painting. What an idiot!" he laughed.

"From there it was a cake walk to find out the schedule and when the security change was supposed to happen."

What had Henry done? Why did he need the money? What was happening with Aimee?

She forced herself back into the present, remembering Aidan and Henry lying outside, "And are they alive?"

"Don't worry." He took his time explaining, "Most of them are fast asleep in the guardhouse, with the help of a little gas that is. And in case you think your night team will save you, I'm sorry to inform you that they've been delayed, thanks to an obstruction in the service road nearest the guardhouse."

"What about Aidan and Henry?" she gulped nervously. She couldn't think about Aimee losing her father, no matter what he'd done.

Josh looked at her quizzically. "If you mean the two men outside, we took care of them. I think they're still alive. Well the one out front should be alive, I think, if he survived the stab wound." Josh didn't seem concerned. "That is if he hasn't bled out yet."

Camille started to walk across the landing. "Estas loco. What are you playing at? What, you're just going to kill everyone and get away?"

"No, no," he waved the gun in his right hand and repositioned it at Audre's temple.

Camille stopped. "What do you want, Josh?" she asked.

"I want my inheritance."

"You got your inheritance years ago, when your father died. Why are you doing this now?"

"That wasn't an inheritance," he spit out. "The man's company was worth a quarter of a *billion* dollars, and when he died it all went to you. The company just became another subsidiary of Cortez Holdings."

Camille crossed her arms, "Josh he left you a trust fund."

Josh laughed. "A *quarter* of a million? That was my trust fund? It all went to you, like you needed it! Your company was worth more than a hundred times that by that point."

"Joshua, your father believed that a man should make his own fortune. Stand on his own two feet. He didn't want to leave you the company, he wanted you to find your own way," Camille explained.

"Well I guess he was right, I found my own way!"

Elizabeth couldn't wrap her head around what was happening. "So wait," she began.

Joshua's eyes went to her, snapping him out of his conversation with Camille, like he'd forgotten Elizabeth was there.

"You want to kill Camille, for an inheritance? You should have consulted an attorney. Because that's not how that works. You were a stepchild."

"Oh, I have an attorney," he said smugly.

"Then you know that's not how that works! Unless . . ." She turned to Cam, "Don't you have a will, Camille?"

"I did," she answered simply.

"But then it went missing," Joshua interjected.

"Yes, it did," Camille wasn't fazed. "And that's what tipped me off. The FBI and NSA, everyone else was busy looking at the information leaks and the account hacks, but I suspected that those attacks might've been a diversion, to gain access to, and destroy my will. And who else would care about such a thing?"

Elizabeth was going into lawyer mode, "No. Even if they hacked the site and managed to delete the scanned copies, if they existed, from your firm's mainframe, the physical copies would still exist."

"That's the thing," Camille said in a light voice. "He broke into the legal department and destroyed the originals."

Elizabeth looked at Joshua. A huge smile was planted on his face.

"Yes, I did," he admitted.

"Did you read it?" Camille asked him. There was something in her voice, the glint of panic, as she realized the full extent of his assault.

"No, should I have? I assumed you would have left me nothing, was I wrong?"

"No," Camille said simply, the smallest hint of relief in her voice.

Joshua didn't seem to notice.

"So, I waited to drop another will," Camille continued. "I had it leaked through a company-wide email, just yesterday. I knew you would see it."

Elizabeth turned to her, "He works for you?"

Camille rolled her eyes, "Yes, he burned through his inheritance quickly, and I was a softy. I gave him a job out of respect for his father. Not one of my finest moments."

"Oh yes," he yelled, starting to lose control. "I suppose you think I should be grateful for your low-level job. You didn't even have the decency to give me a management position!"

Camille shrugged in a *what can you do* gesture, "Well I never really thought you were that smart," Camille said nonchalantly.

Elizabeth's eyes grew wide, she shot her a look that read *don't poke the bear.*

Camille ignored it.

Elizabeth needed more time, more time to figure out how to get out of this, she went back to Camille's initial strategy. "So what did the new will say?" she asked Josh, trying to keep him busy.

Joshua gave her an amused smile. "Oh you'll love this, it involves you actually."

"Me?" Elizabeth turned to Camille.

"Yes, the new will was simple: *I leave everything to my great-niece, Elizabeth Lara.*".

Her head snapped to look at Camille, her jaw dropped. "Did you plant that so he would come looking for me?"

"Yes, I did. But I planted it, so he would come looking for *us*," she corrected.

"But . . . it isn't true, right?" she asked the woman standing next to her.

Camille sighed. "I had hoped to tell you in a different way."

"What do you mean?" Elizabeth turned her body towards Cam, temporarily forgetting about the man with the gun.

"Well, I found out a few years ago that your grandfather, Alejandro, was actually my father."

"What, how?" she was confused.

"Well," Camille shrugged, "my mother Adriana was best friends with your grandmother, Margarita. But Margarita died when the girls were young. So, my mother Adriana was around a lot, and I don't know, I guess a little of this, a little of that, throw in some vino, and poof! I'm here."

Elizabeth shook her head, "No, I mean, how did you find out?"

"Oh, that. I took one of those ancestry tests that are all the rage. I was a close match with someone else. Magdalena. She had also taken the test the year before, so when we matched, we did a further DNA test, and it proved that we were half-sisters." Camille turned to look at Elizabeth, "Lizzie, I am your great-aunt."

Elizabeth didn't know how to feel. What? What was she

talking about? "Secret fathers? Secret affairs? What the hell is wrong with this family?!"

"Yes, so you see," Josh broke through their moment, snapping Elizabeth back to reality. "It became highly imperative for me to dispose of you. But then, on my way here, I was mindlessly scrolling through the inter-webs, and what should I find, but a viral video of some old hags dancing. You can imagine my surprise, when I saw my dear old step-mother amongst them. Alive and well and, in fact, kicking! So you see, offing you two in one go, solves a lot of my problems."

Then why wasn't he getting on with it? She thought through it. He was a talker. He needed to tell his story before he killed them.

So she would keep him talking.

"That's still a long shot," she began, in full lawyer mode now, "for you to stand any chance of inheriting in California, you would have to destroy all copies of the new will so it could not be presented in probate, kill Camille, which apparently you thought you had already done, and kill any blood relations. And even *then* your right to inherit anything from her estate isn't clear. That's an awful lot of trouble for such a long shot."

He let out a deranged laugh. "For *fifty billion*, I was willing to get creative and take the gamble. I could have greased the right palms. Besides, who would have challenged it? She is alone. Once you're gone, there'll be no one," he answered, not giving it a second thought, clearly convinced that it would have all worked out in his favor.

She'd had enough, time was running out. Audre looked like she would faint at any moment, which was probably a good thing. But Aidan and Henry were still outside, dying.

She needed to figure it out now.

But she didn't get the chance.

Out of the corner of her mouth, Camille said, "Cough."

Elizabeth started coughing on command, she didn't know what Camille was planning, but she had to go with it.

She started coughing softly at first, and then she triggered a genuine cough, and then another. Before she knew it she was having a full-blown coughing attack.

Joshua was instantly on edge, "What are you doing? Stop that!" He moved the gun from Audre's temple to point it at Elizabeth, and in doing so he exposed his neck.

It happened so fast, Elizabeth barely caught Camille's quick movement and the glint of the knife, reflecting the chandelier above.

Josh released Audre immediately, she fell to the floor and scrambled away. He dropped the gun and clutched both hands to his throat.

Elizabeth stopped coughing. She stopped breathing as she watched.

He sunk to his knees and fell to the floor. Blood pooled around him.

And then there was silence.

21

THE TRUTH

They found the signal scrambler in Josh's pocket. They had tried to save him, but his injury was too severe. The Garda and the paramedics arrived at the same time as Connor.

He was frantic to find Elizabeth. "Oh my God, thank Jaysus you're all right." He hugged her.

"We're fine, go with Aidan and Henry. Make sure they're all right."

"I spoke with the paramedics before coming in. Henry might have a concussion and Aidan is still unconscious, but the stab wound doesn't look deep. They said he might need surgery, but that he should pull through."

Elizabeth wasn't deterred, "Go with them, and take care of Audre, please."

"Are you sure?" he asked.

She nodded.

They had checked out Audre on the scene and had told them her injury wasn't serious, but they wanted to take her to the hospital to be sure.

Elizabeth and Camille had to stay behind to answer the litany of questions that followed. The FBI was informed, and after a conversation with Agent Jackson, and some other government agency in Ireland, everyone on the scene was instructed to keep quiet about the night's events.

The FBI was flying in that night to liaise with Interpol and all the other organizations which needed to be involved.

Even after Camille had explained, they weren't sold on the idea that it had all been Josh's doing.

They were still conducting their own investigation into the possibility that it was a terrorist plot. So Camille was going to stay dead for a while longer.

Hours later, after the house had been cleared, no sign that anything had ever been a miss, Elizabeth and Camille sat on the couch together.

Camille explained and apologized for putting Elizabeth in harm's way.

"I am sorry that I had to involve you. But at the same time, I'm glad I did. It's been wonderful getting to know you like this, getting to see your life here."

"I understand. So, you planned all of this? You knew this was going to happen?"

"Well, not the particulars. I didn't anticipate joining a

dance group and having a video of us go viral. That wasn't part of the plan," she chuckled. "But I thought that, *strategically*, this was the best idea. And anyway, even if I hadn't planted the new will, he might've found out we were related —and then he would've come after you and you would've been blindsided."

Elizabeth considered that, "Why do you think he didn't know about your granddaughter? If you died intestate—without a will—she would inherit before me."

Camille exhaled. "It was lucky!" she breathed. Sounding shaken for the first time. "Isabelle did an amazing job of scrubbing her connection to me from the public record. Her daughter, my granddaughter, doesn't know who she really is. Stephen knew about our situation, of course, but we never mentioned it around Josh."

"But you mentioned me?"

"Yes, I always saw you as my niece—your entire life. I was excited to find that I had a sister in Magdalena. We already had that type of relationship, of course, but it's another thing to know that the same blood runs in our veins."

"When did you both find out?"

"About two years before Magdalena died."

"Why didn't you tell me?"

"I don't know. It's a simple answer. I think maybe I was worried about disrupting our relationship. I just always thought there would be a right time to tell you. Turns out there wasn't." She reached over and took Elizabeth's hand, "But I am so proud to be your great-aunt."

Elizabeth reached over and hugged Camille, burying her face in Cam's neck and bright blue bob of hair.

"Are you even a little bit sad about Josh?" she mumbled into Cam's hair, before moving away so she could see her face.

Camille looked down at her hands, "Yes, of course. He was always pretty awful, ungrateful, entitled—all of that. I didn't really have any relationship with him, and to be honest, Stephen didn't either. Maybe if he had, Josh wouldn't have turned out the way he did. I'm sad that it had to come to that. I'm sorry that he's gone, especially for Stephen's sake. God rest their souls."

Elizabeth stretched out on the couch with her head in Camille's lap.

They sat together in silence for a few minutes, processing the night, until Elizabeth cleared her throat nervously.

She hesitated, "Do you feel guilty about . . . about taking his life?"

Camille sighed. "Yes, well there's that too. I am only human. But it was Audre's life, and your guards outside. He needed to be stopped. I saw my shot, so I took it."

Elizabeth nodded, her head still in Camille's lap. "Yes, there were no good choices," she said softly. Then she thought of something else, sitting up abruptly, "Where did you have the knife?"

Camille gave her a sad smile, "In the small of my back. That's why I asked you to cough, so his eyes would be on you and he wouldn't see me reaching back to retrieve it."

"Huh," she played the memory back in her head with the new information, remembering the metal of the knife briefly reflecting the light of the chandelier . . . and then . . . she didn't want to think about the rest. A shiver ran up her spine.

It had been a close call for all of them.

Elizabeth leaned over and kissed her cheek, "Thank you for saving us," she whispered, before settling back down on the couch with her head in Camille's lap.

Her great-aunt stroked her hair gently again and again, soothing her.

The heaviness of the day started to overtake her. She felt loved, and cared for, as Camille continued to stroke her head.

She fell asleep and had some vague recollection of Camille carefully maneuvering herself free, laying Elizabeth's head gently down on a pillow.

When Elizabeth was in a state between consciousness and dreaming, she heard the front door open.

She heard Camille talking to Audre and Audre saying that she didn't have a concussion and that she was going to bed.

There were footsteps on the stairs. And then nothing.

A few seconds . . . or minutes later, more voices.

Camille and Connor.

They were standing at the entrance to the living room, or

maybe the foyer, Elizabeth couldn't tell. She wasn't even sure it was really happening. Her eyes were so heavy.

"Connor, I feel I need to intervene. Tomorrow Elizabeth will explain that I am, in fact, her great-aunt—a fact she was only made aware of tonight," Camille said without pomp or circumstance.

A strange noise, perhaps a bit of Irish Gaelic, escaped Connor's lips. Elizabeth thought it might be something akin to, "Wow."

"Now as her aunt, I feel very protective of her," Camille continued. "And even though your marriage is your own, and no one outside of any marriage can really know what it's like, I need to tell you something."

"OK?" he sounded nervous.

Camille took a deep breath. "You're being an ass," she said flatly. "Stop. It's enough. Talk to your wife."

Connor cleared his throat, "Let's . . . talk about this in the kitchen," he lowered his voice.

Fading footsteps. Then silence.

After a few seconds, the sleep came for her more fully and took her away again.

She woke with a start. Her body was curled up in the fetal position, her neck tucked in, almost touching her chest. It was a painful position. She unfurled herself, slowly sitting up, trying to remember where she was and what had happened.

It all came rushing back in an instant. She retrieved her phone from the coffee table in front of her, it was almost four in the morning.

Her body started to move in all the necessary ways, her limbs stretched up towards the ceiling, her neck moved from side to side.

She reconnected with her body slowly. Her eyes were sore, her mouth was dry. A glass of cold water was suddenly all she could think about.

She got up and walked to the kitchen, continuing to stretch her body as she went. The sound of muffled voices reached her ears. Their words took a more clear shape as she approached.

"That's all I'm saying," the woman said.

"You're right, I know y'are," the man agreed.

Elizabeth entered the kitchen.

Camille and Connor were sitting at the table. They stopped talking abruptly as soon as they saw her.

Camille stood up, "Well children I think it's time I found my bed." She turned back to Connor, "Remember what I told you. Don't screw this up," she warned.

She smiled at him, patted his shoulder and walked to Elizabeth. "Buenas noches," she kissed her cheek and was gone.

Elizabeth went to the cupboard to grab a glass, she filled

it with water and went to sit down at the table, across from her husband.

She took a sip and then a large gulp. Before she knew it, she had downed half the glass.

Connor sat with his hands clasped in front of him.

She set the glass down and took a breath, "What did you guys talk about?"

His lips set in a line, "Many things," his voice was strained. "But the short version is that . . . *I'm an ass.*"

Elizabeth rubbed her eyes, she was still groggy. "Tell me something I don't know," she chided.

"Lara," he began, taking a deep breath, "I want to tell you what's been happening."

His words had an immediate effect. She was suddenly completely awake.

Her stomach fell to her feet. He was finally ready to talk, but now that it was time, she found herself more than a little terrified of what he was going to say.

"I'm sorry, I hope it's not too late," he said.

Elizabeth didn't have the words so she motioned with her hand, urging him to speak.

"The auction house in Rome is in trouble," he breathed, staring down at his hands. "It's been in trouble for a couple of months now. I've been desperately trying to save it, but . . . to make a long story short I haven't been able to come up with a solution."

Elizabeth tried to place the emotion in his voice.

Sadness? No. Something else . . . she couldn't quite put her finger on it. She wasn't sure she'd ever heard it from him before. Was it shame?

"OK," she said slowly, still waiting for the other shoe to drop. "Yes, I knew that, you kept running off. Get to the main part, the reason you haven't been talking to me, not giving me details of why you had to keep leaving. Why you've been so distant." Her words came out in a rush.

She was desperate to know already. All the terrible possibilities, the ones every woman thinks about at one time or another, were now flooding her brain.

Would they survive it?

"The auction house is failing," he said again slowly, in a flat voice that seemed to carry another meaning. His eyes narrowed. He gave her a *don't you get it?* look. Like she hadn't understood the first time.

And? Why wasn't he getting to the main part? The reason he'd been so distant.

They stared at each other. Elizabeth narrowed her eyes and shook her head, not knowing how to ferret out the rest. He wanted to talk about the auction house failing. Maybe that's how he needed to start the conversation before moving on to the more difficult bits—*whatever they were?*

"Okaaay?" she struggled to stay with him. For a moment, she envisioned herself reaching across the table, grabbing him by the shoulders and shaking the rest out of him. She gritted her teeth, "So what are you going to do?" she asked, still confused, and more than a little impatient.

"Well," he began moving his head, his eyes trying to find a place to land, before settling on her face, "I can't fail." His voice was grave.

OK. It seemed that if she was going to get answers, she was going to have to deal with the troubled auction house first.

She took a deep breath. "What do you mean? It's a business. Just close it?" Her impatience now on full display.

He stared at her frozen in place, eyes wide.

What was she missing? "How are the other auction houses doing?"

The question roused him, "London and Paris are fine, all three houses operate independently from each other." He ran his fingers through his hair.

"Okaaay," she shook her head, "so just close the auction house in Rome, what's the problem?"

He was maddening. The business issue was so obvious to her . . . why wasn't he getting to the important part?

"Lara, you don't understand."

Clearly.

He got up and started pacing. "The Rome house was the first auction house I opened. It was the first time I did anything on my own. It didn't matter who my father was, or how much money I inherited. I built that house from the ground up, with money *I* had worked for. It was mine, completely mine. It existed solely from my talents and my efforts."

She nodded, encouraging him to continue.

"It was the proof—that I was good at something. That I was *worth* something. Me, Connor Bannon. Not Lord Bannon or Keanan Grail's son. *Just me*. For that house to fail?"

He stopped pacing and gripped the back of the chair, his head bowed. "It means that *I'm a failure*."

She waited for him to continue.

But he just stared at the floor. The weight of it seemed to crush him.

A realization was starting to dawn. Anger and relief mixed together and started to rise in her, "Wait," she was trying to keep up, "*this* is what you were keeping from me?"

He nodded, still looking down.

"So this is about your pride?" her voice crescendoed.

His head snapped up, "It's not about pride, Lara," his voice was harsh, "it's about *self-worth*," he corrected. "Everything I have in my life is because of someone else, because of an inheritance. The auction houses were about me."

"You still have London and Paris, right?"

"Yes, but I failed. I failed at the only thing that was ever just mine."

Elizabeth took a deep breath, she was trying to stay calm. Trying to see his side of things, but it was a hard pill to swallow. Hearing that he had stopped communicating with her, put her through so much . . . *all because he had been too proud to admit that his business was in trouble?!*

"And that's it? There's nothing else?" she tried again.

Connor breathed, "That's it. Isn't that enough? I'm a failure," his voice was dripping with disdain and self-loathing.

Jesus.

Was this his midlife crisis? She closed her eyes and focused on her breathing. Her poor husband. Even after all these years, the feelings of insecurity from his childhood—which stemmed from his father's treatment of him, from being Keanan Grail's bastard son—still weighed him down.

Her voice softened, "Failure is a part of life, Connor."

He held her gaze. "I didn't want you to see me that way," he admitted. "You're so good at everything you do, everything you try, it all comes easily to you. But that hasn't been my life."

Elizabeth considered that, "Things don't come easily to me," she contradicted him quickly. "I mean some things sure, but everyone has those different talents—I'm good at what I do because I work my ass off!"

Connor's expression changed. A look of appreciation and devotion transformed his features. "I know," his voice was more calm, no longer strained. "Lara, you're amazing. Every day I think about how lucky I am to have you. I just want to be . . . *good enough.*"

She felt like she'd been slapped. What had she ever done

to make him feel not good enough? With a sinking sensation she realized that she had done nothing.

It wasn't about her. It was about him and his demons. His childhood trauma. His own fears and insecurities. All she could do was stand by his side when they rose to the surface, hold his hand when he needed to wrestle with them all over again.

His eyes reflected the light behind her, they almost glistened.

She wasn't sure if she wanted to slap him or hug him.

Relief started to dawn, but she was weary. "And that is really it? There's nothing else?"

He shook his head.

"You didn't want to tell me that your business was failing because you didn't want me to think of you differently?"

He nodded simply, and in that moment he looked like a little boy. She could see his vulnerability. As asinine as it all seemed to her, it was clear that Connor believed every word. The fear of failure was crushing him. The issues from his past had manifested in new and different ways.

He'd stopped communicating with her because, *he was afraid.*

She exhaled all at once. The tension was finally starting to leave her body. "Ugh, you daft man, you *did* fail me." Her words were serious, but her tone was light.

He looked down at his hands, *"I know,"* his voice was hard. He started to fall back into the self-loathing.

She shook her head. "No, that's not what I mean."

His eyes found hers.

"You failed me when you stopped talking to me. When you stopped communicating. When you flat out refused to tell me what was going on! Not talking was eating me alive.

"I was ready to go to sleep by ten tonight, because I was so depressed. I thought this was the beginning of the end. I thought that this was how we drifted apart. *That's* how you failed me."

Blood rushed to his face, his eyes were electric. "I'm sorry," he was flustered, his voice was something beyond strained. "I shouldn't have kept it from you."

After a few moments, his face relaxed and some new emotion took hold.

Acceptance . . . ? Surrender . . . ? Peace?

He released his grip on the chair opposite her and moved to sit down in the chair diagonally adjacent to hers.

The proximity softened her another degree.

She was used to seeing him be tough, intense, confident. It shook her to see him so affected by the thought of failing her.

Her beautiful, strong Connor. The abandoned boy, the broken teen—still carrying the weight of the world on his shoulders.

Still trying to prove to the world that he was good enough.

"No, you shouldn't have kept it from me," she agreed, her voice stern, but gentle.

She reached over to squeeze his hand. He accepted her eagerly.

His entire body relaxed under her touch.

She kept her voice soft, "I love you. You *are* enough. Your business is only one part of you, it doesn't define you."

He didn't say anything in response.

"Besides, you don't think I felt like a failure after my lost decade? For not coming to Ireland with Mags when she asked? For not listening to her sooner? We all have our stuff."

He nodded, still listening.

"All we can do is try our best and rely on each other. Isn't that what this whole marriage thing is supposed to be about?"

He let out a soft chuckle, "I guess so," he agreed. "I've been an eejit, I'm sorry."

She gave his hand another reassuring squeeze.

His fingers were long, powerful. He drew small circles against her skin with his thumb.

After a few minutes, he brought his other hand up to her forearm, stroking her flesh in slow, deliberate movements.

Something started to change in her body.

Something started to change between them.

The electricity.

Her breathing became shallow.

His lips parted a degree, his eyes were on her mouth.

The look he was giving her . . . he was fully himself. His power, his thirst, it was radiating off of him in waves.

Her heart stopped. All she could see were his sapphire eyes. All she could think about was the strength of his chest, of her body melting into his. . . .

Suddenly, they were on their feet, crashing into each other.

His lips came down on her, hard. They were forceful, unyielding. He was hungry, desperate to taste her, to envelope her.

She accepted him eagerly, wanting nothing more than to feel him, to reestablish their connection.

His arms formed a protective steel cage around her, bound her to him, while their lips came together feverishly. Their tongues tangled again and again, like their lives depended on it.

It was Connor who broke away, but only to take her hand and lead her out of the kitchen.

They ascended the stairs quickly and found themselves alone in their bedroom.

Silvery moon beams floated in through the windows, casting a magical glow that made their passion turn primal.

Connor began to undress her, one piece of clothing at a time, until she was standing there completely naked.

Her husband took her in. Let his eyes rove over her body, let the electricity and lust build between them.

She went to him, undressing him in kind, letting her

fingertips trail down the rippled curves of his bare chest and down to the stronger curve of his backside.

In one lithe movement, he reached for her, pressing her against him, crushing her soft breasts against the hard line of his body.

They stood there, flesh on flesh, holding each other, breathing into one another, until their primal need for each other overtook them.

Connor scooped her up and carried her to their bed.

He placed himself over her, allowing her to feel his energy, to anticipate his possession.

And then he was kissing her again.

She accepted him eagerly, wrapping herself around him.

They became one again and again, making love with reckless abandon. Elizabeth had no thought, no sense of anything but the feel of her husband.

They both surrendered to their bodies, swearing to the high heavens as they collapsed.

Their blissful reunion complete.

22

THE VOICES

"Where will you go?" Elizabeth asked Camille.

Connor took her aunt's giant suitcase and rolled it to the car where Agent Jackson was waiting.

"I think I'll be going through it all with the FBI and whoever else again. They're a bit on the slow side, it might take them a second to catch up."

"What if they're right and there is something bigger going on?"

"Mmmm . . . I don't think so," Camille said.

But Elizabeth detected a glint in her eye.

"You're not going to tell me what you're thinking, are you?" Elizabeth concluded.

Camille just gave her a knowing smile. "You're so smart, my love." She kissed Elizabeth on the cheek.

"Here," Cam handed her a phone and a card. "This is a

burner phone—my number is already programmed in it. And that," she pointed to the card, "is a second number in case you need to reach me. If you call that number, someone will find me, and I'll find a way to contact you."

Elizabeth nodded. "You make it sound like you're going into deep cover. Can't I just use your regular cell or call Agent Jackson?"

Camille looked at her for a second, and then answered with a simple, "No."

Elizabeth shook her head and tried not to laugh. "Well, where will you go after they're done debriefing you?"

Camille considered. A mischievous laugh escaped her lips, "I think I'll stay dead for a while. I'm having such fun not being me!"

Elizabeth smiled back, she reached out and fiddled with Camille's blue hair. "Having fun suits you," she agreed.

"It does, doesn't it? Anyway, after all of this," she motioned back to the black sedan waiting for her, "I think I need to go to Scotland. I'm told my granddaughter is there and I think it's time some things were said."

Elizabeth nodded, piecing some of it together and letting go of what she couldn't. She'd given up trying to completely understand the inner workings of Camille's brain.

"Goodbye my darling, Lizzie." Camille hugged her fiercely and then walked away.

She grabbed Connor's cheek hard enough to make him

wince, "You be good now, you hear? And don't ever stop talking to your wife again, do you understand me?"

Camille could sound very scary when she wanted to.

Connor nodded, rubbing his cheek with his palm as soon as she released him.

With one final wave through the window of the sedan, Camille was gone.

Elizabeth walked aimlessly through the trees, trying to rid herself of the horrors from the night before, trying to process the life-altering revelations, and her feelings about Camille's departure.

Her marital reconciliation and the fact that she had a living great-aunt were bright spots.

Although, she *was* starting to become numb to it. It seemed that she discovered new relatives every few years.

"What a family," she said under her breath. She shook her head as she thought through all that had come before.

She hadn't paid attention to where her feet were taking her, and before long she found herself in the blue butterfly clearing; the meadow she had started to think of as her very own fairy glen.

She walked to the center of the clearing and sat down on the luscious grass. She remembered the thought she'd had then. The thought for another day.

She looked around and thought about how it might be

possible. And in that moment, she was certain. Her voices came back to her loud and clear. She knew exactly what she wanted, exactly what she needed to do.

Without a second thought, her phone was in her hand, her plan set in motion. She wrote the email and then dialed the number.

The phone in New York rang several times before the machine picked up.

"Hi, this is Elizabeth Lara. I'm calling to thank you for your offer for the Met residency, but I'm afraid I can't accept. I'd be happy to talk to you about an exhibition, but please offer the residency to the next person on your list. Thank you very much for the honor."

She hung up and took a deep, cleansing breath. A strange noise filled the air. It erupted from her chest and came out through her mouth. It was a wild sort of laugh. Before she knew it, she was laughing hysterically, with only the flowers, birds, and trees to bear witness.

It was freedom. She scrambled to her feet and screamed into the sky, "Yeeesss!"

Her glorious voices, her connection to the Universe, was restored.

Again.

The thoughts came quickly after that. Her heart was pounding, her head was buzzing. Everything fell into place.

She planned the build in her mind, saw the little studio.

It would be unique and cozy . . . and completely hers. Her little piece of Ireland, her getaway.

She was making her own rules now and it was up to her to figure out what she needed.

She walked back to the house with a spring in her step, feeling every bit herself, and fully connected to the Universe.

When she was nearly there, she found Declan also walking up to the castle.

"Hello, Lady Elizabeth," he said to her with a broad smile.

"Declan!" she closed the distance between them quickly, giving him a bear hug.

Although it had taken him a couple of years to get used to her openness and affection, she had eventually worn him down.

He returned her hug.

She released him, "Did you have a good time at training?"

"Oh, yes. It was splendid, thank you. How has Castle Bannon kept without me? Have I missed anything?" he asked.

She pursed her lips together, trying to stifle a laugh.

He looked at her quizzically, before remembering something else, "Oh, Lady Elizabeth, there is a shipment in for you. I directed the lorry myself just now. They're putting everything into the warehouse by the garage."

Elizabeth remembered the shipment she had sent to herself from California. The one that included the larger items she had wanted to keep from Mags' house in Berkeley. "Thanks, I'll go have a look."

He nodded and walked briskly towards the house.

She followed Declan slowly, mentally going over all of the items she'd had shipped, remembering her favorite blue couch.

Just then, the front door opened; Audre took a few steps out into the sunshine.

Elizabeth stopped walking as she registered her friend. A small bruise had formed over her cheekbone, beneath her eye.

It was a great relief to see her awake and OK.

Elizabeth broke into a run and brought Audre into a bear hug. "Oh my God, I'm so glad you're all right!"

After a moment she let go, remembering, "I didn't hurt you, did I?"

Audre gave a short laugh, "No, Babes, I'm fine. Where's Camille, I haven't seen her yet today?"

"She's gone. I'll fill you in later." She was still examining her friend.

"Damn! I wanted to hug that bloody woman and thank her for being such a badass. I want to be her when I grow up."

Elizabeth chuckled, "Me too." She took in the bruise more fully. It looked painful. "How are you feeling?"

"Like I've been bopped over the head and held at

gunpoint, but other than that, I'm fantastic," Audre smiled, most of her swagger returning in an instant.

"Seriously, though, are you OK?"

She nodded. "I'm fine. A little bruised . . . a little traumatized, but I'm alive," she said in that same self-effacing tone. "Certainly puts the daft things we worry about into perspective. . . ."

She took a breath, "I'm not afraid anymore."

The sound of screeching tires suddenly interrupted their exchange. A speeding car came racing down the gravel path and screeched to a stop in front of the house.

Elizabeth took a few steps back, away from Audre. Kilian jumped out of the car and started running towards them.

Connor appeared then too, coming out from the side of the house, reaching Elizabeth and pulling her to the side, just as Kilian shot past them and launched himself straight into Audre.

He picked her up and moved in a circle, her feet fanned out behind her. After a moment, he set her down again, "Jaysus, are you all right? I just heard Connor's voicemail. Those feckin' bastards!"

Kilian examined every inch of Audre's face, using the back of his hand to gently caress her bruise. He hugged her again, "I don't know what I would do without you!" He was frantic.

He released her a degree, just enough to see her face again. His eyebrows were drawn together, his eyes burned with a fire that was torture, pain, passion, and love all melted together.

The world stopped. Before any of them knew it, he was closing the distance, taking her lips in his, recklessly forgetting himself.

After a few seconds he realized what he was doing and broke away, "Feck me, I'm sorry, I don't know what came over me. I'm just so glad you're all—" but he didn't get a chance to finish.

Audre grabbed his face and started kissing him in a fierce, manic sort of way.

Kilian responded instantly. Taking her more fully into his arms and pressing her to him. His lips devoured her, his hands ran the length of her back.

They remained enveloped in each other's arms for several seconds, completely forgetting about their friends bearing witness.

Connor looked at Elizabeth, he smiled and laced his fingers through hers.

They both rejoiced as their best friends finally found each other.

Audre wrapped her arms around Kilian's neck, bringing him closer still, while he encircled her protectively in his powerful embrace. They pressed their entire bodies into one another, like they were trying to bind themselves.

It was evident to both Elizabeth and Connor, that Kilian would never let go of Audre again.

. . .

In addition to the castle, grounds, forest, garage, guard station, and cottage, the estate was also home to a large warehouse. Although she'd technically "lived" on the estate off and on for years, she'd never actually stepped foot inside.

It was a large building, large enough that a film buff might think it housed the Ark of the Covenant.

Crates and boxes and furniture took up a sizable portion of the floor and a significant number of the industrial steel shelving units.

Many things seemed to be cataloged, but a great deal of the contents were still in boxes and piles waiting to be unearthed and rediscovered.

"What's all this?" she asked him, pointing to the stacks and boxes and antique furniture congregating near the shelves, but clearly not organized in any particular order.

He shrugged, "I had to put the old man's stuff somewhere when I renovated it the first time. I couldn't just get rid of it, there could be some valuable items in here." He scanned the space around him, "But I couldn't bring myself to go through any of it or to get it valued, so I just . . . left it."

She briefly surveyed the area, eyeing Tiffany lamps and expensive looking couches, tables, paintings, and large trunks with locks. There were a few safes and stacks of old-looking documents.

It was a lot—an entire castle's worth of pieces. "When was the last time you were in here?"

He shrugged again, giving her a sheepish grin, "When I instructed the movers to empty the house completely and showed them where to put it?"

"Sooo . . . you just told them to clear the house, and then you renovated it?"

"Yep," he stuffed his hands in his pockets and swayed in place.

Her eyes returned to the paintings, most looked like originals. "Uhhh, shouldn't those be professionally archived or on walls? It can't be good for them to be in here during the winter or the warmer days of summer." She couldn't help it, the historian in her was rising up, potentially horrified by the treatment of historically significant pieces or artifacts.

Connor smiled, he was amused. "Have I told you lately how sexy your brain is?"

She narrowed her eyes, but smiled back, "I'm serious."

He let out a short laugh, "No worries, Lara," he motioned to the walls and ceiling, "the whole place is insulated, and temperature controlled."

"Good," she was satisfied, now free to focus on the matter at hand.

She found her shipment at the front of the massive space, on the right side near one of the industrial-sized doors.

The boxes of albums, and diaries, and porcelain dishes,

and framed pictures were carefully stacked to one side next to the larger pieces of furniture.

Elizabeth found Mags' blue couch and unwrapped it quickly. The sight of the soft deep blue fabric and the weathered, but comfortable cushions, made her feel like a piece of her own ancestral home had finally made it to Ireland.

She sat down, took off her shoes, and curled up on it like she used to growing up.

It smelled of lavender, peppermint, and sunshine—just like Mags. She breathed in the scent letting it take her back to the house in Berkeley and all the times she'd sat on it to do her homework, watch a movie with her great-aunt, or stare out the large window that looked out onto the street to watch the people go by.

Connor watched her for a minute and then walked away, his eyes trained on something in the distance.

It was a comfortable couch, but after a few minutes she noticed something wasn't quite right. She moved this way and that, finally detecting that something was poking at her. She reached down between the cushions to discover the culprit.

Her fingers closed in on a thick piece of paper. She extracted it carefully.

It was a photograph. A very *old* photograph.

A twenty-something Mags stood next to a plane wearing a pilot's uniform. From the visual markers, it looked like

World War II. There was a young woman standing next to her.

They both smiled broadly for the camera.

"Mags was a pilot? In World War II?" she said to herself.

"What was that?" Connor looked up and walked over, but he was distracted. "What d'ya say, Luv?" he asked again absently, completely engrossed in something else.

Elizabeth shook her head, "Never mind." She was lost in her own thoughts.

A new idea was beginning to form.

She was vaguely aware that Connor was holding something in his hands, a set of papers maybe. "What did you find?" she called out to him.

"I'm not sure yet," he said in that same absent tone. "Are you OK here?"

"Yep," she answered her eyes still fixed on the picture.

Connor started walking back to the castle, leaving Elizabeth to examine Mags' face and wonder why she'd never told her about the war.

She wasn't sure what she was looking at or what it meant. This was a part of her story she never knew existed.

And so it was that Elizabeth Lara began to wonder what secrets Mags had taken with her to the grave, and what else her great-aunt still had to tell her.

A NOTE FROM JULES

If you enjoyed reading *The Irish Castle,* then please leave a review. Reviews go a long way to helping a small fish like me! You have no idea the type of impact your words can have—both on me personally and on the all-powerful algorithms that decide which authors to promote or keep visible.

Thanks in advance for helping me to stay in the game and keep writing for a living.

♥ With a grateful heart, Jules ♥

Keep reading for an exclusive preview of the next book, *The Irish Secret. . . .*

THE IRISH SECRET EXCLUSIVE PREVIEW

Prologue: The Choice

The car turned onto the small road. She looked up for the first time since leaving the Creative Quarter. The impressive stands of Croke Park peeked out and framed the sky. A hodgepodge of buildings made from brick, concrete, and glass, formed the base of the stadium that lined the left half of the street.

Thousands of people walked past, busy and excited, on their way to enter the temple of music and entertainment. She could hear the general buzz of excitement, even through her windows.

The sleek black car pulled into the side entrance and into the backstage area that she had visited the day before. A few seconds later she was in a massive underground structure, the wall of sound from the outside was muted, replaced by a new hum of energy. Everywhere she looked, people dressed in black were rushing around the large enclosed space, busy with last minute preparations.

Security checked her badge three more times before she was allowed into the innermost sanctum of the staging area.

The cacophony started to build. She readied her camera and said goodbye to Noah. The white walls and black signs guided her towards the last series of corridors and finally up the steps to the side of the stage.

Elizabeth checked her watch. She'd barely made it—only twenty minutes left.

A small group of people surrounded a man, fussing with the collar of his tight white shirt, and carefully tending to the mop of curls on his head. She reached him just as the glam squad dispersed.

Kilian turned around and caught her eyes. His cheeks were flushed, and his body was tense. "Oh Liz, finally, thank God!"

"Sorry, I'm late—"

He waved her off, "No, it's not that. I can't tell you what a relief it is to see a face I know well." He smoothed his shirt. Unsure about where to place his hands, he balled them up and brought them awkwardly to his side.

He was restless or nervous, she couldn't quite tell. She wanted to hug him, but she was afraid of undoing the efforts of the group that had just left. She reached out and squeezed his arm, "I take it you don't know many of these people?"

He shook his head, "Audre contracted them especially for this."

Elizabeth looked around at all the people buzzing about, but didn't see her best friend. "Haven't you seen Dree? Where is she?"

"Yes, I've seen her, but only briefly. She's around, I think on the other side of the stage." He motioned vaguely in that direction before suddenly placing his hands on his knees and expelling all the air from his lungs.

The quick motion startled her, she felt the change in her own body—now her pulse was starting to race. "Kil, what's wrong? Are you really that nervous?"

He was a natural on stage, he loved performing. She'd never seen him get nervous.

He straightened, focusing on her face.

"Just breathe," she instructed, trying to calm herself as well. It was a big day. The culmination of so many dreams.

She waited for him to speak.

"It's not stage fright . . . or maybe it is . . . I don't know anymore, Liz. It's Croke *bleedin'* Park!"

"I know," she said softly. It had been the focus of his summer—getting ready for the biggest gig of his life.

After a few moments, he continued, "It *is* the show, but it isn't what's got me going mental. It's, you know . . . the *other* thing," he said pointedly.

He started looking around to see if anyone was in earshot. "Am I barmy for doing this?" he whispered.

"The concert?" she started, and then she remembered. "Oh, you mean . . . *right.*"

She reached for his hand, pried his fingers open, and squeezed reassuringly, "I think it is . . . *definitely* bold, and will make for quite a story." She smiled with a certainty she didn't feel.

He waited for her to say something else. When nothing came, his eyebrows shot up, he could see through her. "Oh Jaysus, I *am* barmy! Feck!" He looked away out towards the stage. "Maybe I won't do it."

The wall of sound coming from the stadium was getting louder and louder as the hour approached.

"Is that what you want? Because you can absolutely go out there and give these people a great show and not do . . . the *other* thing."

He didn't speak.

"What does your heart tell you?"

He brought his lips together in a straight line, weighing the decision. He took in another deep breath; his eyes found a woman with sleek black hair and a headset motioning wildly and directing everyone around her. Elizabeth watched as his chest stilled and his energy changed. A general calm overtook him. He stood up straight, shifting his powerful 6'2 frame until he looked every bit the confident rock star.

He turned back to Elizabeth, eyes sparkling, "No, I may be mad, but I'm goin' for it." He beamed just as Audre looked up from the other side of the stage. She gave them a dazzling smile and waved.

Chapter 1: The Irish Meadow
Six Weeks Earlier

The sun warmed the soft green grass under her bare feet. Elizabeth took a long blade between her thumb and forefinger. She stroked it absently, feeling its smoothness as she looked at the white structure she'd built.

It was the first thing she had ever dreamed up from scratch and brought into the world.

From somewhere nearby an excitable bird began to sing. She looked to the trees and took in the space for the hundredth time, it was impossible not to smile.

Her very own fairy glen was teeming with lush verdant grass and wildflowers. It was her secret garden, her vibrant meadow, her ancient forest.

From the instant she'd found it weeks ago, she'd felt at home, like it was some magical escape from the real world where time stood still, and the cares of life couldn't reach her.

A gentle breeze flowed in and around the circular clearing and through the mature woodland that surrounded it. She took a deep breath, filling her lungs with fresh Irish air.

It was another beautiful summer day. They'd been lucky with the weather, it was the reason they'd been able to complete the white structure in front of her in only three weeks.

It wasn't finished, there was still a good deal to do on the inside—electrical, plumbing, some of the drywall, as well as painting and the final touches, but Elizabeth was elated that they had managed to make her dream a reality in such a short period of time.

She lay back on the blanket she had strewn across the grass and stared up at the blue sky and the white puffy clouds as they floated serenely by. The sunshine seeped into her skin.

She took a deep breath and relaxed further, melting into the soft pink fabric.

She listened to the breeze and the birds, and the trees as they swayed. Every so often the scent from the flowers near the edge of the meadow wafted in her direction, especially the Wild Jasmine.

She breathed it in, let it wash over her.

julietgauvin.com/books/the-irish-secret/

BUY NOW

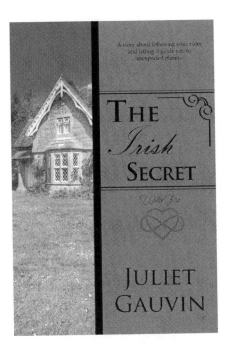

JULIET GAUVIN

feel-good romantic trilogies with spice.
epic love. life-altering journeys.
IRELAND.

FOR DELETED SCENES, RELEASE NEWS & EXCLUSIVE
GIVEAWAYS

JOIN THE READERS GROUP

julietgauvin.com/contact-jules

ACKNOWLEDGMENTS

This book (and every other) would not have been possible without the unwavering love, support, and belief of my mother, Martha.

I'd also like to thank my family, my writer friends at Virtual Pub, on Clubhouse, the BFA, and the readers who wanted more Elizabeth & Connor.

ABOUT THE AUTHOR

Jules is originally from California. She is a true, hopeless, all-in romantic. Her first kiss was with a Frenchman in Paris, her first love was an Eagle Scout, her first crash and burn was with someone from Harvard (Jules studied history at Yale-- she should have known better).

The Irish Cottage: Finding Elizabeth was inspired by Jules' love for all things Irish. A love sparked in her teens by Riverdance; fanned into a flame when she befriended a group of Irish kids in France; and blazed into a wildfire by a visit to the Emerald Isle.

Recently, she flew to Scotland for book research, met a fella, and moved to Edinburgh where she lives today.

ALSO BY JULIET GAUVIN

THE IRISH HEART SERIES

THE ORIGINAL TRILOGY

THE IRISH COTTAGE: FINDING ELIZABETH

THE LONDON FLAT: SECOND CHANCES

THE PARIS APARTMENT: FATED JOURNEY

THE CONTINUING TRILOGY

5 YEARS LATER

THE IRISH CASTLE: KEEPING ELIZABETH

THE IRISH SECRET: WILD FIRE

THE IRISH WEDDING: A NOVEL ROMANCE

Made in the USA
Columbia, SC
29 July 2022

64294867R00214